Ex-teacher, university sports officer and tour guide, who took to writing when a teenager and who then got ambushed by marriage, divorce and life in general before deciding to write a miscellaneous collection of short stories.

To Cathie Louise

D. E. Ceit

OF WOE, WONDER AND WHIMSY

AUSTIN MACAULEY PUBLISHERS

LONDON • CAMBRIDGE • NEW YORK • SHARJAH

A CIP catalogue record for this title is available from the British Library.

ISBN 9781788786355 (Paperback)
ISBN 9781528955799 (ePub e-book)

www.austinmacauley.com

First Published (2020)
Austin Macauley Publishers Ltd
25 Canada Square
Canary Wharf
London
E14 5LQ

Thanks to Austin Macaulay Publishers for their help with this book.

Table of Contents

The Bowling Green! (Stewart Utterthwaite!)

Not long after he'd sat down upon the bench by the Bowling Green, and just as his mind was beginning to wander away upon the gentle summer breeze, the pretty little dragonfly (vivid red and green iridescence) landed upon his outstretched leg and perched delicately, almost acrobatically, on the material of his faded khaki shorts flexing its fragile lace-like wings. The 'ruddy darter' that now rested serenely upon his leg was, to all intents and purposes, her mischievous familiar, its vivid red and green little body triggering all the hapless memories inside his head. And before he could object, before he was able to eject her memory from within his perplexed mind, her ghost ambushed him, grabbing him by the scruff of his neck and thrusting him back into the playground of his past. His heart suddenly skipped a beat and he stifled and swallowed a rising sob as his brain was switched back to the past. It was as if the insect had turned a light on inside his dusty and cobwebby head. And as his thoughts hurdled back the many years past, he knew that he was powerless to stop them doing so. He had to go with the flow now. He couldn't resist. It was futile to even try!

"What a load of codswallop! What a load of old rubbish! Twaddle! What a complete waste of time, and more importantly, precious money!"

She stopped him (for they were walking up the old 'Packhorse' Road towards 'The Fleece Inn') in his tracks and looked earnestly, deploringly, into his eyes, his clown-like smile beamed from ear to ear.

"Stewart, listen to me, there are millions, maybe billions even, of starving people out there in the world right now. Men, women and children, what about them? And what about what's going on in Vietnam, is that right? How do you square all that imperialist aggression with your precious, glorious 'space race', your silly little man on the moon, you, you, you capitalist pig!"

Now whenever Maggie derided him and called him names, he couldn't help himself but laugh back at her, which in turn was like pouring petrol onto an already flaming blaze. But if the truth be known, neither of them were anything like politically aware in a decade that had been a veritable hotbed of political issues for the youth of the world. They were in fact just a couple of struggling, clueless teenagers. Small and ineffectual cogs in a massive machine of that was the radical youthfulness of the 1960's. Naïve little satellites in a topsy-turvy universe that bubbled and spat trouble like a witch's cauldron.

By the late summer of 1970, they were both nineteen and, on the face of it, nothing appeared to have changed much. Man was now firmly established on the surface of the moon. President Kennedy's prophecy had proved correct and he'd won hands down so-to-speak. His eternal flame was assured forever. But then nothing really followed, and the 'Apollo' programme soon fizzled out in rather less glory than when it had commenced a few years earlier. The 'Beatles' had split up and gone their separate ways, and all that remained of the 60's were the distant echoes that were themselves fast becoming the past, as 'glam-rock' reared its ugly and glitzy head. The 1960's were indeed very much over and so was the flower power, and yet the misery, that was Vietnam, rumbled on regardless for a few more years yet.

Stewart, like his father, began drifting from job to job: from mill to farm and from farm to mill and back again. Whatever he found himself doing he was never very settled; he couldn't quite find a suitable niche for himself. His itchy feet always took him to some other place but never to somewhere that he felt able, or more importantly, comfortable enough to put his roots down. He began to mistrust many of those around him and in reality he became well and truly a 'loner'. But as long as he had enough money in his pocket for his beer, tobacco and eventually, his rent, nothing really mattered anymore and he stayed exactly the same.

Maggie Habergam's dreams, ambitions and great expectations also resulted in nothing. All became grey, dull and decidedly sodden with self-pity, and it all became a bit of a damp squib, and what's more she knew it! She was painfully aware that she had sold herself short, but felt that there was really nothing that she could actually do about it. But behind the 'grin and bearing' of it all her dark fears and realisations were beginning to take a definite shape now, and she knew that sooner or later she'd have to confront and face them. But not just yet as she has one last hurdle to surmount and that would be the big ultimate test for her. But in the meantime, she carried on with her humdrum way of life with its everyday routine – just like everyone else. She didn't go to join V.S.O, she didn't even send for an application form, for the thought of even the slightest inconvenience and discomfort in foreign climes absolutely appalled her. The awful food. The disgusting sanitary conditions. And all those nasty creepy-crawlies didn't even bare thinking about, let alone actually having to face them for real on a daily basis. In her fickle heart she knew that she liked her steaming hot baths and crisp clean bed sheets far too much, not to mention her clean 'Marks and Spencer' underwear. Moreover, her other great desire, the farmed 'Time For Tea' café that she had dreamt up in her mind, and would one day eventually own as her own, became nothing more than a childish whim, a silly fantasy, and resulted only in her inner embarrassment whenever she happened to think about it, which in actually fact was hardly ever nowadays. Whenever he was with her, Stewart could sense her discomfort so, very sensibly, kept his mouth shut and never brought it up again in passing conversation. In the end, she ended up getting a job in the offices at 'Ripponden and District' motor carriers and trained to be (of all things) a junior typist! She really didn't like it very much and found her tasks monotonous, but the people she worked with were kind to her and were good fun when they went out to the pub after work on a Friday afternoon. And she especially liked the colour of the blue and cream lorries and vans that she saw in the works yard beyond her office window. Very smart indeed. She also carried on living at home on the 'Oldham Road' so her work was in easy walking distance and meant that she had no travelling expenses to fork out for. And this in turn meant that she was able to save money on regular weekly basis, something that was completely alien to Stewart's way of thinking. Therefore, her life was pleasingly tolerable for the time being, although her 'bogey-man' was never too far away from her waking and sleeping thoughts now.

It was in the heat of the day, late on in the summer, when they once more (and for the last time for a very long time) shared each other's company. Until late that August they had hardly seen anything at all of each other throughout the whole of that summer. Indeed, they had only met in passing where they'd exchange the obligatory 'how are you doing?' and 'what have you been up to?' As well as all the usual mundane questions related to their places of work. But during that late August month Stewart received a letter which impressed his mother to no end, from Maggie asking him to meet her on the old Packhorse Bridge that spanned the River Ryburn at the bottom of the 'Priest Lane'. She gave a specific day and a time when they should meet, and she further stipulated that if she wasn't there by such and such a time, he wasn't to wait a minute longer but to get himself off and that she'd be in touch. The day came. It was a Friday and he found himself on the old bridge looking down into the fast-flowing water for brown trout and was fascinated by the 'dippers' diving into the water searching for their food amongst the stones and rocks, walking upright on their little legs. He was mesmerised by two in particular dipper birds that flew with a flick of white back and forth up a culverted outpouring that ran along under St Bartholomew's grave yard. He glanced at his watch again, it was bang on five-thirty and she suddenly came into sight. He straightaway noticed that she didn't appear to be her usual self, and at first she hardly talked at all and she seemed quietly agitated. They had planned to go up the old Packhorse Road to the 'Fleece' for a drink but in actual fact they never got past the church's graveyard. At first their talk was clumsy and disjointed and even he could sense she was trying to find a way of getting something off her chest. He came to her aid. He asked her what was the matter. She turned to him and took hold of his hand in her own. She looked him straight in the eye and asked him straight out.

"Stewart, have you ever done it?"

He was dumbfounded and flushed instantly, as red as a beetroot. She persisted regardless.

"You know done it, I mean really done it? Really had full sex? Tell me the truth now, whatever you do don't lie to me, please Stewart!"

He jumped to his feet, still as red as a puce. He exclaimed vehemently and begged her to stop messing him about. He told her to stop being a silly bugger, and that you don't joke about things like that, and that it was really serious, grown-up sort of stuff. However, she pleaded with him.

"But we are grown-up, sort of, aren't we? Please tell me the truth now. Have you ever had sexual intercourse, or tried to do it for real?"

He grew really angry now probably out of sheer embarrassment. He told her in no uncertain terms that she was acting stupid, and what kind of a lad did she take him for. He walked around the graveyard trying to sort his thoughts out, trying to wonder what she was getting at and why she'd asked him such a question as that in the first place. He eventually calmed down, as she knew he would do, and came and sat back down next to her. His curiosity, as she also knew it would do, got the better of him, it always did. He asked her why she'd asked him such a serious and personal question. Her answer flew back at him.

"Well I've never done it you see, and I don't think you have either, have you? But I want to try it, I've got to try it, and I want to try and do it with you, Stewart!"

She paused for she was out of breath.

"Will you do it with me, please Stewart?"

He shot to his feet once again and told her again in no uncertain terms that he wasn't going to get involved in all this hanky-panky rubbish, and what sort of bloke did she take him for anyway. And besides, he certainly wasn't ready to be a father, and he definitely wasn't ready to get married.

"I'm not asking you to give me a baby, Stewart! I don't want one as well, you know, and I really don't want to get married either, especially to you! All I'm asking is that you'll do it with me, after all, we've been friends with each other since we were little kids. I need to know what it's like you see, what it really feels like, doing it with a man! And I trust you Stewart, and I know that you won't hurt me if we do try it together. And hey, don't worry, I've managed to get hold of some contraceptives for us to use if we do it together."

And as true as her word, she pulled them from out of her pocket and displayed them proudly in the palm of her hand right in front of his very eyes. She was very cleverly backing him into a corner and she hoped that her feminine reasoning was wearing his defences, as well as his embarrassed outrage, down to a thin veneer, ready to be shattered.

"It will be dead safe, I promise you, Please Stewart, do this for me. I'm begging you to help me, please!"

He was flabbergasted and dumbfounded into an astonished silence! He couldn't believe that she had managed to get hold of some contraceptives. Real rubber condoms! He felt a cold clammy sweat coming trickling down his back. Even he didn't know how (or let alone dare) to get hold of some of those things. He shook his head in disbelief. She really was truly amazing. And that is why he'd always truly loved her. He sat back down, but only after she'd put 'them' back in her coat pocket. He wiped the sweat from his brow and stared before him, lost for words. She left him alone.

She let him mull it over in his mind, as she knew he would do. Presently he spoke and asked to see 'them' again. She placed them in his hand and smiled at him tenderly. He scrutinised them carefully, almost in awe of them, and he asked her where she'd really got them from.

"One of the girls at work got them for me. Her boyfriend gets them from the barber's shop where he goes to get his hair cut."

There was a slight pause as he turned the packet over and over in his fingers as though challenging their validity. She snatched it back out of his hand.

"Don't worry, they're new ones you know, they're not out of date, honestly! Believe me!"

Stewart nodded in reply and by the look on his face she knew that she'd won the day, his curiosity, as well as his hormones were well and truly aroused, and they were definitely on her side now.

They continued to talk and their talk was clumsily centred around all the aspects of sex that they were aware of and actually knew about – which, as it happens, wasn't a great deal at all, but just enough to arouse their latent lust and curiosity for one another. In actual fact, to all intents and purposes, they were sexual virgins and they were fumbling completely in the dark with the help of one another. She further explained to him that she needed to know what 'it' was really like, what 'it' actually felt like for a woman to have a man inside her body. She went on to say that it was different for a woman because they developed and matured much sooner than boys therefore she needed to know what it was like from actual experience, and that because she was still a virgin; she was already way behind where she should be as a 'flowering' young woman. She felt that she needed to catch as it were. He saw her point of view. And then she further convinced him that it made good common sense for them to try do 'it' together because they were friends and went back a long way with each other, because they'd grown up together and because they'd shared so much together. She once again very cleverly didn't give him any time to think about the value of that last statement, but moved him and her argument on quickly and decisively in the direction that she wanted it to go. She still further convinced him that it would be a good life experience for them both and that it couldn't do them any real harm at all in the long run, and what's more, they might really like 'doing it' and if they did they could do 'it' again wherever they liked, except 'for that time of the month' of course. Game, set and match! So it was all agreed then, and a day and place were also agreed upon. They agreed that they would meet well away from prying eyes, and the place they agreed to meet at was Shibden Hall Park, just north-east of 'Halifax' town centre. Yes, they were both aware that it was a very popular place with local people, but it was big, very big, and the solitary woods that abounded in its country park would be ideal and comfortable enough for them both. Lots of bushes everywhere. So they were bound to find somewhere to hide themselves away, somewhere dark and somewhere hidden!

The following Saturday (the day of their tryst) seemed like a lifetime away. Time dragged, like an anchor, towards the planned, fateful encounter. Both thought about backing out more than once. Both prayed for a sudden illness that would let them 'off the hook', but none came and the days passed. And as the day drew nearer, their carnal desires grew stronger and sleep was erratic and dreams interspersed with erotic images with waking sweaty bodies in beds that were far too hot to contain their growing excitement. At long last, Saturday morning arrived and Stewart was up with the larks bright and early and downstairs having his breakfast when the post arrived, and 'another' letter was placed before him. He gulped down his food and made an excuse to go to the newsagents to buy a morning paper. On the road he hastily tore open the envelope and read the letter within.

Dear Stewart

Sorry, can't meet at Shibden Hall today, impossible, someone knows, someone knows about us, someone will be waiting for me. Will explain later. Please meet me up at 'Flints Moor', the old air-raid bunker, about 3:00pm.

Maggie .XXX.
PS Don't you dare be late!!!

At home, hidden away, amongst all his official documents and savings certificates, as well as the meagre collection of old family photographs that he'd somehow managed to garner, he still had Maggie's letter together with its hastily torn envelope. He treasured it. He had nothing else of hers, and no photograph to remember her by. Just the memory of her voice as it was then and those images of her that were carefully tucked away and hidden deep within his mind.

Stewart now looked all around him. It appeared that there was no one else in the park, which struck him as strange as it was such a beautiful day. (Although the dark clouds of an impending summer storm were already gathering, ganging up, ready to unleash their worst just beyond his immediate horizon.) He realised by the position of the sun behind him that it must be getting on into late afternoon. The lengthening shadows that were swallowing the bowling green before him were merging and blotted together. A strengthening wind was also brewing and was already rustling the leaves into song as it skipped over the tops of the surrounding hills. He wanted to leave now, go and have his pint of beer, but also knew that the memory had to be fully re-called when suddenly, as if out of thin air, the dazzlingly beautiful red and green dragonfly re-appeared and rested delicately upon the metal arm of the bench he was sitting on. Flicking its lace-like wings up and down to catch his attention, to draw him back once more. He knew that his beer would have to wait a little while longer yet. And as the warm summer wind caressed his weather-beaten face, and ruffled his silver thinning hair, the events and images of that fateful encounter merged into clarity before his wistful, staring eyes.

The day of the tryst came bright and hot. Indeed, the heat of the previous day had hardly dissipated and continued throughout the night and was already making its searing presence known as soon as the sun poked its eager head above the hills as the majority of the 'Ryburn Valley' still slumbered. Dew had already begun to dry on grass and leaves and those nocturnal animals still at large and roaming, very soon disappeared into burrows, shrubs and undergrowth, and the cool shade of safety as the daytime 'shift' duly reported for work and came on duty and filled everywhere with a cacophony of birdsong, loud and sweet to the ear.

He'd not been able to eat a thing since coming downstairs bright and early as his stomach churned incessantly and gave him no respite at all, and worst of all he was, as he always was first thing in the morning, absolutely ravenous! But now, not to be caught out later on, he cut and buttered two thick wedges of his mum's homemade granary bread and put them, along with some caramel wafers (his favourite) and a bottle of orangeade pop, safely inside his saddlebag and made ready to leave. When the actual time came for him to go, he left good and early, with plenty of time to spare all around. He had also decided to take his bicycle along with him on the journey because it would (to all intents and purposes) make his journey easier and give him more time to prepare and enable him to give himself a thorough good talking to so as to bolster his confidence and 'prep' his pride if need be. He already had butterflies in his stomach and waves of nausea very nearly got the better of him every time he tried to calm down and relax. What's more, he couldn't stop himself from perspiring. He'd already changed tops twice as he drifted from hot to clammy and back again without warning. He planned a long circuitous route to the place of their rendezvous. He felt it would be safer in the long run, fewer prying eyes to mark his passing by. And even before he embarked upon his journey, he already felt that he was being sly, treacherous even, that it was all wrong and that he was about to commit and do something fundamentally bad! And yet, he had repeatedly reasoned with himself, that he, 'they', were not doing anything wrong at all! And so, he left the house and the adventure began in earnest.

He began the long trek up the 'Rochdale Road' quaking in his shoes. Indeed, his feet were already steaming like a pair of kippers. A grave sense of trepidation came and went with the nausea, but there was also a new and growing sensation, albeit somewhat subdued at first, a marked stirring in his loins. He, more than once, stopped dead in his tracks and dismounted from his bicycle and thought seriously about turning back and giving it all up as a bad lot. But every time he did so, the very thought of Maggie, up on 'Flint's Moor' all alone, pushed him onwards and steeled his nerve. He couldn't, mustn't and wouldn't let her down come what may. He pressed on, his fears (for the time being at least) assuaged and at long last he began to calm down and relax and his brain registered and appreciated the breath-taking beauty, which surrounded him on every side. The fields and the hills, wherever he looked, appeared to glow and shimmer (especially those on the other side of the valley) in the almost glowing heat of the late morning sunshine. The light that bombarded the land and hit his own eyes lent a great clarity to his vision and everything appeared to be perfect in every detail, from the sheep and cows in the not so distant fields, to the lumps of weathered rock that made up the dry-stone walls that criss-crossed the entire landscape. The only thing that truly spoilt it for him were the ugly and ungainly electricity pylons that seemingly marched across the land like giant emaciated men. But then again on such a beautiful day as this, it didn't seem to matter all that much. After all he had far more important things to think about. He could forgive them their intrusion for today at least.

He passed the 'White Hart', and the 'Butcher's Arms' pubs on his right and left respectively, still walking, still pushing his bicycle patiently. He decided, though, that he'd mount it and peddle the rest of the way up the 'Rochdale Road' as soon as he had reached the 'Stones Methodist Chapel'. From this point onwards, the road levelled off somewhat and it would be much easier to ride along comfortably without sweating-cobs. He'd already decided as well that he wouldn't stop for a break, and that his bread and butter and orangeade pop, would have to wait a little while longer, until he'd reached and taken, the top road. Or better still, with a sudden flash of inspiration, just before then. He'd sit on one of the stone banks of the dam that adjoined the 'Blue Ball Road' and take his break there instead. The dam was really quite small, but its deep and dark waters would hopefully, at least, give off a cool and refreshing breeze. Furthermore, he would be able to immerse his pop into its depths and cool it off to his liking. He smiled to himself; it was a good idea indeed.

He reached the 'Stones Methodist Chapel' a few minutes later and mounted his bicycle and was off. Speeding towards a life-changing encounter that was to be his first and his last in a young life that was too rudely awakened, and his innocence compromised. But all that was still ahead of him as yet. True, not very far away. But still all to come nonetheless.

Peddling along, with the warm air pushing past his body, brought the famous Utterthwaite smile to his glowing face. The road stretched out ahead of him, on and on it appeared to go as did the wide and open landscape to the left and right of him. He felt that he could really live anywhere around these immediate valleys and hills and he never wanted to live anywhere else. He could never live in a town or city no matter what, not for all the tea in China! And what's more he had no inclination whatsoever to travel further afield, (well definitely not beyond his beloved 'Yorkshire', that is, at least) let alone to foreign climes, nasty places, when he had all this exploring to do, as much as he wanted, right here at his fingertips. He felt himself to be a very lucky man indeed, but in the very near future, 'lucky' was something he wasn't going to feel again for a very long time. But not quite just yet!

He passed the 'Hollin Lane' and the old 'Gigg Mill' peddling easily and flying round the sharp dogs–leg bend in the road; he approached the little row of cottages on his right. Sat outside the middle one was an elderly man and woman, probably man and wife. He had a shock of silver–grey hair, the woman next to him wearing a little white summer hat with a bright orange band around the middle of it. They were both sat outside their open front door in striped deck chairs obviously enjoying the sun. Both drinking, what appeared to be, wine out of glass tumblers. Stewart smiled and waved as he passed by and they nodded and waved back in return. And as he passed them, the old man shot out of his deck chair and shouted after him urgently.

"Hey mister! Look out! Your back wheel's following your front!"

He said this gesticulating frantically and pointing at Stewart's back wheel. Suddenly panicking, Stewart arched round and glanced down at his rear wheel. Unsteady now, he wobbled and lost balance, turning around he tried to straighten himself but over compensated and hit the curb, wobbling left and right he sort of fell off onto the pavement in a one-legged and pathetic kind of manner and as he let the bike fall away, his leg gave way at the knee and he fell to the ground with more of a 'plop' than a 'bump'. And as he fell, he heard a raucous, almost manic laugh behind him and he got to his feet as quickly as he could. As he turned round and looked back, the scene was empty. Completely deserted! There was no one to be seen. The people and the deck chairs had gone, vanished into thin air. He propped his bicycle against a wall and crossed the road and stood before the middle cottage where the old man and woman had been sitting in their deck chairs, drinking wine only moments before. There was nothing to be seen, not a trace of them at all. He edged closer to the front window and cupping his hands to his eyes peered into the dark and gloomy room beyond. To his shock and surprise, it was completely empty. Devoid of all furniture. A shell. The house was empty, and from the look of the empty room, it hadn't been lived in for quite some time at that, for he could just about see the piles of mail on the other side of the front door. For some inexplicable reason he suddenly decided to knock on the front door. It sounded loud and hollow and emptily futile. With a puzzled look upon his face, he re-crossed the road and retrieved his bicycle, but as he mounted and moved away off towards 'Blue Ball Lane', the curtain in the upstairs window twitched and the sliver of a chink closed to the light of day. The whole incident had completely unnerved him and jangled his already jittery nerves, and as he turned right off the

'Rochdale Road', the hairs were still standing on the back of his neck. He dismounted, now in no mood at all to attempt to cycle up the short, but decidedly steep cobbled lane, he shivered uncontrollably, right down to the marrow in his bones, and began the climb to the top. Now, had Stewart bothered to look back the way he'd just travelled, back to the place of the incident, he might well have seen the hazy outline of an elderly man and woman sat on deck chairs just outside the front door of their cottage, shimmering indistinctly in the summer sunshine. But he never looked back and the ghosts, if that is what indeed they were, were left in peace once more to go about their ways.

At the top of the lane, he turned right waving a cheery hello to Tony and Rosemary Foster, the 'Fozzies' to all who knew and loved them, they were cheerful hosts of the 'Blue Ball Inn', and good friends of his father's, and who were now outside their beloved pub watering their prize flowering tubs. Passing by the opening to the road that would ultimately take him up to the 'Flints Moor' and to Maggie Habergam, Stewart dismounted and leant his bicycle against the gate of the 'Black House' dam, Ripponden's water supply. Retrieving his 'little picnic' from out of his saddlebag, he hopped smartly over the wall and made his way to the far side and sat down cross-legged as close as he could to the water's edge, and to where the cool inviting breeze wafted over his hot and sticky body. Before opening the grease-proof packet of bread and butter, he unwound the little ball of string which he always carried in his saddlebag (along with three old forks for removing a punctured tyre whenever necessary, a small tool kit, a spare inner tube and the all-important puncture repair kit) and he carefully tied one end round his ankle and the other round the neck of the bottle of warm orangeade and carefully lowered it down into the deep dark water to cool. The wafers biscuits, already badly affected by being enclosed within the saddlebag, were far too soft to eat, and so once the pop had sufficiently cooled for the bubbles to sting the back of his throat, he'd subject the caramel wafers to the same water-cooling treatment that he'd personally and proudly invented.

He now, being only a couple of miles or so from the place of their meeting, couldn't help but ponder on what (hopefully) lay ahead of him. And even if Stewart had wanted to push the thoughts to the back of his mind, the growing sensation in his loins wouldn't let him do so. He had been a late learner throughout his adolescence (as Maggie very well knew), and as a beginner, he was slow to take up the baton of his burgeoning manhood. It all felt awkward to him. He seemed to stumble and fall at every hurdle. And if the truth be known, he felt scared of it all. Although now, the growing urges to explore and to know (like Maggie herself) what it actually felt like, fascinated him, and almost completely overwhelmed him at times. His erections became more and more embarrassing. They came out of the blue and took him completely by surprise, and he did whatever he could to hide and conceal them from sight, which only made his predicament more ludicrous and obvious to those who witnessed his awkward behaviour. On his Sunday evening bath time, a time when he hoped he wouldn't be disturbed and he'd be left in relative peace, he studied his erection with a mixture of awe and amazement, and with a little bit of trepidation. But the overwhelming urge to touch was too great a temptation and had to be answered. He was amazed at how natural the process of the masturbation that followed, actually felt. It was almost as if he'd known how to 'do it' from birth. An inherent instinct. As the sensation of self-pleasing powered itself towards its inevitable climax the sudden fear of ejaculation took a hold of him, and like so many before him he really tried to stop, but again, like the many before him have experienced 'first hand', the momentum couldn't be stopped no matter what! And when his viscid ejaculation exploded, he was both amazed and shocked. It shot into the air and he desperately tried to control its eruption. But as he reached in vain for the toilet paper and then in desperation for his discarded underwear (the bath towels were most definitely out of the question) in order to stem the flow of his blossoming manhood, he simply stood over the bath and released the rest of his longing into the empty bath tub which he then hurriedly and guiltily washed away before running his early evening bath. And this was the first and only time that this sort of thing occurred at home, the longing and desire were there but not the determination. But not long after this particular episode, the erection issue raised its ugly head again, but this time not at home but at his present place of work, a dyeing mill down by the woods at 'Kebroyd'. Whilst repairing and cleaning a particular machine amongst the ladies, who were having their morning break at the time, he felt a throbbing, pulsating sensation rising in his loins, as the all too familiar erection inflamed and filled the groin of his overalls. He tried anxiously to conceal it but it was spotted by the lazy-eyed junior (who always seemed to appear at the wrong time and catch him unawares) as he inadvertently rubbed at his aching crotch trying to make the swelling go away. She was a seventeen-year-old rosy-cheeked, healthy and plump individual, who often looked at him with side-long glances, her face framed by a curly mop of deep chestnut hair. Her lazy-eye seemed glued to his swelling and there was the very faintest trace of a smile at the edges of her full red lips, and then it flittered away again and she was gone. Leaving him alone and red faced and incredibly uncomfortable, but self-consciously aroused. He found himself increasingly attracted to her lazy-eyed beauty, for she was undoubtedly a handsome young woman. She was earthy in a way that drew him to her like a magnet, and he followed her every movement whenever he could. From the way the cheeks of her firm youthful behind flexed and relaxed, and sometimes clenched when she was walking past him, to the soft bounce of her full breasts, which lay deliciously concealed beneath her work blouse. Her whole body exuded a raw, ingenuous, animal magnetism, and he found himself (for once in his short life) looking forward to going to work of a morning just to see her, although he didn't even know her name nor did he dare ask anyone what it was. He just sort of hoped that one day soon they'd eventually bump into one another, that the fates might bring them together. But they never did. And had he any semblance of common sense, or indeed, had he been brave enough, he'd have sunk all his money and invested it heavily into her and left Maggie Habergam well alone, and ran with what actually felt right and natural to him at the time. But soon afterwards, she disappeared completely from the mill. Vanished into thin air so to speak. He never ever saw her again and for a time, he was left wondering what on earth had happened to her. But he sort of knew that he'd had his chance and lost it. He sighed deeply. It was a long careworn sigh for once so young and its audible sound belied his age. But all that was long ago now, water under his bridge of life. She was nothing but a memory, whereas Maggie was still very real and would very soon be within his reach. However, that haunting lazy-eye would never completely fade away and it was only ever just a blink away from his mind's eye.

He finished off his granary bread and butter and took a good long pull at the orangeade bottle until the fizzy bubbles stung the back of his mouth and he had to stop drinking to catch his breath. Pulling the chocolate from the water, he broke a piece off the little block and munched away at it slowly. He looked down at this watch. There was still plenty of time to spare. He stared straight ahead of him quietly munching the chocolate into a gooey pulp and noticed away in the distance a distinct change in the weather that was heading towards him now, and it was coming over the hills, and it appeared to be coming fast. Way off in the distance, the darkening sky appeared to be growing increasingly unsettled and the great billowing clouds towered thousands of feet above the hills and rose higher and higher into the bright blue sky. He stared at them intensely as they imperceptibly changed their shape before his very eyes. They were slowly changing their colour too. Just marginally above the crest of the hills they were a dense, deep grey, and above that, they glowed angrily, reddish-pink, as though on fire, then rising to a fluffy white way above, blissfully ignorant to the transformation that was taking place below. He knew from experience that a storm was coming and that it was heading their way. It was inevitable. But hopefully it wouldn't break until after they had met and done what they set out to do. And if the worst came to the worst, he knew that he could easily give Maggie a ride home on the back of his bicycle after they'd finished. If the weather broke sooner than expected then there were plenty of spreading trees to shelter underneath until the storm had passed. He finished off his chocolate, and gathered up his things, he had to make a move now. As soon as he stood up, the butterflies attacked his stomach with a vengeance and made him belch repeatedly, he rubbed his stomach trying to ease and calm the wind and his growing sense of nerves. As he made his way back to his bicycle, he lit himself a cigarette, and exhaling the sweet-smelling smoke, he noticed just how heavy with heat the air actually was. He could have cut it with a knife. There wasn't a breath of air to be had anywhere and a strange silence reigned over everything, including the cows and sheep in the surrounding fields, which now sat chewing the cud staring towards the impending storm. They too were now deathly silent. No bleating or lowing could be heard anywhere. They knew what was coming. After stowing his things back inside the saddlebag, he moved off with a heightened sense of urgency. As he hit the 'Coal Gate Road' he dismounted (the incline was instantaneous and he didn't really want to sweat anymore) and marched up through the funnelling dry-stone walls that seemingly fenced him in on either side like a man possessed. Strangely, hereabouts, probably because he was unable to see over and above the walls, the air was completely still and he couldn't hear a thing. He felt he could have heard a pin drop, so quiet, in fact, that he could really hear his ears working and straining to the silence. Then suddenly, as he neared the top of the rise in the road, the haunting call of the curlew rent the air close by as if in alarm. He stopped walking and looking up, and all about him, saw nothing, save only the clouds of midges hovering above the walls here and there, but nothing else. He finished off his cigarette and carefully stubbed it out beneath his foot then moved off once more. Now back on the flat he whizzed on and away down the road with the burgeoning storm over his left shoulder and, for the time being at least, somewhat way behind him. But coming on fast nonetheless! In fact, much faster than either he or anyone else, for that matter, thought at that time!

He peddled faster and faster now, as fast as he possibly could. He saw the haunted wood looming up on his left-hand side. He'd always promised himself that one day he would explore every inch of its secret mystery, ghosts or no ghosts, but for one reason or another, he never ever got around to it. Maybe one day he would.

Way over on the other side of the valley, to his right, lay the 'Norland Moor', with its deadly hidden bog, and just beyond that he could easily make out the 'Wainwright's Tower', dark and tall like some sinister phallic symbol. He grimaced. For some unknown reason he didn't like the 'Wainwright's Tower' at all, it gave him the willies. Then way ahead of him, in the distance, and on a far hillside still bathed in summer sunshine, was 'Warley Town'. It appeared friendly and all too inviting to him. He wished that he were there for some unknown reason. Having himself a quiet drink in 'The Maypole', instead of peddling like a madman headlong to his unavoidable doom!

As he looked over his shoulder, he saw that the storm clouds were rolling towards him and that they were almost upon him now so he peddled faster. He left the trees of the wood well behind him and as the skies darkened ever more ominously, the heather that blanketed the moor on either side of the road looked like black and grey spongy stuff, alien almost, when suddenly in the near distance, 'Flints Moor' suddenly came into sight, as did the old air raid bunker! And as he fixed his eyes upon his fate the first vivid flash of summer lightning lit up the sky above and behind him, followed some few seconds later by a subdued rumble of grumbling thunder. He knew then that the storm had almost caught him up. It was now a race against it flat out! He put his head down and stood on the peddles just as a startled deer leapt across his path in alarm. He swerved violently to one side, and then to the other, as the wide-eyed animal flew past him and bound with an effortless grace and agility over the roadside wall and disappeared just as the next great flash came and illuminated the ever-darkening sky. But this time, close upon its heels came the crashing thunderclap, which told him, in no uncertain terms, that the storm was indeed now with him, with them both, and at the bunker! Reaching the highest point of the 'Coal Gate Road', which was just ahead of him now, it was all downhill and he raced along as though he too was a part of the storm. Up on the moor, by the track leading up to the bunker itself, which still lay some considerable distance ahead of him, he spotted a husk of hares dashing, ears flattened, eyes bulging, for the cover of safety. He suddenly screeched to a skidding stop in a cloud of dust and loose stones and amid an acrid smell of burning rubber, at the gate, which would lead him up to the bunker and hopefully, the waiting Maggie Habergam. The track was far too rough and strewn with sharp-edged stones and small rocks to cycle along, so he ran with the bicycle alongside of him. As he reached the walled bend in the track, a hissing bolt of lightning discharged itself like just above his head. Any lower and it would have parted the middle of his hair forever. He let go of the bicycle and flung himself against the side of the dry-stone wall, scared to death. The distinct smell of electricity pervaded the air all about him and he could even taste it in his mouth. He'd only counted to two inside his head before the almighty crash of thunder erupted overhead. But he had to move on regardless, he couldn't stay where he was, cowering like a mardy-pants. He couldn't leave Maggie all alone. She'd be scared stiff, he was sure, he knew he was. So, grasping his bicycle off he went again. The track was so rough now that the wheels rattled and bounced into the air as he ran along making it difficult to keep up his pace, so he decided that he'd have to leave it behind. He propped it up against the side of the wall and left it alone with the storm, he knew it would be safe to do so today. There was no one around to steal it. So, head down, and slightly hunched over, he ran the final couple of hundred yards up the remainder of the track and up to the brick bunker that was situated on a slight hillock upon his left. He reached it in near total darkness, for the storm was right above them now and just as the first heavy drops of rain began to fall.

He ran around to the entrance that lay just in front of the protective outer wall that was supposed to have been its war-time shield. The whole complex (or what was indeed left of it), so real in its imitation that it had certainly fooled the enemy in war, as it still continued to fool anyone who unexpectedly came across its slowly disappearing mass, awaited him solemnly, seemingly brooding over its own authenticity, the passage of time having eroded the memory and its once keen-edged brickwork as the sly, moor land winds rattled through its emptiness whispering their deceptions. He paused in the doorway entrance, hesitating as he thought he saw a movement in the interior's gloomy depths. He stepped back a couple of paces whilst craning his neck and thrusting his head forward before committing his body fully to the dark. Then it came again. The vivid flash of lightning, electric luminosity so intense and seemingly brighter than natural sunshine itself. It dazzled him. Then into this light stepped Maggie Habergam. The clothes that she wore were, for the briefest of moments, brilliantly illuminated in the flaring light. Brilliant bright green denim jacket and flared blood-red corduroys. He would never forget those colours ever! They became the colours of thunder and lightning forever! Her bosom, rising and falling beneath her white t-shirt, was clearly visible as was the prominent erection now showing in the groin of his jeans. In an instant, while still in the dazzling light, he saw the look upon her face. It was a mixture of determination, fear and wonderment. The explosion of thunder was instantaneous, deafeningly loud, and it shook the very fabric of the old bunker so that dust and grit fell from its concrete roof onto them both like a sprinkling of confetti. Then complete darkness and semi-blindness after the dazzling flash. The thunder hammered the earth and frightened the worms still deeper into the soil. It shattered the shells of snails still out in the light and slithering far too slowly to find shelter and safety. And as the thunder still pounded the air above, he heard her voice call out to him.

"Come here. Come here, Stewart!"

Excited by the storm, excited and exhilarated by the smell and taste of the lightning's lingering electrical charge, excited of what lay ahead, he moved towards her. The storm above them berated and admonished them but they were now oblivious to it and it could no longer do them any harm. They came together, or more truthfully, she leapt at him and fixed her mouth on his. For a split second he didn't know what to do or how to respond to her. Then he did! He kissed her back on the mouth and found her tongue as hers found his and his arms enveloped her in a passionate embrace as the storm embraced the earth above them. Maggie broke free from his arms and stepped back. In the flash of lightning that followed, he clearly saw the wild look in her eyes, then in one swift movement, she pulled up her top revealing her full, braless breasts. They bounced seductively as the hem of her top caught them just underneath her nipples. Now it was his turn to be wide-eyed. It suddenly felt like his swelling in the groin was going to burst through the material of his jeans. And he felt the sweat running down the middle of his back. She stepped closer, but stopped short of his reach. She looked down at his waistline and back into his eyes, her voice growled at him.

"Show me!"

With shaking hands and fumbling fingers, he hastily unbuckled his belt. He undid his jeans and pulled down the fly zip as she, with heaving bosom, looked on with her wide-eyed anticipation. He pulled down his jeans hooking his thumbs under the elastic of his underpants but found himself struggling clumsily to pull them down over his erection. He smiled stupidly, his old familiar smile, as his swollen member suddenly sprang free and into view as the brightest flash of lightning he'd ever seen, or indeed would ever see in his life, dazzled in a sudden burst of light just as his jeans and briefs fell down to his ankles. Maggie screamed, it pierced and rent the air louder, much louder, than even the cascading thunderclap that accompanied the shocking flash. She yanked down her top with a look of abject horror upon her face as Stewart, his erection standing proudly to attention, and his dumb smile somehow glued or frozen to his face, beckoning to her with the bemused, no terrified, look upon his face like some grotesque ventriloquist's doll. In one swift movement, that took him completely by surprise, she barged past him screaming at him at the top of her voice.

"Oh God it's horrible! It's really horrible! It's a monster! Put it away. Put it away! Please, put it away!"

She was now almost out of the shelter. But before she vanished, she turned briefly and screamed, almost spitting at him.

"Oh God, I should never have come! I knew it was all a mistake!"

Then she was gone, out into the raging storm. He stood all alone. For a couple of seconds he stood there, trembling violently, (her words resounding in his ears) then his sobs shook him even more, consuming his whole body. He pulled up his clothes as best as could, but what with the sobs that were now racking his body and the tears streaming from his eyes, and an erection that wouldn't go away, his trembling fingers couldn't fasten his jeans up properly and so it was in this state that Stewart emerged from the bunker to find himself instantly soaked to the skin in the storm's deluge. The raindrops were as big as marbles and bombarded every inch of his body. He ran back down the track the way he'd come to the bunker as best as he could. Still sobbing his heart out, the noise of which made him sound like a distressed or wounded animal, tears and rain blinding him completely, he ran bumbling along until the unfastened jeans, now sodden, fell back down to his ankles, tripping him up. He stumbled on a pace or two until he fell with a crash into a pool of rapidly swelling peaty mud. He quickly got to his feet still not understanding why he'd fallen; he took two more strangled steps before lumbering into the side of a dry-stone wall cutting his forehead quite badly just above his right eye. Still sobbing, he pulled up his jeans and fastened them as best he could and ran on not realising that he'd injured himself, and that his flowing tears were now mixed with his oozing blood. He staggered on. Eventually, he somehow reached the bend in the track and found his bicycle propped against the wall where he'd left it. Man and machine made their confused and stumbling way to the gated entrance and back onto the road just as the storm crescendoed and reached the pinnacle of its intensity. He flung the gate wide open and mounted his bicycle like a drunken man, his feet slipping from the pedals and twice stumbling onto the road. He tried again and again to find his balance and eventually he somehow managed it as he headed off down the road, with thunder and lightning and the pouring down rain all around him and enveloping him completely. He was just in time to see the sparkly red rear lights of a car speeding away round a not too distant bend in the road. He yelled out to it as loud as he could, his voice distorted by the sobs, which rose up from his heaving chest and into his throat.

"Maggie! Maggie! Come back! I'm sorry! I'm really sorry!"

Why he felt sure she was in that car he couldn't explain. Why Maggie should be fleeing in a car was inexplicable. She could well be on any one of the many tracks or bridle ways close by, speeding her troubled way back home. But nonetheless he followed in its direction. The road to 'Eccles Parlour' was predominantly all down hill and he sped along, again standing on the pedals, grinding the wheels into the road with all his might, as his jeans slipped down his backside and hindered his movement until, once again, blinded by the rain and his tears, he momentarily took his eyes off the road. He skidded and skewed violently across the road on a raft of loose stones that were being washed down and away by the savage rain that was pelting down. He ran slap-bang into the side of the drystone wall and was catapulted clean over the handle-bars of his bicycle, down into a steep wooded gully ending up unconscious at the bottom, lying on the muddy bank of a fast-flowing stream and with his unfastened jeans once more round his ankles. And that is exactly where and how he was found a little later on that day when the storm had abated and died away. And of the incident, for a very long time thereafter, he could (or refused to) remember nothing at all.

He was off work for two whole weeks. His mother and father repeatedly questioned him. What on earth had gone on? What had really happened to him on that fateful afternoon? But luckily for him, his (temporary) amnesia let him off the hook. Even the local village constable ('Bobby Nobby' aka Sergeant Norbert Ramage) had had words with him but all to no avail. On descending the stairs from his bedroom, the officer of the law had just simply shrugged his shoulders towards the pensive mother and father, saying repeatedly that it was "a mystery all round, you mark my words, a mystery all round". And that was the end of the matter. Life went on as usual. Everything got back to normal. But not for Stewart Utterthwaite, not never ever again!

Time passes. Time passed. And so did the years. And Stewart reached middle-age without any further female attachment, or anymore female adventures. His first was most definitely his last intimate exposure with the opposite sex. The events of 1970, it is true to say had not only burned his fingers, but scorched his brain and seared the very fabric of his subsequent life. From that moment on he completely withdrew into himself, and his depressions became an ever-present companion. The incident should have conferred legendary status upon him, but in actual fact, all it did was elevate him to an unfavourable level of notoriety within the village as whisperings of his escapade leaked out like poison gas. And if he had been viewed as strange before, well now, he was most definitely a weirdo! From that moment in time, people saw what they wanted to see in him. But more importantly, from that moment in time, they only truly saw what he allowed them to see of him. And that was strictly rationed.

By 1990, at the age of very nearly forty, Stewart Utterthwaite found himself working at The Beehive (renowned for its fine country dining and its friendly atmosphere), as a waiter-on at table, glass collector and washer, cleaner, and all-round dogsbody. He'd eventually found his niche in life and he'd worked there for close on ten years now. All the mills had closed, and his old way of life, as an itinerant mill worker, had gone for good. The pub, and its customers, treated him well and were, on the whole, outwardly friendly towards him, and for the most part he was left alone to get on with his work. He liked working at The Beehive. It wasn't exacting, nor was it monotonous like mill work, and every day was as different as the people who came through the front door to dine and drink there. Of course, there were the regular clientele, a disparate bunch, from all the varied professions and backgrounds of life. Confident, complex and often shocking people, men and women alike. But all of them fascinating and beguiling, and he listened in to their colourful conversations unobtrusively whenever he could, spellbound. So far up to then it had been a beautiful summer, and it was almost forty years to the very day since the events of that fateful August storm, the old bunker up on Flint's Moor, and the catastrophic bicycle ride away from his sudden and unexpected life-changing humiliation. When, who should walk into the pub, in at the side entrance, as bold as brass, grey-haired and bobbed, and as large as life, but Maggie Habergam that was, and had been. He saw her straight away. Tears came instantly to his eyes and the heart within him, that had remained so placid for so many years, leapt to his throat and pounded so loudly that he eyed the customers standing at the bar close by him sure that they could hear its rapid beating. In a split second he was awash with perspiration and the sudden feeling of nausea very nearly overcame him. However, propping himself up against the corner of the bar, he somehow managed to remain standing. But to say that he felt decidedly strange, uncomfortable and perplexed, was a gross understatement. Now Stewart might well have been standing at the other end of the bar but he recognised her straight away. Her features, although definitely and obviously older, hadn't really changed at all. Same eyes, same ears, same slender neck, (although a little bit loose now) same smile. She stood at the top end of the bar waiting to be served and hadn't as yet spotted him. It being early evening, and the pub already full of diners, all the bar staff were busy, moreover, he couldn't have served her even if he had wanted to as he wasn't allowed to serve customers at the bar, or use the till for that matter. She grew impatient (a trait that he well remembered) and glanced down the bar towards where he was standing and looked straight into his smiling face and looked away. Then she did an instant doubletake. She'd recognised him now. She smiled and then burst out laughing as she made her way towards him. He blushed. His face so red and ablaze that he felt it was about to explode! If he could have done, he would gladly have fled the place right there and then, but there was nowhere to run and (again!) she had him boxed and cornered. When level with him she clearly noticed the tears that still welled and shone in his eyes, but just as clearly she cleverly hid her recognition of them. Maybe it was the light inside the pub? Maybe not! Or maybe she chose not to see them or the truth behind them.

She stood before him laughing, her head thrown back confidently (he'd never remembered her ever doing that before) displaying two rows of perfectly straight, still pearly white teeth. (Stewart's were now decidedly yellowing to say the very least, and he kept his mouth firmly shut tight.) She was dressed in a very smart business-like summer frock, and he clearly saw her middle-aged, tummy pressing against the material. Apart from the banal and formal pleasantries to which he stutteringly replied red-faced, as the bar customers looked on amazed that he, mere glass collector and washer, could ever know anyone half so pretty and so well dressed, and so very obviously well to do. Their exchange suddenly ground to a halt as he was called away to wait on table. Maggie paid for her drink and went away and sat down at a corner table over by a window, obviously waiting to meet someone.

As he cleared away two big tables, he stole furtive glances in her direction whenever he could, more often than not she caught him looking at her, he waved pathetically and she smiled in return. Twice he was told, in no uncertain terms, to get a move on and to stop daydreaming. Eventually, after about an hour or so The Beehive settled down and he managed to sidle over to where she was sitting, waiting patiently. She looked truly lovely in the slightly hazy pub light, a light that mellowed the overall atmosphere at any time of the day. He wiped her table (although it didn't need cleaning at all) and smiled down at her. She spoke clearly and graciously to him, her eyes genuinely expressing sincerity and warmth.

"I never got chance to thank you, I mean after the last time we met. It was unfortunate, I know, but I never saw you again, anywhere around, I mean. You sort of disappeared altogether. You kind of vanished off the face of the earth so to speak!" Cleaning the table yet again, he simply smiled and nodded in reply. She carried on, her voice now gentle, soothing.

"Not long afterwards I moved away, did you know that, to Pickering. I got a job. With a company in Malton. I'm still there, well actually in both, I mean in Pickering and in Malton. I like where I live and what I do, I'm happy, very happy you see. But I will move back home eventually, one day, quite soon maybe. It's on the cards actually."

She obviously felt awkward now, but clearly wanted to continue, but just as she was about to carry on, he moved abruptly away and left her open-mouthed, and slightly embarrassed. A few minutes later Stewart returned with a clean cloth and six new beer mats. She smiled, he smiled, customers at the bar close by smiled, and she carried on where she'd left off.

"I should have said sorry, I should have got in touch before now, I should have tried to explain, but the time never seemed right and what with moving away... And, well, it's been so long! My, it must be very nearly twenty years, mustn't it!"

She fidgeted in her seat and he noticed a slight film of perspiration at her hairline, she crossed and uncrossed her legs somewhat nervously and he saw the sheen of her tanned, freckly skin.

"The truth is I certainly didn't expect to find you working in here, of all places, in a pub I mean."

He quickly explained that all the mills in Ripponden, and the surrounding area, had closed down, and most of them pulled down, many of them years before. He further explained that work, of any kind, was hard to find in the area and that he was very lucky to have any work at all, especially at his age. She nodded her understanding. He went on and gave her a potted history of his life, (a very small pot indeed!) making a wide detour of any difficult periods and events, especially his continuing depressions, and his increasing reliance on alcohol to get him through the dark and gloomy periods of his isolation. The more they talked the more they seemed like complete strangers to one another, with nothing in common at all anymore, other than a brief period of a tenuous friendship now lost and forgotten in their distant and murky past. Once again he had to leave her alone as he was called on to serve at two separate family tables celebrating a golden wedding anniversary and a twenty-first birthday, both tables full of beaming faces, mirth and joy, both very happy occasions. But happiness was not something that he was feeling at that particular moment. Now that he'd got over the initial shock of seeing her again after so very long, he found that there was so much that he wanted to say to her, to ask her, and to demand of her, and it was imperative that he did so while he still had the chance. He helped serve up the meals. Cleared away a couple of tables of their empty glasses and wiped them down until they shone like glass then, back behind the bar, he washed and put away a whole load of glasses of all descriptions, shapes and sizes. Then once more made his way round the bar back to where Maggie was sitting. She eyed him intently. She sensed his urgency immediately, she could see it in his eyes, recognised his awkwardness from years before, but remained outwardly patient towards him. He tried desperately to broach the subject that they both knew was important to them, to him in particular. He rolled the thoughts and the words around his brain and just as they dropped down into his mouth, she very quickly interrupted him, stopped him dead in his tracks.

"We both did things and said things that we shouldn't have said and done. But that was a very long time ago! Wasn't it Stewart! But I do want to thank you for helping me in, and through, a very difficult period of my life. Helping me to find out who I really was! I don't think that I could have done it without you, you know. I mean gone through it all, the trials and tribulations."

She smiled up at him. She had robbed him of his moment, (again!) and of what he'd very clearly wanted to say, what he'd wanted to say to her for so very long and now it was lost and gone forever! Or so he thought.

"We're dining here you know, tonight, this evening. I'm just waiting for her to arrive. We've been to see my mother, she's in a home now you know."

He simply smiled and nodded. Then she suddenly rose to her feet very quickly. He stepped back a pace in alarm thinking, for a brief moment, that she was about to hit him, just like she had done before in the past after one of their heated and silly arguments about nothing in particular. But she didn't strike him, but simply held out both her hands, almost in supplication, and smiling effusively, addressed someone who had just arrived and who was now standing directly behind him.

"Wendy my darling, how are you? This is Stewart, Stewart Utterthwaite. Stewart, I'd like you to meet my partner Wendy, Wendy Tyler."

He turned around and looked up into the face of a tall, very well-tanned, serious, but decidedly good-looking woman somewhere in her mid to late sixties. She had short silvery-blonde hair that glistened in the light under which she now stood, and only served to enhance the overall look of her face and lent a framework to her lovely features. Moreover, she had vivid green eyes that shone with kindness and good humour, and on looking into his own, her rather large mouth blossomed into a rich, warm, and attractive smile and the seriousness that he had at first encountered on turning around, completely vanished.

"Well, well, well! So you're Stewart Utterthwaite, are you? I'm very pleased to meet you at long last! I've heard so much about you off Maggie. I was beginning to think that you were a figment of her very fertile imagination. I felt that I was never ever going to meet you. But bless my soul, here you are flesh and blood at long last, standing right in front of me, and working here too!"

She held out her beautifully manicured hand, with long and slender fingers, in a no-nonsense sort of fashion which demanded that it be shook without any further hesitation whatsoever. Which he duly did still wearing the silly smile upon his beetroot, and clearly glowing face. (The little group of on-looking customers, standing close by at the bar, sniggered privately amidst a round of raised eyebrows and knowing looks and a volley of crude, vulgar remarks which gladly, and indeed luckily for their sakes at least, the said parties concerned didn't hear or even suspect.) All of which sowed the seeds of many future jokes made on his behalf, and galvanised the legend surrounding his 'manly' qualities, his sexual inadequacy, and his overall stupidity. But more importantly this famed meeting formed the basis of his final defeat in life, the complete and utter acceptance of his fate. Or so he believed.

He now desperately needed to get away from the two women as fast as possible but couldn't move, he didn't know what to say, or how to extricate himself from their presence. And had he not been angrily summoned back to work by the pub's owner, he would undoubtedly have remained where he was standing all night long, rooted and glued helplessly to the spot. But back to work he went. Maggie Habergam, and her life-long partner Wendy Tyler, sat down to their meal oblivious to his insufferable discomfort. Before they finished their food and drank their vintage, and very expensive, red wine, Stewart Utterthwaite had come to the end of his evening shift of duty and signed off work. He hastily left The Beehive without saying goodbye to either of the two women, or a word to anyone else for that matter, and hurriedly made his way back to Ripponden village down the Royd Lane, half-walking, half-running. Every now and again stopping in his tracks and looking back over his shoulder, somehow suspecting that he was being followed. He never went back to work there, indeed, he knew that he would never be able to set foot in The Beehive public house ever again! And that was definitely as far as Maggie Habergam was concerned (Or was it!). And that was how it would have remained had the beautiful dragonfly not suddenly rested upon the leg of his old and tatty khaki shorts down at the bowling green, on that lovely late summer's afternoon. But then, without warning, the ruddy darter, its job now done, took to the air again and flew away from him.

He watched its flight intently as it flew away dipping and rising erratically, on across the bowling green it flew towards the park that lay upon the other side of the narrow road, until even its vivid red and green hues were lost to sight as it merged naturally into the changing light of its surroundings and thus released him from the troublesome memories of his past. Far, far the first rumblings of thunder made themselves heard, but they were too far distant as yet to be of any real threat to him. He rose unsteadily to his feet. The painful recollections had wearied his body, as well as his mind, and it ached in protest as he stood straightening his back. Stewart looked around him and took in his deserted surroundings, then looking down at his watch realised that the Conservative Club had already been open for quite some time and his beer was already waiting for him. And so off he went, clutching his cherished 'woods', as the ghosts from his past rose up into the gloaming and vanished back into the thin air from whence they came.

THE END

COMPLETED TYPING ON 18th MARCH 2016

Savage Revenge! (The Wind!)

Far, far away, away in the lands of the distant north, a tiny wisp of a wind, a wind that was destined to be great, a great wind of terrible power and havoc, that was to make desolate anything that lay in its path, was born. And once born, like an infant, it grew and was nurtured and suckled and jealously guarded, and protected by its mother, Mother Nature.

The lands of its birth were cold and barren. Inhospitable to all mankind and, to all but a few exceptional, and hardy animals, which its wastes tolerated and allowed them to live in relative peace and quiet…as long as they could find a way to survive without scratching the tips of its icebergs. This then was its nursery, its playground and its school. And this is where it grew from a baby, to an infant, into a powerful adolescence and ultimately, into a terrible power-seeking adulthood. Then, not long afterwards, breaking free from the shackles of its mother's dominance; it was unleashed into the world of all men, where destruction and death awaited its embrace with open arms. But as yet, for the moment, the world was unsuspecting, even from the furthest reaches of outer space, from where the world tracked Mother Nature's every movement and caught wind of her every breath. Forewarned was forearmed, or so the scientists and the politicians, the world over, all said, but not in this particular case, not this time!

For much of its time the little wisp of wind was left to its own devices. To roam alone unaided among the vast wastes of ice and snow, both near and far. It would be wrong to assume that this little wind had been maternally abandoned, that would be unjust in the extreme. Nor that this little fledgling breath, this movement of air was uncared for, un-nurtured, unloved or un-mothered. Nothing, indeed, could be further from the truth. This little will-o-the-wisp of gustiness was in its mother's playground, its front and back garden both, and was always under her watchful, caring eye and guarded fiercely with her all-encompassing protection. Here it was to be left alone to learn, to bruise its limbs, to cut its teeth, to tumble and to cry. But more importantly, to grow, ever daily, from strength to awesome, awe-inspiring strength. Here in these, its domestic wastes, it gambolled laughingly, haughtily and peevishly under the all-watchful, all-knowing and all-seeing protective eye of its mother. The matriarch of the planet. And so, it was here that it learnt of its terrible role in times still to come and was taught everything it would need to know in later life, whilst being mothered and kept warm under unimaginable protective wings of air.

As a child it was boisterous. As a young girl it was tempestuous. And she roamed the wastes causing mischief and mayhem wherever she went. As she grew in strength, so did her boldness and she bullied anything and everything that she came across, or that unwisely stood in her breath's way, animate or inanimate! Her blossoming alchemy knew no bounds and she arrogantly displayed it at each and every turn whenever and wherever she could. She battered and pounded ice and snow together. She raced around snow covered mountains and hills. She raised waves, as much as her adolescent strength allowed her to do so, and she split the delicate ice-sheets and dashed them to pieces on the wastes and laughed back down at her handiwork as it quickly passed behind her. She laughed scornfully at the wreckage she so happily created, never giving the havoc and destruction she so wilfully caused a second thought, and so moved on joyfully, her senses abandoned to pleasure. She spiralled down and twisted, shot up into the air thousands of feet at every second, and came crashing down to earth in vented fury. She pummelled the compacted snow and ice just inches above its surface and scoured it like the coarsest of sandpaper. She looped-the-loop and somersaulted to her heart's content, showing off to no one but herself, and to the ever-watchful mother who never took at least one weather-eye off her daughter's teenage movements. She danced, moving one way then the other, at one moment tamely unremarkable, and then, at the next turn, bewilderingly, astoundingly, unpredictable and unstoppable. Unsparing with every breath and gust of air. And as she cavorted and caterwauled, like a veritable banshee from the bowels of hell, her stately and dignified mother looked down upon her from on high and laughed to herself with sheer pleasure, and in honour of her delightful offspring. Indeed, she laughed so loud and so long and so hard, that she submitted the entire world to share in her happiness and carefree mirth as storms and adverse weather battered and harangued the planet. In her subsequent merriment, she unleashed her rejoicing across the globe, and accepted the resulting human and animal sacrifice in due course as tokens in awe of her all-inspiring greatness. Her roars of laughter resounded throughout the northern lands causing temperatures to drop to never before seen, or recorded levels. Laying waste to lands whose histories of temperatures were smashed, lashed and frozen to smithereens, while their stupid and pathetic inhabitants got down on their red-raw knees and prayed for forgiveness and deliverance. To nothing in particular or important! Across the desert wastes around the Equator, her searing peals resounded and blasted the already barren lands of sand and torched with her unforgiving forked tongue anything that dared to move or even breathe. While in the southern oceans and seas, her raucous laughter whipped up the waves to do her bidding and sent their towering masses in search of land and life in tempests, typhoons and hurricanes, so that they too could share in her unbounded pleasure and unbridled joy. And when she had taken her fill of all the intense jubilation, she turned her back upon her exaltation and rapture and cast all her attentions back upon the trials and tribulations of her demanding daughter with a loving, motherly eye.

The youngster was so enamoured in her own pursuits that she hardly noticed the preoccupations and the brief abandonment by her mother. But now encouraged, and maternally urged on by her, the youngster wind was goaded on by her mother to display her growing prowess. It was now time for her to show off and cast all her cautions to the devil. In a show of bravado and sheer exuberance; she exploded into life and hurled herself whole-heartedly into the task ahead with gay abandon. She charged around helter-skelter hammering and pulverising everything that stood in her path. And in the time that she had grown from a teenager into a fierce, vicious, young woman of a wind, she'd also found her voice in full, and in all its fury she gave it to the earth as her gift. It howled, it screamed and screeched and froze the blood and stopped the hearts of all the living things that were unlucky enough to hear its unearthly voice. She sought out her victims with a lively sense of amusement and when she espied them in all their helplessness, she showed them no mercy and gave them no quarter whatsoever, but vented all her terrible power and vindictiveness in a show of utter contempt. (Hell hath no fury like a woman's wind!) In a show of magnificence, purely for the sake of her adoring mother, she snuffed out the scent of a gigantic polar bear, a huge muscled beast, every bit as arrogant as she herself. It had heard her coming, it had smelt her power and in alarm it now raised itself up upon its hind legs in what would have been on any other day and at any other time but this, an awesome show of power, aggression and strength, but today it was little more than a pathetic display of animal brutality, and futile! It roared its defiance and stood its full height on legs like tree-trunks, open-mouthed, huge yellow teeth flashing and its razor-sharp claws standing out like beacons in the blinding white, roaring its massive head off for all it was worth. But today, on this day, it was all worth nothing at all!

She picked him up like a feather and flung his colossal weight up in the air as if he weighed nothing more than a mere piece of straw. Up into the air he went, spinning over and over again, helplessly fragile. This once all mighty beast of the wastes, an animal to be feared and respected and avoided at all costs, now reduced to little more than a ball of saggy fur, soaring up through the sky like a whimpering mouse with a bemused look upon its face, that is if a creature can ever look bemused that is. Up, up it went, until it reached the zenith of its ascent, then gravity pulled it back down to earth with a velocity that instinctively caused it fear of its own death, and raised the hackles on the back of its neck. And as it fell back down to earth, free-falling with frightening speed, it instinctively splayed its huge limbs in a vain effort to secure its safety. Its giant paws and dense fur puffed out and with the passing of rushing air it did slow its descent somewhat, but only marginally, and never enough to prevent its inevitable death. It crashed back down to earth with a sickening, body smashing boom that resounded across the icy wastes, its once proud bones shattered into many pieces. Beneath the snowy hummock onto which it had fallen, lay hidden, jagged rock, which made a mockery of the beast's once indomitable presence and strength. And there it lay, left to be frozen, and left as carrion for those animals it had once forced to bow down to its prowling terror.

But our headstrong and hoity-toity wind witnessed none of this. She'd long since moved on and had left the beast to its own destruction, and its rapidly freezing carcass was already far behind even its lesser trailing wisps of airy tendrils.

She raced on and on regardless of everything and anything. She next hit upon an exploratory polar camp that was searching the virgin terrain for gas and oil. Arch enemies of her mother indeed. Human specimens scaring, exploiting and destroying the pristine land with a total disregard for 'Mother Nature', her mother, and destroying the very wastes themselves without as much as a by-or-leave, or kiss my veritable backside. She fell upon the camp with all her fury, and like an unwanted guest, she was totally unexpected, and completely undetected by the camp's computer-driven weather station. She smashed into the flimsy prefabricated buildings with ease, egged on by her applauding, ever-watchful mother, and scattered everything before her to her outstretched and waiting winds. Everything was utterly smashed to pieces. Man and machines irrevocably destroyed beyond description and recognition. Flesh and metal was pulverised and twisted before even the most rudimentary of warnings were able to escape the camp and so alert to the outside world of the impending dangers still to come. Next, she came across a whole series of snowy mounds, cairns to the forgotten and the foolish, or merely to the intrepid stupidity of human kind. She blasted them to bits and flung the bones and pieces of mummified flesh to the heavens, all except one skull that is. For this was the monstrous cranium belonging to Baron Frankenstein's hideous, abominable creature, whose massive nodular skull was irreverently, laughably, bandied about the wastelands from snow mound to ice sheet and back again like some medieval pig's bladder. So much for the infamy of the past! Nevertheless, so much carnage for one so young, such as our developing little wind clearly was, was tiring and draining to say the very least. Close to exhaustion she sought her mother's solace and sat down by her side panting, licking her lips, calmly and quietly getting her breath back. Being taught and learning how to achieve her second wind with consummate skill. Whilst silently absorbing her mother's love and admiration. 'Mother Nature' imbued her doting daughter with hypnotic, sibilant whispers of encouragement and venom and cajoled her on to her task of mayhem and destruction. By the time our young wind had rested and calmed herself she had reached her maturity, and was even a gale whilst she slept. Mother and daughter were now no longer bound by family ties but bound by rivalries of boundless chaos and catastrophic ruination. And so, with a good swift kick up her daughter's behind 'Mother Nature', in all her fury, rose up high into the sky, pursued by her savagely beautiful sibling hot on the heels of her trailing breath, and embarked on their relentless quests for revenge. And a savage revenge lay ahead of their rampant, gleeful rampage, and in their terrible trailing wakes lay the inordinate misery for the millions who had stirred and awakened their wrath. An orgy of wanton death for all!

Over the northern ocean like dragons they roared split apart and blew their separate ways. 'Mother Nature' hurtled down to the southern hemisphere and scoured the lands and seas with a seemingly manic delight. Whilst our newly matured wind made the northern hemisphere her playground, where she schooled herself in the arts of sheer devilment and where she wreaked havoc on everything and anything that lay in her path. She crashed through the northern seas whipping up the waves to unbelievable heights never before seen by man or beast. At one point the base of the waves she created reached to the very seabed itself and purged wrecks of their bones and their souls until 'Davy Jones' locker was empty. And all of this was done in the name of fun. Sand and rock, not exposed, or having seen the light of the sun for millions, and in some cases, hundreds of millions of years, looked clean and incredibly fresh in the bright light for the first time in any living memory. And then, in the blink of an eye, it had all gone once more. Irrepressibly covered! But all this meant very little, indeed, it actually meant nothing at all to our little wind as she flew onwards searching for fresh and vulnerable victims that undoubtedly lay before her. But here she was to be disappointed. Word and warnings had now gone out across the northern and southern hemispheres and alarm bells were now ringing out loud and clear everywhere alerting all and sundry that dire mischief was in the air! But none of this was of any concern or consequence to our little wind, for with every passing second she grew in maturity and above all, in awesome strength. She powered off the northern Atlantic and she hit the North Sea furiously angry. Her ferocity was ready to explode. And then she espied her fleeing victims in the distance, coming into view on the rising waves. Hundreds of them, maybe thousands, of all shapes and sizes. Ships, all of them fleeing, in mortal fear of their lives, all steaming and powering for the cover and safety of harbour, any harbour! But little did they know (or did they?) that none of them were going to make it. They were all doomed, as were the souls of all on board. She bore down on them all with wind and water and with demonic laughter in her howling screams. And they were all hit and battered, swamped and deluged with such power and mountainous waves never before recorded in any of the illustrious annals of the sea. Vessels simply disappeared. Others fought the attacking elements as bravely as they could, but to no avail. No quarter would be given on this day.

Others were flung together with a sickening crash which could be heard even over our little wind's terrible 'whooping whoops' of victory. The twisted and tangled wreckage sank like a stone without ever a trace to come. The larger vessels fared no better, in fact their fate was to be worse all round. She caught two deep-sea ships dashing, at breakneck speed, towards the 'Shetlands' and the 'Orkney Islands', seemingly to find safe haven away from the storm that now threatened to engulf them. She wrapped her tendrils round the hull of a Norwegian cruise liner and hurled it onto the decks of a 'North Sea' ferry with sickening ease. In the seconds before they perished, victims looked with surprise and horror into each other's eyes just before they gazed into the eyes of their own individual death, as the vessels they were on exploded and momentarily illuminated the angry sky above, before they to disappeared into the watery abyss that lay waiting for them beneath their keels. And then they were no more. (Obviously such a terrible calamity, with the resulting loss of life had, to say the very least, a most serious and effect on the cruise-line industry as a whole, and it was to be many a year before it was able to report even the slightest sign of recovery!) Shetland, as well as the Orkney Islands, were swept clean of civilisation and were once again returned to the birds and to the few sheep that remained alive, and to the ruins of the past and of the present. On, and on forever on, our little wind swept down towards The English Channel causing tidal surges, as well as all manner of tidal defences against the sea to be breached wherever they lay. Seaside resorts that had stood the test of time were completely engulfed, as was any land that lay below, or slightly raised itself just above the sea's level. The emergency services everywhere were inundated with desperate pleas for help, but they too were bombarded and battered by our wind and her allies, the rain and the seas, and were rendered almost useless. Churches opened their doors for refuge only to be themselves washed away, in the sight of God, by the flood wherever the waves could swamp them. Further down the Channel she suddenly changed direction, sweeping inland at the entrance to a huge estuary, and with the bit between her teeth she charged inland for all she was worth. By now the alarm bells were ringing everywhere as people fled for cover like rats wherever they were able to, or simply cowered in garden sheds and garages, and in their motor-cars, or more sillier still, in cupboards under the stairs, and quivered and shook like jellies awaiting their particular fates, whatever they might be.

Thoroughly enjoying herself now our beautiful little wind, not long before just an 'enfant terrible', was now reaching her full devastating maturity. And as she winged her way up north, she found herself to be in possession of all her strength and vented it with arrogance and sheer disdain on anything that roused her displeasure, which in reality, was absolutely everything she came across. The 'great' metropolis, now laid waste behind her, had witnessed, had been subjected to many eventful calamities (of varying fortune) throughout its chequered past. 'Boudica', 'The Black Death', 'The Great Fire', 'The Luftwaffe', and wholesale redevelopment in the name of progress. But it had never ever before been visited by an 'Armageddon' on such a magnitude and accompanied by such a near total loss of life! But nevertheless, our gusty harpy cared little for the devastation and misery that she was indisputably causing. She was much too busy revelling in her new found enjoyment and carefree power, far too much, to worry about what were to her anyway, such minor irritations and trivialities.

On, on, and on she went, hurling herself forever northwards. On her travels the minions trailing in her wake aped and copied her infamous example by destroying the land's second metropolis (as she had done the first) by raising it to the ground, flinging its wanton destruction high into the sky in triumphant elation as the vanquished perished wholesale. But like many young and arrogant adults our little wind grew bored, ennui set in upon her all-powerful and all-consuming progress. She abated somewhat. And as she calmed down, she lessoned her speed and enjoyed the freedom of her movements, somersaulting, spiralling, rising up skywards and then plunging back down to earth. Her anger somewhat assuaged and sated.

Way behind her now all hell broke loose. Flames and water consumed the land. What was left of human life struggled to cope with the state of the devastation now swamping and threatening its very existence. And what was left of the emergency services panicked in dismay at the sorry and dauntless task now facing them 'en masse', and did what very little they could, and remained for a very long time afterwards, ineffectual to bring relief to the suffering that overwhelmed its minute by minute operations. But what, if anything, did our beautiful little wind care? What was it all to her anyway? What did anything matter to her now? She trundled up along through the middle of the land in a matter-of-fact sort of way, consequently flattening all that lay in her road, until that is, she spied the island's backbone, which suddenly seemed to offer her something fresh, challenging and new in the realms of pleasure. She craftily slowed her pace to something akin to a stiff freshening breeze, camouflaging her real intent and designs. As a result, the people of the northern lands breathed an uneasy sigh of relief and were cleverly hoodwinked. They ventured out of doors and chatted at the garden gateposts, in the shops and in the pubs, on trains and on the buses, and at the school gates too, all in hushed tones, and above all, all the time with wary, suspicious eyes, scanning the weather, searching for the telltale signs of even the slightest change in the strength of the wind or the clouds in the sky. They knew little of what fate awaited them or the dilemmas that lay in store for them all. Like the many before them, especially after an earth-shattering calamity, they believed the worst to be over now and they silently, secretly, rejoiced in their miraculous and lucky escape. And even the non-believers amongst them all privately prayed to an Almighty, thankful of their deliverance, and begged His (or Hers) merciful blessing and forgiveness on the inestimable suffering of those 'down south' still reeling under our little wind's stormy battering, and for all those (now numbering countless thousands) who had fallen and perished, never to return.

Oh dear me, how all the churches across the northern lands would have been filled to bursting point, had only Sunday come around sooner for the many millions now thinking themselves safe and free from out of harm's tentacled reach. But then it just goes to show that you never know what lies just around the corner of life. The catch phrase "We're doomed, we're doomed, I tell ye!" suddenly sprang to mind. But there was nothing remotely laughable or comic about the 'doom' that was about to fall explodingly on the timorous and unsuspecting inhabitants of Rishworth and Ripponden and their surrounding environs. They all believed to a one that everything was back to normal again. That the worst had passed them by. That they'd got away with it all unscathed, and that compared to everyone else, as well as the rest of the land as a whole, they'd got off lightly. That they'd all done rather well out of it all, and they all felt rather smug with themselves, and so they rejoiced. Little did they know or understand what now actually lay in store for them all.

It was a bright, beautiful day. A brilliant, blue sky dominated the heavens above and cheered up the people to no end. The pubs were packed to the rafters. The Conservative Club in Ripponden village was holding a family fun day and was absolutely heaving, bulging at the seams, much to the delight of the steward and his stewardess. Luckily for its patrons (young and old alike) the 'Royd' and 'Stony' lanes were close at hand and would proffer salvation when the time came. The atmosphere all around was electric and crackled with pent-up excitement. It was like the 'Mad Friday' of all 'Mad Fridays'! Yes, and so it was. It was indeed the day before the Sabbath, and if anything, it should have been the churches that should have been 'packed to the gills' not the ale houses and bars! And yet those lonely and neglected places of worship remained largely empty and devoid of human life, except for a very few 'true' believers who huddled somewhat closer together to savour every ounce of religious comfort. But then, for all the others, for what they were about to receive, maybe it was the 'hop' and the 'grain' that in reality would actually prove more beneficial at the beginning of their journey to heaven (knows where), than the grape of the reverential holy wine! And furthermore besides, pizza and chips at the bar, tasted so much better than the 'Holy Wafer' could ever hope to taste altogether! But I digress. Forgive me please. For by now, our little wind was parched and her terrible thirst was about to be slaked in the near total devastation, and in the flesh, blood and bone of her awaiting flock. But as yet they were still unsuspecting and remained completely in the dark as to their respective fates. For the present moment, our little wind lay many miles distant to the south (but she was now travelling fast) and her victims still had some precious time left yet in which to enjoy their wine, women and song, before their deaths came-a-calling.

'The Boothwood' and 'The Malt House' (they were to be the lucky ones in what was still to come) were enjoying an exceptional summer's afternoon trade. As was 'The Cinnamon Lounge', reaping the rewards of its traditional Indian buffet. Further along the 'Oldham Road', the 'Silk Mill', and, a little further on, 'The Fox', were absolutely jam-packed to the very rafters. Even the 'Green Door' café had opened its doors to hopefully capitalise on what appeared to be a happy and joyous occasion. Its proprietor ever pleasant and accommodating as always, and ever tireless. The local tapas bar, 'Elgatto Negro', that splendid den of small portions, very ordinary cuisine, and inflated prices, had opened its doors to suck into its tiny bowels the hungry, but more importantly, those who had more money in their pockets than they had common sense.

And so, as we complete our little tour of the surrounding area, our little wind had suddenly and quite ecstatically picked up the victims' scent and her nostrils flared in joyous expectation. The little zephyrs, that gently danced and played around the feet and the bodies of the blissfully ignorant, and which rose into the surrounding environs many, many miles distant from her searching eyes, now sent their mischievous message to their mighty, gusty mistress, in dutiful compliance. (The game was now up! Their fate sealed!) And she, in her turn, responded to her minions by screeching and screaming her acknowledgement, and by rearing up in frightful, hellish fury, full of renewed purpose and vigour. And so off she went again, on her adventures of rampage and wanton annihilation. She chased and harried sheep and cow in fields, (the numerous horses in her path smelt the wind of her coming and bolted for cover and safety wherever they could find it) and on catching them up she gleefully flung them hundreds of feet into the air then left them to their respective fates. An already edgy populace gave warnings at the first hints of her second coming, and in towns and villages alike, the Second World War sirens sounded their alarm far and wide, and their wailings sent shivers down the spines of all who heard them. Their dire songs travelled along with, and were woven in between the awesome gusts of wind to unsuspecting and disbelieving ears. At first, in both Rishworth and Ripponden, no one heard a thing. The warnings went unheeded. It was only in the various states of inebriation that patrons drinking and carousing in 'The Fox', and only some of those who'd ventured outside to smoke a cigarette, all smiles and all jokes, who suddenly caught the slightest of whiffs and the briefest of notes upon the still distant wind and who, in sudden abject panic, suddenly flew back inside and raised the alarm and gave a garbled warning of the imminent danger to come. The pub was instantly filled with the screams of panic-stricken, terrified women, as man after man yelled, "Fire! Fire! Run for your life! Every man for himself!" Instant, total mayhem. In no time at all the pub emptied, exploded onto the 'Oldham Road' and what then ensued was utter confusion and chaos amidst all the shouting, screaming and frantic calls of help to goodness only knows who. The panic was instantaneous and infectious and spread throughout the entire area faster than the blink of an eye and was truly marvellous to behold. Ripponden village hadn't seen so many of its inhabitants spilling out onto its main street (and such dynamic movement hither and thither) since the celebrations of 'November

1918 and V.E.Day. In fact, motorcars came to a halt despite all their toot tooting. There was one stupid collision just outside 'The Co-operative' building, which brought any hope of further movement to an abrupt and definite stop. Men and women clambered over the bonnets of cars, much to the boiling rage of their respective owners. But in the end, there was very little that anyone could actually do about it. The throng was now blind to any and every kind of reason. Children screamed as they do when they are uncontrollably excited. Others, more frighteningly, became detached from their parents and wailed blue murder in sheer terror of the situation unfolding before their very eyes. Mums and Dads desperately, frantically, tried to relocate their lost bantlings, and some, in their motionless callings out, were violently shoved to one side or were simply trampled under fleeing feet. It was all a spontaneous reaction to, and a result, of the terror that now pervaded the very air that they were now trying to breathe. The fear was like a drug! No! No, it wasn't at all! The fear was like the deadliest of germs, and it was murderously infectious! Bodies that had gone to the ground were helplessly pulverised with no attempt whatsoever to offer aid or assistance. They were simply rendered 'goners' and that was that. Entire families wiped out in the blink of an eye! And then there came a noise. A terrible noise. Like no other ever heard before. The people were suddenly transfixed. It was like something straight out of a film. All those who heard it were aghast, wide-eyed, goggle-eyed, mouths agape and yet the strangest thing about it all was the complete silence that it was heard in. The screaming and the yelling had now all momentarily stopped. You could have heard a veritable pin drop to the ground. The whole scene was pure tragicomedy. There then came an even bigger noise, a noise much more ominous, a noise which blasted the stillness to smithereens and stirred the stillness into one of instant human motion. And then once again panic and fear reigned supreme. Utter mayhem ensued. Above the screams, the shouts, and all the yelling, all that now was heard were the terrible screeches of the wind. No! No I say! Not just any old 'wind'! But 'our' little wind! And it was heard clearly, and distinctly, coming and relentlessly heading their way! For yes it was indeed she, in all her indomitable glory, that was now wreaking a terrible, savage revenge, for one last victorious time before she returned to the (now dear longed for) northern wastes. There to be re-united with her darling, doting mother, and where she could then rest, grow and mature into her womanhood. And there to mate with a lesser, but nonetheless, suitable 'gust' and to become a 'mother wind' of all mother winds. But that was still some little time off as yet. It was not to be just yet—not quite just yet! For in the meantime she had just one more little mission to fulfil. One more little trick up her sleeve. Our 'little' wind's final coup-de-grâce was to be at the expense of all the life that she could find within the 'Ryburn Valley'. The noises that had been clearly heard just moments before, all along the Oldham Road and along the entire valley, noises that had struck a fearful chill into the hearts and bones of all those who heard their strident sounds, were, in fact, the shockwaves of the nearby reservoirs being cracked open, and their sudden catastrophic failure, as our little wind rammed their now mountainous waters against their once solid walls and split them asunder! And how on earth had she achieved all this with such apparent ease?

She had roared onto the hills and moors past the little town of Littleborough flattening The White House hostelry as she crested the summit. And once there, she scented water, and lots of it, as she hurtled across the tops of the moors with the bit of mischief firmly between teeth. The 'Blackstone Edge' reservoir was emptied and dumped unceremoniously onto The Turvin Road, which was subsequently washed away without a trace of its past existence. Such was the all-encompassing tour de force of our awesome little wind compared with the utterly pathetic little 'tour' that had previously slogged along that very same road not all that long before. But nothing now would pass along that road for a very long time, save only ghosts and wandering memories. She now rallied all her strength and surged over the bleak hilly moorland with a renewed sense of purpose and vigour ideally suited for a last hurrah. Her strength was such that she stripped the heather and the fern from the heath by their very roots (never seen or known before) as she blasted everything to kingdom come. Cows and sheep, cowering by dry-stone walls, were flung willy-nilly thousands of feet into the sky never to be seen again. In fact, she hit them so hard that she fleeced them raw of both hide and wool! And then, a little way in the distance, she saw the beginnings of the 'Baitings' reservoir and she roared forth towards it like no other wind had ever done before, or since, with pure wickedness in her eyes. As she passed over the water, she whipped up the already considerable wavelets into a watery frenzy and sent them chasing one another towards the dam wall where they crashed against it in all their pent-up fury cascading themselves over its stone lip down the hundreds of feet to the valley below. She flung herself down with falling water, then with the sheer mischief in her rage-filled eyes, she suddenly rose again and sucked herself high up into the sky and somersaulted back upon herself and took another run at the 'Baitings' reservoir. The air surrounding the entire area suddenly found itself in a vacuum and in an instant the angry water found itself becalmed, astonishingly enough, like a lily pond! The gentle couple who lived in the house adjacent to the dam wall, on the Rochdale Road, left off cowering behind the flimsy protection of their living room curtains and beheld the perfectly still waters in wide-eyed amazement, unable to comprehend the meaning of the sight now being played out before their very eyes. Believing, quite rightly, and indeed, innocently, that all imminent danger had now passed, they tentatively ventured outside by way of their front door and stood hand in hand upon their drive way and stared out across the dam and over its glass-like body of water, to the trees along its far edge, and then to the surrounding hills and above all, to the soaring sky that was mirrored ghost-like in the water's reflection. They both breathed easily and smiled tenderly into one another's eyes. It was a smile that had taken many years of practice to perfect. And for just a brief moment, all seemed well with the world. Until, that is, our little wind turned and took another turn at the reservoir as the becalmed waters awaited the touch of her terrifying tendrils once more. And she now let rip with all the strength that she could muster. Our gentle couple were just about to turn away and go back inside their house for that cup of tea that would have put the world to rights when the screaming, the awful screeching sounds, (that actually sounded like a jet-airliner gone terribly wrong) filled the air and their ears with a fearful din that rooted them to the spot and froze the very marrow in their bones. The woman suddenly screamed (which almost killed her spouse stone dead in sudden fright) as she saw the mountainous wall of water surging towards them, rising clear into the air above. In a fit of pure terror, she turned and ran wailing into the supposed safety of her abode. Her husband, in a confused state of delirium, turned to follow his doting mate, but instead of actually following in her footsteps, he turned in the opposite direction and ran slap-bang into the cast-iron pole of the garden washing line and knocked himself clean out, and with a heavy thud he dropped to the ground like a ten-ton rock as though he'd been shot dead by a bullet from a gun. Missing her darling spouse she suddenly re-emerged from the house in search of her life-long love, and when she saw him lying prostrate, and twitching, an even louder blood-curdling scream rent the air as the water and the wind burst open the dam wall with a crack of thunder, which, to all who heard it, was like the very crack of doom itself! In a blind panic she grabbed a firm hold of her beloved's leg and pulled for all she was worth but only managed to pull his shoe off just as the water's wave was cascading down upon the scene. Shoe in hand, she made it back upstairs and hid underneath the matrimonial bed, curled up in the foetal position sobbing for all she was worth uncontrollably, kissing her spouse's shoe as though it were some long-lost child suddenly reunited to her. Outside, suddenly coming round to his senses, he opened his eyes to a fury of wind and water that was just about to overwhelm him completely, and so clinically dispatch him from his mortal coil, and indeed, which was going to be his last living sight on this earth, and so his final words were befittingly poignant.

"Where's my shoe? I've lost my shoe!" And that was pathetically that.

Our little wind blasted apart the dam wall as though it were made of nothing more than straw and twigs. Stone and concrete were hurled away at astonishing speeds and distances in an arch of sheer beauty. Chunks of all imaginable sizes were flung outwards at an incredible velocity, killing and flattening anything that stood in its path. Obliteration everywhere. The water, so long a subdued prisoner behind its barricade, suddenly exploded into life in joyous excitement and enthusiasm, and with its new found friend and partner 'our little wind' now holding its many hands, burst forth in an awesome exuberance ready to embrace everything it met on its journey of discovery. And so off they went together, hands in many hands, lost friends seemingly reunited. Their glorious malevolence now girding one another completely, they were ready to achieve new heights of infamy. Their song of celebration was heard far and wide and brought forth curses from all those who now heard its dulcet tones.

The water and the wind thundered and churned their way down the valley with extraordinary speed (farms and homesteads that were dotted along its sides were erased from the face of the earth in the blink of an eye) and they very soon came upon the trembling waters of the smaller 'Ryburn Reservoir' in a matter of seconds. Its waters were sucked up en masse and dumped down, with colossal force, at the reservoir's dam wall, which cracked open and was accompanied by the delightful sounds likened to a hard-boiled egg being broken, or dropped onto something firm. Its once hard outer shell now totally compromised forever. And its breech and subsequent failure was hardly heard by anyone at all!

The combined forces of wind and water now ripped down the valley, its momentum unstoppable, scouring clean the entire valley before it, wiping out men, women and children, not to mention, all forms of wildlife and livestock. But they (the animals) could at least start again with 'Mother Nature's' blessing. The other forms of life, well, they would be left to their own devices to survive as best they could.

The deluge hit the Cinnamon Lounge Indian restaurant with all the force of an atomic (Vindaloo) bomb. Its deadly waters, now containing the flotsam and jetsam of its carnage, flattened the restaurant, including all the buildings immediately adjacent to it, down to their very foundations. Gone forever, never again to be rebuilt. Shattered stumps of stone, nothing more. The massive wave now carried on regardless and slammed into the opposite hillside with a sickening force and momentarily shuddered like a gigantic jelly before rebounding upon itself seemingly to regroup before making its inexorable way along the 'Ryburn Valley' with unbridled force. Pummelling and punching its way towards the village of Ripponden. The said population now knew of its coming and fled before it whither they could. Their only hope now of salvation was their being able to attain higher ground. But their best efforts were entirely confounded by the insane panic and chaos that now gripped the populace—not to mention the abandoned vehicles that clogged all the roads, which in reality were their only means of affecting a viable escape. In other words, they were doomed to face a dreadful death.

The wind (our little beauty) now raced ahead of the surging and enveloping waters and caused mayhem and blue murder all along the 'Oldham Road', tossing people, regardless of who or what they were, (and indeed some of them fully deserved a good tossing!) as well as their vehicles high up into the sky. One such victim, cowering behind the steering wheel of her wonderful high performance, and ridiculously expensive box of tricks, but which was now rendered utterly useless, stared all about her, her eyes agog, darting hither and thither. The huge wad of grubby banknotes, that she held between her sweating palms, were sucked out of the window like cheap confetti as the vehicle she was quaking in was plucked up and whisked away on torrents of wind like a piece of random straw. They were spun around like a merry-go-round out of control, with such a phenomenal speed that her goggle-eyes actually started out of her head and she saw no more, but all the time whining like a stricken beast and stupidly pressing the horn of her car as she flew through the air towards her inevitable death. The vehicle was catapulted across what was left of the village rooftops and slammed into the spire of 'St Bartholomew's' church, which subsequently crumpled under the impact like crumbly 'Wensleydale' cheese. Seconds later, the waters engulfed everything, including the ancient 'Bridge Inn' and its Packhorse Bridge, thus wiping out centuries of history and tradition, off cultural maps and out of memories alike, as the tidal-wave continued to surge down the valley, all the time running, imperceptibly, out of steam and momentum. Not that that bequeathed any real salvation for those still fleeing before its horrendous devilry. But by the time it had reached 'Triangle' it had, in reality, flogged itself to death and was now nothing more than an exceptional flood. And even though there were still more victims to be claimed, mainly the inquisitive, the plain stupid and the elderly, the power of the now weakening wind and water had considerably abated. In fact, what had once been 'our' little wind, had now ran completely out of breath, and for this particular visit she had most definitely done her very worst. In a matter of fact, she was now breathless! And as quickly as her awesome strength and power had come than, it had gone and waned away to nothing. And what was once a mighty force to be reckoned with, and above all feared, was once again rendered nothing more annoying than wilful wisps of air. In reality, she was now a spent force and it was time for her to go back home to the lands of the northern wastes. To the place where she could seek shelter and rest in peace and quiet. To the lands where she could re-group and gather her strength once more. To where she could and would seek her mother's love and comforting embrace. In time she would recover. And like her mother before her, she would find a mate and breed afresh and thus, be herself: the mother of other great winds to come. But she would live to fight another day. However, the devastation that she and her watery ally had left behind would take many, many years to allay. And even when all the physical reminders had been swept away and removed, the psychological remembrances would remain and scar the memory right up until death, and indeed, sometimes beyond.

But generally, on the whole, people are good and more often than not, kind hearted towards the suffering of others that they see before them. Ripponden and Rishworth and their surrounding communities all rallied round and pulled together, and as one they buried their dead and their guilt. They prayed together and sang hymns together and nursed their injured and soothed their young and vulnerable. But was it all enough? Could that ever be enough? New memorials would now be needed, commissioned, and duly erected, as annual remembrance of recent past events became the respected focal point for communal grief and sorrow. But how long would they, and how long could they remember for? Could there ever be an allotted length of time in which to grieve and learn? And would they, and could they learn from their past mistakes? Although indelibly embedded in the consciousness and sub-consciousness of all those who survived the calamitous events that very nearly wiped them out, how soon would they succumb to the joys and sheer thrill of being alive again? How soon, after having survived all the odds stacked against them, would the joys of life dim their recent recollections and thus assuage their fears, and so weaken their resolve? And what of the young still to be born, would they, in future, heed the lessons of the past? Or would they to prostrate themselves before the pleasures of wanton greed and negligent exploitation, and go the way of their forefathers? Would they learn or would they to deserve to perish? Whatever the answer, they wouldn't have all that long to decide. For the 'old' earth was changing fast, grown sick and tired of neglect. Things were definitely changing, and damage limitation was now the way forward, if survival was indeed meant to be. But they would have to hurry! For many, many miles away, miles from the nearest civilisation, in the lands of the northern wastes, a little wisp of a breathless, adolescent wind began to stretch her limbs and find her feet, and playfully toyed with the skull of a gigantic polar bear, that lay atop of a snowy mound. Tossing it up high into the sky, up into the star-spangled night sky above her. And when she grew up (and she was growing up very fast) whom would she choose and take to be her friend and companion to see and travel the world?

THE END
COMPLETED TYPING ON 7th APRIL 2016

Pillars of Sand! (Fred Walker!)

He woke up early, much too early to be of any use, too early for his own good. He knew straight away that he wouldn't be able to get back to sleep. So he decided to get up, although he didn't really want to. He turned off his back and onto his side and rolled out of bed like a beached and blubbery whale (although if the truth be known there wasn't an ounce of blubber on him, in fact his body was quite the opposite, a veritable 'Fred Astaire' of a man!) and huffed and puffed and groaned his way onto his stocking feet. He'd not slept well at all. In fact, he'd tossed and turned for half the night, and just when he found himself drifting off to sleep, he suddenly found himself waking up again. Frustratingly, wide-awake. His mind full of all sorts of stuff, jumbled thoughts and memories. Consequently, he woke up tired, more tired in fact than when he'd finally retired for the night. This was not a very good start to the day. His day. The big day. And now, shuffling along the brightly sunlit landing towards the bathroom, with the night's lack of sleep stuck glutinously in the corners of his eyes, he found himself to be somewhat angry, irritatingly annoyed with himself for no apparent reason that he could quite put his finger on. He stood before the toilet more closely nowadays, his legs almost touching the sides of the bowl, a sure sign of his growing older and weakening prostrate, ready to relieve the aching sensation that he'd awoken to. He passed water with great pleasure, almost ecstatic relief. He gazed down and watched intently as the yellowish stream of liquid churned the toilet water into a mass of frothing bubbles. The last drop dripped, and the immediate feeling of joyous relief was shaken away and done with for the moment. He turned away from the toilet and stepped over to the sink to wash his hands and peered into the bathroom cabinet mirror. He stared back at his image and believed that he'd actually aged quite well. But in truth, he had not aged that well at all. However, he always managed to brush that fact to one side without any real bother. As he contorted his face first one way then the other, opening his eyes

56

as wide as they would go then squinting them almost shut, his tongue suddenly found the nagging sore situated in the roof of his mouth and he winced back at his reflection. He opened his mouth and tried to locate the source of the pain but, his eyesight not being what it was, he saw nothing untoward even in the bright light streaming into the bathroom. Had he taken the time to find his spectacles he would clearly have seen the sore that had been irritating him for so long now. But just at that moment he couldn't be bothered. So, he made a mental note to get it sorted out as soon as possible. He stared back at his reflection. Yes, he thought to himself contentedly, "I don't look a day over fifty-five! And a damn good-looking fifty-five at that!" But in truth the reality was very, very different. He looked very much like a man in his late seventies, indeed, he looked worn, weathered and ragged around the edges, aged. And aged very badly at that. His reflection knew that. It knew the truth. But his eyes didn't. They masked the lie and hoodwinked him completely. Indeed, there now were only two mirrors left in the whole house. True, there had been more at one time, a lot more in fact. But when his wife had died, he had decimated them in the aftermath, and now there were just two of them. Yes, of course he agreed, and would always accept that he'd grown considerably older, (like everybody else that he knew and saw all around him) but he'd aged well, like a quality bottle of wine, a vintage malt whisky. He looked into the slightly bemused reflection that hovered before him and winked at his self as if to say

"Aye aye mate, what's your game then? What are you up to now?" And as the wink came straight back at him, he gave the world a wry smile.

But as already stated, the lie concerning his actual appearance belonged only to himself. He couldn't fool the world for the world knew differently. Everyone else saw the truth and knew a completely different Fred Walker. His whole face was heavily lined and sagged here and there in bags, folds and crevices of flabby pallid skin. Its unhealthy pallor at times changed chameleon-like, varying from puce to a blood-pumping red, depending on what and how much he'd been drinking that particular day or night. The blotches came and went like scudding clouds, there one minute and gone the next. His eyes, the windows to his soul, were now always partially bloodshot, and what remained of the whites of those eyes were little more than a watery, yellowish liquid, so much so that his pupils appeared to be forever swimming within them. The two front teeth that he'd somehow managed to retain, like a pair of defiant tusks, were now nothing more than yellow spikes, nicotine stained over the many years of his smoking, protruded somewhat obscenely whenever he opened his mouth or laughed out loud, and Fred Walker laughed a lot, almost all of the time at anything and everything. True, it must be said, that for a man of his age he sported a very good head of hair, but that to, like his two front teeth, through all the years of prolonged contact with tobacco, had surrendered to the yellowish tint of a heavy smoker. It was combed straight back from the forehead and plastered to his skull with his favourite hair tonic, 'bay rum', which he purchased from 'Boots' the chemist. But the crowning glory of Fred Walker's face was undoubtedly a nose that seemed to explode out from the surface of his face. It was his most notable feature. It was deeply purple and heavily veined, bulbous and veritably throbbing as if it had a life all of its very own. Altogether it was the telltale drinker's nose. And Fred Walker would be the first to admit that he had always been a heavy drinker. He was still a heavy drinker! That was something that would never change, moreover, that was something he couldn't change even if he wanted to, and he didn't. Like the cigarettes that he still smoked with great relish, it, the drink, would surely one day very soon, be the death of him. But he being the man he undoubtedly was (seemingly invincible!) Fred hoped and believed that that day was still a very long way away as yet. But days are fleeting and pass all too quickly, even the Fred Walker days!

Once he'd shaved, (the most satisfying of all his bodily functions, for he couldn't even begin to contemplate facing the beginnings of a day with the stubble of the night before clouding his face) he combed his hair, and when he was suitably dressed he made his way downstairs to the kitchen. He filled the kettle and then turned on the radio, both done automatically and without conscious effort or thought. Whilst the tea was mashing and his breakfast was cooking, he settled down at the kitchen table. The kitchen was warm and cosy, it was his favourite room in the small cottage, and he spent most of his time there since his wife had died very nearly ten years before. It caught and trapped the sun for most of the day and if it ever felt cold, then he soon warmed it up by switching on the under-floor heating. In reality he had abandoned the rest of the house to the past and most of it was little used by him now. Especially as he had to keep an ever-watchful eye on the money coming in and the money going out much more closely these days. He had a strict budget nowadays. And since his wife had died, he had implemented a whole range of cost-cutting measures. He had closed down the back bedroom and turned the radiator down to a low setting, with just enough heat to keep it from freezing on a bitter winter's night. He hardly ever entered into it nowadays unless to dump something unwanted, or unused in it, something that he didn't want to throw away quite just yet, something that he just might need a little later on. He'd also gotten rid of the spare single bed as soon as his wife was gone. No one had ever slept in it anyway, and he certainly didn't want anyone to stay now. Moreover, they had never had children, well none that the other ever knew about, so closing down the spare room didn't matter at all. And the little dining room, adjacent to the lounge and kitchen, was now nothing more than a pass-through room. Its once expensive oak-leaf dining table, a repository for anything from unopened junk mail to no longer used or worn items of clothing. The lounge, fronting the main road, housed the only television (now very rarely watched, or indeed, switched on), and a once very expensive pair of Italian two-seater settees, and greatly deliberated over, like the television, were never used if at all ever sat upon. So it was the bedroom, the bathroom, and the kitchen, and in the summer (weather permitting) the tiny rear garden, that formed the extent of his entire life and had done so since his late wife had so unexpectedly passed away. His life, like everything else within its compass, had significantly shrunk, as had his wants, needs and desires.

With great relish he ate his boiled eggs and toasted soldiers. He still loved dipping them into a runny yolk and savouring the taste of egg and toasted bread within his mouth. Then sitting back on the high-backed stool, he poured himself another cup of tea and contemplated the funeral that now lay before him. He always drank a pot of leaf-tea first thing of a morning. It set the day off just right. It set him off just right as well. It was akin to his morning shave, a daily necessity, and he simply couldn't do without one and the other to start the day. He stared out of the kitchen window into his little garden which was now flooded with brilliant early morning sunshine. He listened to the birds singing and chirruping away to themselves through the open kitchen door, each and every one of them getting on with their busy little lives, all of them oblivious to Fred and his head so crammed full of thoughts. For a brief moment the hint of a smile could be discerned playing at the corners of his mouth, puckering the saggy jowls that hung there, and there was most definitely a little twinkle to his eyes. Yes, it was indeed going to be a most beautiful summer's day, one of the very best. A beautiful day for a funeral.

Suited and booted—to use the vulgar parlance—he left the cottage, with plenty of time to spare, sporting his R.A.F. regimental tie. The one thing he was still immensely proud of wearing. Kept spotlessly clean in a cellophane sleeve inside his wardrobe. Pristine! It was his one and only treasured possession. And whenever he happened to wear it, his shoulders automatically squared themselves across and he rose a good inch in height. Just as Fred was about to close the front door, he suddenly paused on the threshold, one foot on the door mat just outside the front door and the other on the door mat just inside the tiny hallway, a hallway that smelt strongly of home and of everything he knew and cared about. He was momentarily transfixed, rooted to the spot as they say, just as the old mantle clock struck its 'Westminster' chime and then, after a brief pause, promptly struck the hour of eight o' clock in the morning. Its sounds always reminded him of his childhood and the very happiest of all the many memories that were stored within his head. Especially hot, lazy, summer afternoons, in the old, big house that belonged to his beloved grandmother when there was nothing to do but sit quietly and daydream the minutes and hours away. When there was nothing to do but sit quietly and sip your ice-cold lemonade, sucking the ice cubes at the end and crunching them between your teeth whilst watching the dust motes dancing and playing for fun in the rays of the sun powering through the brilliantly white net curtains. A summer's Sunday and all the shops shut up tight like 'bible-basher's' blouse! As its sounds faded into the next hour, he left the house (for good this time unbeknown to him) without even an inkling that he'd never hear it sing its chimes again. He stood for a moment on the driveway by the side of his motor car and stared intently at the cottage. He gazed at the doorway, the windows, towards the guttering and the drainpipes, and at the chimney up upon the heavily stone-tiled roof and finally, at the very stones themselves that made up the building, as though casting the images to his memory forever. He stared long and hard. There was an uneasy churning deep within him and a feeling of uneasiness griped his stomach. And then from nowhere a near overwhelming sense of trepidation threatened to overcome him completely. He shivered right down to the marrow in his bones as though someone had just passed over his grave. He shook the shiver and foreboding away like a dog shaking the shower from its coat, and then suddenly annoyed with himself he climbed, without more ado, into his motorcar and sat behind the steering wheel and realised that there were tears in his eyes. He'd actually been crying. He couldn't, for the life of him, fathom out what on earth had happened. What on earth had caused him to cry in the first place? He felt totally disconcerted. Unnerved to the extent that his hands were shaking uncontrollably and the palms of his hands were sweating profusely. When eventually he calmed himself down somewhat, he reasoned that it was all down to the impending funeral. The funeral of his comrade and life-long friend. Yes! It was the funeral, Dennis's funeral! Indeed it had to be the funeral, it couldn't be anything else after all, now could it?

Fred had met Dennis a good two years at least before the outbreak of war in 1939. In actual fact they had known of each other's existence, as casual acquaintances, for a good deal longer than that. But not as friends, and never with a thought regards one another. At first their paths simply did not cross. And when they did meet, it was in a public library of all places in the early summer of 1937. In fact, it was the library in 'Sowerby Bridge' situated close by the slow-moving river 'Calder'. On that day their friendship was forged on the anvil of external events and upon situations way beyond their control and comprehension. For far away in central Europe and the Far East, peoples and their ideologies were surfing on the crest of a wave that would lead to their ultimate destruction, and to the deaths of the innocent and the naïve like Fred and Dennis, little lives in a big wide world.

Libraries were very different back then. They were valued and esteemed to a far greater extent than they are today. They were the fonts of all knowledge, repositories of learning and the means of raising oneself out of the gutter and onto the ladder of greater things. They gave hope to those who wanted to strive and improve their miserable lives and put within their grasp the seemingly unattainable. For one thing they were quiet! One could digest countless snippets of wisdom and absorb the millions of facts that enveloped the thirsty for knowledge without interruption. Back then one could mull over the very greatest of writings without the slightest of disruptions. Noise would not be tolerated! Rules were rules and were obeyed to the strict letter of the law. The homeless and the smelly were 'booted' out before they could fall asleep in the free warmth! Chatterboxes and those on a mission of assignation were summarily frogmarched from behind the towering shelves (ever so quietly of course) to the main door and ejected with great aplomb. Librarians back then, like their teacher colleagues, were the local community's municipal gods and were to be feared and respected if seldom ever loved or revered. Parents, especially mothers, (unlike mothers today) would never have allowed their children to run around, let alone run riot, in the open spaces and beckoning bookshelves, as if it were little more than a corporation playground. Children didn't scream or bellow out aloud much to the general amusement of their owners and of those around them. Moreover, library users never engaged in lengthy conversations with the librarians serving them as though they were conversing with some long-lost friend and wished the whole world to share in it with them. Heated discussions, the taking and making of telephone calls, argument and disagreement, inane gossip and whispered words loud enough to be heard even across the densest of shelves, and goodness only knows what else, would never ever have occurred back then, in 1937, when Fred and Dennis bumped into one another. No! Not at all! Back then libraries were principled, they were the bastions of silence, reading and knowledge, the places of learning and understanding. Above all they were the places that contained the stillness of time, and never changed. Places where the only words that were ever spoken were couched in sibilant whispers, but above all, they were the places if you were very, very crafty indeed, where you went to keep warm, and doze undisturbed on a cold wet winter's day!

He put the motor car into gear and carefully edged off the driveway and onto the main road and began his journey to the 'Park Wood Crematorium' in 'Elland', deep in contemplation. A million and one different things seemed to be buzzing around his mind all at once, and yet there wasn't one clearly distinct thought that he could actually pin down. The air inside of his motor car was stuffy and decidedly stale and used. He let the both of the front windows right down and the early morning fresh air flooded the cabin and suddenly cleared his mind of all the buzzing-bees of mixed up thought. He lit himself a cigarette as he turned at the milestone and charged down the 'Elland Road', commonly known as 'Ripponden Bank'. He still foolishly believed that a good 'head-of-steam' (increased speed to you and I) made it easier for the engine to climb the tortuously steep and seemingly relentless hill that lay ahead. He always enjoyed his first morning cigarette. He liked to savour its taste and aroma. It usually made him feel really good. But not this one. Not this time. This one tasted and smelt annoyingly foul and he angrily, carelessly even, flicked it out of the window to goodness knows where. The sore in his mouth made him wince and he couldn't help his tongue finding it, repeatedly, like finding a broken tooth or a missing filling. On the way back home, after the funeral, he'd call in at the 'Brig Royd' surgery and make an appointment to see his doctor right away, get it sorted out, once and for all. He made a mental note.

It was a truly beautiful 'Calderdale' morning. The valleys and the rolling hills stunningly beautiful in the slightly hazy early morning sunshine. It was glorious to be alive on such a morning like this. He turned the car radio (which was never on louder than a murmur in any case) completely off. He didn't wish to hear any other sound other than the rushing of air past his ears and into the motor car's interior. He positively rolled along past the 'Spring Rock' public house, past a row of quite quaint looking stone-built cottages and on along the deserted road eventually passing 'The Sportsman Inn' without anything really of any consequence lodged inside his mind, especially not the impending funeral that was before him. The rest of his journey proceeded without anything untoward occurring, and eventually he turned a sharp left off the 'Park Road', his being now in 'Elland', into and onto the driveway of the 'Park Wood' crematorium. He was now feeling decidedly uneasy. And it showed. He, unusually for him, dithered as to where to park the motor car. He reversed twice and failed, he revved the engine needlessly making one hell of a racket in the deathly silence of the place, and he even went much too near to another parked car forcing him to pull out and start all over again, causing him to swear and blaspheme much too loudly for his own salvation. After he'd parked the 'bloody thing' somewhat nervously, and rather cack-handedly, he switched off the engine with a huge sigh of relief and lit himself another cigarette. And there he stayed and smoked his cigarette until he had calmed down and suitably composed himself.

Entering the front of the building he made his way straight to the gentleman's toilet, (it was a building that he had become very familiar with over recent years).

And once safely inside he carefully checked his image thoroughly in the mirror above the washbasin making sure that everything was spick and span and as it should be for such an occasion. Satisfied with his dress he fastidiously combed his hair and when done and when everything was as it should be, he left the room ready to face what now lay before him. And so it was with a great sense of trepidation that he re-entered the crematorium. The antechamber, or entrance hall, was now completely lit by blazing sunlight that swamped the entire space. It was bright, airy, fresh smelling (thank god) and above all, clean. Spotlessly clean, brilliantly clean, and far too clean for its own good, or anybody else's for that matter. So clean in fact that it made a person feel decidedly uneasy and out of place. It appeared utterly sterile. No single germ could ever dare hope to survive its sparkle and shine. And what's more, its sterility irritated him still further and soured his mood to the point that his stare could have curdled milk at one-hundred paces. He crossed the floor (passing the chapel) and entered into the adjoining waiting area set aside for the relatives and friends of the deceased. And although the blue fabric covered chairs looked positively comfortable in the extreme, he decided to remain standing on the matching blue pile carpet. He was in fact the first to arrive to his old friend's funeral. He was pleased about that, and he felt relieved that he wouldn't have to make an awkward entrance when all eyes would be upon him. Suddenly, and from nowhere in particular, an innocuous piped music seemed to buzz ever so softly all around the room like an unseen insect and it enveloped him completely, it came from goodness only knows where, and it was only faintly audible above the soft and gentle hum of hidden and seemingly distant machinery. He couldn't spot the whereabouts of the concealed speakers for love nor money, although he scanned every conceivable nook and cranny and so after a little while he gave up looking. And just in time. For as he gazed out of the big glass window, he saw the first cars of the mourners arriving, soon followed by Dennis himself. He quickly composed himself, straightening his tie and polishing his shoes on the back of his trouser legs, and then braced himself ready for action. Within a matter of minutes, the waiting room was full of people standing, and seated. However, he held his ground and remained standing by the entrance to the room. A discreet, and yet indistinct murmur suddenly filled the entire room and drowned out the background music. Fred talked and chatted to numerous people. A few of them he liked and might (on a good day) have called his friends. But most of the people that he conversed with were little more than general acquaintances, and more than just a few of them he didn't downright like at all! But for the sake of propriety he shook all the hands that were offered to him and made all the necessary small talk when it was appropriate. Then, after about twenty minutes or so the room was brought to sudden and deathly silence as the chief mourner duly announced that it was time for them all to make their way into the chapel. It was time for Dennis's funeral service to begin. The brief movement of people from the waiting room across the antechamber and into the chapel was solemn and dignified as befitting the moment and executed in complete silence. Like the rest of the building, the chapel was brilliantly illuminated by the summer sunshine streaming in through the modern, yet decorative, stained glass windows. And the air within the room was growing hotter and hotter by the minute. As Fred walked down the centre aisle, he reckoned that the atmosphere would soon be stuffy and unbearable and he became uneasy and decidedly uncomfortable even before he'd seated himself. However, his thoughts were soon elsewhere, for as the mourners in front of him peeled away left and right, he saw his friend. For there, in all its crowning glory, lying in state atop a plinth-like bier was the coffin awaiting them all. The last throw of the dice before oblivion! The rest of the mourners made their way to their appropriate seats accompanied by the sounds of concealed organ music that was both nondescript yet reverentially formal. And as the mourners seated themselves with as little fuss and noise as humanly possible and then adjusted both themselves and their somewhat tight and formal dress, the organ music abruptly stopped and the regimental band of the R.A.F. struck up the theme tune of 'The Dambusters'. Fred raised his eyes from the floor and his gaze was met by that of Dennis himself whose photographic portrait, placed just before his coffin, was looking straight back at him. Fred smiled and nodded back towards the image of his once great friend. His best mate in life. But above all, his comrade in war and peace. Fred had been invited to say a few words, memories of Dennis, of their friendship, that sort of thing, but he'd categorically refused. He'd always hated that sort of thing. It had always made him feel incredibly uncomfortable, and although he had at first given the suggestion long and hard consideration in the end, he'd respectfully, but adamantly, refused. He wasn't at all a competent speaker, and as he'd mulled it over and over in his mind, he'd grown more and more terrified at the prospect of fluffing his lines and making a complete and utter fool of himself. No! He quickly decided that he wasn't going to say a word. He'd leave all that sort of thing to others better suited than himself. And anyway, he hated funerals, detested them, simply because he couldn't handle them at all. In fact, he hardly ever went to any of them. He didn't know how to act properly, didn't know what to say or do, but above all, he couldn't cope with the emotional side of it all, the tears and the sobbing, the vacant looks on people's faces, the silences. No! The quicker Dennis's corpse was disposed of, the better, as far as he was concerned. And if Dennis had been around to speak for himself, Fred was absolutely certain that he would have fully agreed with him on that point. "Get the bloody thing over and done with, and good riddance to this paraphernalia!" He could hear him saying those very words as he looked towards the coffin. He'd always prided himself on his atheism and of his not being baptised in a church. His father, a devout socialist, and an active member of his trade's union, had never allowed any sort of religion to enter into his house either by the front or the back door, and Fred had followed happily in his wake. Much to his mother's growing consternation. When his father had eventually died (to everyone's great relief), and his body committed to the ground, it was to the resounding words of trade union rule 66, sub-section 4a, paragraph 14, and as his coffin was disappearing into the earth, his friends and work mates sang the 'Red Flag', rather dourly in the biting wind and cold pouring down rain. The young shivering Fred had clutched his mother's hand for dear life and cried his heart out. They were the last to leave the graveside, and as they turned away (and he could still see this in his mind's eye) his mother looked back towards the open grave and spat a mouthful of saliva onto the coffin with venom. He distinctly heard it plop, like earth, onto his dead father's wooden lid. And that was that as they say. Later on in life when he too had married in the registry office, not long after the war had finished, he made absolutely sure that the service was devoid of any religious connotations altogether—no mention of God at all. His lovely wife to be hadn't given a damn as long as they were actually married; she couldn't care a jot. And anyway, on that particular morning (they'd managed to book the very first slot) she'd turned up awash and sodden with gin and the new-fangled pills prescribed by her doctor, and incidentally, of all things, wearing odd shoes! However, that's another story altogether. Now many, many years later, Fred (like countless others of his generation) had already arranged his own funeral right down to the very last detail. No fuss or bother. Cremation! No words to be spoken or said. Strictly no mourners. And strictly no religion! In and out and up the chimney so to speak. Gone in a puff of smoke!

The minister's voice droned on and on like the constant buzzing of a sleepy bee. He didn't hear a single word that she spoke to the gathered congregation. He felt himself slipping away. He couldn't help himself. He tried opening his eyes as wide as they would go but the respite lasted mere seconds that's all. His head, top-heavy with drowsiness, dropped to his chest. The second time that it did this, his chin snapped his open mouth shut causing him to bite down hard on his lolling tongue. He came to with a start and a clatter, the order of service and the hymn book falling noisily to the floor. The pause made by the minister was barely discernable to all those who happened to be paying any real attention to what she was saying. But the look she shot towards Fred was one of professional disdain and tore him to shreds. He felt the blood blister beneath his tongue swelling and momentarily he appeared, to all intents and purposes, wide-awake. But as the minister's voice sunk to new depths of monotony, his mind drifted away on the tide of memory and he was transported back into the past, and Dennis was there waiting for him.

Two days after they had met in the library in Sowerby Bridge, they arranged to meet at the town's railway station to catch an early train to Leeds, where they planned to make their way to the R.A.F.'s recruiting office and join up. Neither of the young men had really fancied the idea of flying, but wished rather to enlist as 'groundcrew', learn a decent trade, leave, and then return to the Ryburn Valley and start up their own respective businesses, whatever they might be. Almost straight away their plans were scuppered as Dennis was sent away to an airbase deep in Wales to train as an aircraft armourer, whereas Fred was sent off to train as an airfield engineer and packed off (with a few other miserable recruits) to somewhere deep in the remote wilds of Scotland. Thank the gods for malt whisky! However, within two years of their joining, fate brought them back together again, thanks to the wishes and desires of one particular German gentleman. They met up again at a newly built aerodrome in the beautiful Hampshire countryside just a couple of months before the outbreak of formal hostilities, and awaited nervously, but also with an unmistakeable bubbling, youthful excitement, for Mr. Hitler's opening gambit. For seemingly months on end, which included an Indian summer, nothing at all happened for them. Except that is, training and preparation upon preparation and training. Everyone, including our two heroes, believed and hoped, that the ensuing conflict would indeed be solved by political negotiation. But come the dawning of 1940, all 'hell' broke loose, and modern, technological warfare made the 'Black Death' resemble nothing more than a mere rash upon the skin of Europe!

By the late summer of the following year, both men along with their squadron, and two others, were shipped out to the 'Middle East', to Egypt to be exact. The heat very nearly killed them! And they both struggled to adapt to their new surroundings from the outset. Like the majority of their comrades, they hated the food, the dust, the sun, the desert and the indigenous people they had to deal with on a day-to-day basis. But above all, they hated the watery beer and the flies that constantly buzzed around their glasses. Fred, even when given prolonged periods of 'off-duty' time, never left the confines of the base. Dennis, on the other hand, embraced the Egyptian culture whenever and wherever he possibly could. He tried to remain positive and make a go of things. He made the best of a bad job so to speak. He made more than one visit to the 'Valley of the Kings'. He saw 'King Tutankhamun's tomb and was mesmerised. Now an officer, in charge of all weapons and ammunition, he was fascinated by the caves that were used by the 'Pharaoh's' workers and craftsmen, and which were now back in use as the R.A.F.'s chief ordinance dump in Egypt. He was amazed at all the ancient graffiti that adorned the walls and the extant monuments without Egyptian, Greek and Roman, Napoleonic French and British. When he was able to get a place on a transport to Cairo, he made a point of wandering around the city's museums for hours upon end, soaking in everything relating to ancient Egypt. A historical love and fascination he maintained right up until the end of his life. Fred, on the other hand, when off-duty, simply hung about the N.A.A.F.I. and was morose and bad-tempered and got on everyone's nerves, including most of all, his own!

But now as he dozed, and the minister's voice was lost on him, one distinct memory fluttered to fore in his mind's eye. As it battled for prominence in his subconscious, the sun's rays without suddenly reached a new intensity and the light against his closed eyelids was blinding and the desert peninsula, where he'd been sent to complete a very important task, burst back into life. His mission was to blow-up a rocky outcrop that jutted out into the sea at the extreme end of the smallish peninsula. It was going to be flattened and the base's runway thus extended in order that the squadrons based there could successfully operate the new American 'Liberator' bombers. These aeroplanes, along with their longer range and heavier payloads, meant that Fred's squadron would now be able to attack both Italian, and the much more troublesome, German targets with relative ease. As the officer in charge of the task, Fred's commanding officer had repeatedly reminded him of the grave responsibility that was now being placed in his hands, not to mention the strategic importance to the war effort in the Middle East's theatre of war. Indeed, the campaign's very success might well be resting upon his shoulders! He shrugged them as the C.O. reiterated his dire warning,

"Now don't let me or the squadron down. Do you hear me, Walker? Don't let me down now, we're all depending on you! Do you hear me, Walker?"

The C.O. twirled his swagger stick round and round in his finely manicured fingers as Fred stared straight over his head and out the window to the ominous runway beyond the aerodrome's buildings. It appeared to be beckoning to him.

"Get this right and there could well be a medal and promotion in this for you. Now there's a good chap, off you go man."

Fred saluted and left the C.O.'s office and walked back into the dazzling sunshine. He didn't give a damn about either a medal or promotion for that matter. But professional pride, now that was a different matter altogether. From the stores he requisitioned very nearly two tons of high explosive and had it packed with great care onto two canvas-topped lorries. He spent close on two days in the sweltering heat carefully planning and laying the charges. He laid the majority of the high explosive underneath the rotting hulks of two ancient dhows that lay half submerged upon either side of the rocky peninsula. Everyone at the base was in awe of his work, especially his tunnelling skills. On the day of detonation, after breakfasting in the officer's mess, Fred strode with a jaunty swagger towards the spot that he'd made his centre of operations. He personally oversaw all aspects of the impending explosion and, it being 'his baby', he was to depress the charge's plunger and detonate the explosion. As he strode purposely past the end of the existing runway, his cap at a rakish tilt, he knew that all eyes were upon him. At precisely the designated time and in the blistering heat of midday, cowering behind a big desert boulder, he plunged the handle of the detonator downwards and eased off the biggest bang the entire region had ever witnessed, in peace or war! It was said that it could be heard in Cairo, and within the 'Officer's Club' there, all the glasses tinkled and the tables wobbled slightly. It was obvious to all who saw it (and none more-so than Fred) that he'd far too much high explosive. The cloud of smoke and debris from the explosion carried on rising up into clear, bright blue sky for three or four minutes or more. The biggest mushroom cloud anyone could ever remember having seen. In Berlin and Rome respectively, the 'Army High Commands' were duly informed that the British were up to something big, and consequently spies and spotter planes were immediately despatched to investigate further. Later that day Fred stood once again before his profusely perspiring and now manic C.O.

"Well, you've really done it this time, Walker!" He mopped his brow with an already saturated handkerchief.

"Churchill wants you shot immediately! In fact, I've got a good mind to bloody well shoot you myself! I mean, what in God's name were you playing at, man? And by the way, the American's want you shot as well I might add. I mean what possessed you, man? Why on earth did you do it? I mean, after all you're supposed to be the bloody expert with all this kind of stuff, well, aren't you!"

Fred shrugged and looked over the C.O.'s head out of the window towards the sea and the now non-existent peninsula.

"The 'Air Chief Marshal's' going to have my guts for garters over this, you mark my words! I'm done for! I mean good God, man, what the bloody hell were you thinking? Why there wasn't enough wood left from those old dhows to make a bloody match stick with!!! Well don't just stand there you blithering idiot, get out man! Get out of my sight!"

The commanding officer's voice followed him out of the room even after he'd shut the door.

"You'll pay for this, Walker, do you hear me? You'll pay for this—you'll be for the high jump, you mark my words!"

Outside the C.O.'s office the air was still heavy with the acrid smell of explosive and he could distinctly taste cordite on his tongue. Seeing him emerge, Dennis ran across the parade square forgetting to salute the ensign that hung lifelessly upon its mast and running straight up to Fred asked him breathlessly.

"Well, Fred, what happened? What did the C.O. say to you... Come on Fred, what did he say?"

He carried on walking without once looking down towards his best friend, but then half turning towards him he replied rather succinctly.

"Well, I don't think we'll be getting 'Liberators' any time too soon!"

And that was the end of Fred Walker's commission in the R.A.F. Shortly afterwards he received orders transferring him back to Scotland where he was to be part of a new team, permanently land-based, training junior weapons and engineering officers. And there he remained (and he didn't see Dennis again) until the end of hostilities in May 1945.

The recalling of this memory had clearly dumped him into a deepening sleep, and just as he was about to snore out aloud he got a good firm push on the shoulder. He came to with a start and pulled himself upright on the pew. His backside was as numb as the wood he was sitting on. He turned slightly and nodded his appreciation for his being awoken. The minister now flatly refused to acknowledge him with even the slightest look askance in his direction. And she appeared to now make his misery even worse by reiterating a whole host of sugary memories and anecdotes concerning Dennis that bore no real semblance to the man that Fred actually knew so well. Well, that did it for him. He'd had just about enough of all this nonsense and couldn't stomach another word that was now being sprouted. He couldn't remain there a moment longer, not even for Dennis, and he knew that he'd understand anyway. He shot to his feet (which momentarily dumbfounded the minister), bowed his head towards his friend's coffin, and walked briskly out of the chapel, out of the crematorium, and into the bright summer sunshine and back into all things living. He shook his body as though shaking himself free of death and its inevitable decay and shivered right down to the marrow in his bones. It was as though someone had just walked across his own grave! He lit himself a much-needed cigarette and casually strolled along the driveway that led towards his motor car, debating whether or not to go back to Dennis's wake now that he'd made a complete spectacle of himself, or whether to make his own way somewhere else and have himself a quiet pint or two. He'd leave the decision to chance and when he started the journey back home, he'd let the car decide which way to take him. He stepped off the tarmac and onto a beautifully manicured piece of lawn refusing to look down at the myriad of small commemorative plaques that adorned the borders and flowerbeds everywhere, seemingly springing out of the very earth itself, but instead he looked back down the valley towards the distant hills. He'd suddenly changed his mind. He decided right there and then that as soon as he'd been to the doctor's he'd go for a good, long leisurely walk along the moors and into the windswept hills. Forget

Dennis's wake, and forget his couple of pints for the time being, he'd have a quiet drink with his old friend some other time, after all there was no rush now, was there? His friend wasn't going anywhere too soon. Besides he wanted the fresh clean air to wash the smell of death from his clothes, to scour his nostrils of the cleanliness of the crematorium. He'd take a flask of tea (and maybe a little something to put in it for later on), some sandwiches and some dark chocolate biscuits, not forgetting his book to read when he needed a little rest. And up there alone, in the middle of nowhere, he would be able to remember a life-long friendship as it should be remembered, as it truly had been. Suddenly, he felt much better. Refreshed of mind. Smiling to himself he pulled deeply on the cigarette to finish it off and was just about to step off the grass and onto the curb-stone when he was suddenly aware of something terribly wrong inside of his mouth. He immediately thought that it was a hard piece of tobacco (he still smoked plain cigarettes), or worse, a little piece of filling. It then seemed much bigger than either and he fished for it with his tongue and pushed it to his lips. He pulled it clear of his mouth and held it before his eyes—it was a tooth! A full back tooth! A molar! His mouth instantly filled with the taste of blood. Shocked, he staggered off the grass and onto what he thought was the curb. Missing it completely he stepped instead onto a curb-side drain and anchored his foot in one of its openings, as he lurched forward, he turned his foot over snapping it cleanly at the ankle. The pain that ran through his entire body was tremendous and rendered him instantly unconscious. Luckily for Fred a groundsman happened to be nearby and witnessed the whole episode and immediately radioed to the crematorium office for help. The ambulance was there in a matter of minutes and whisked him off to 'A&E' where he was promptly despatched to the operating theatre and thereafter admitted in to hospital. And that was that, really. There isn't really much more to add to the story. Save that it was a swift end to a relatively long life. An episode over and done with, so to speak. A closure that ultimately resulted in the death (whether indeed it was timely or untimely) of one Fred Walker. No fuss, no mess, and absolutely no squabbling. Short and sweet. His body was cremated and duly dispatched within a week of his death. For whilst being operated on, the surgeon in charge checked the source of the bleeding from Fred's mouth and immediately sent for a specialist consultant for a second opinion. She expertly diagnosed an extremely advanced form of oral cancer, inoperable and terminal.

The operation on Fred's ankle was thereby cancelled and he was quickly patched-up and packed off somewhere to die with as little expense to the N.H.S. as humanly possible. And that turned out to be very little indeed in actual fact. For on his way to the ward, he suffered a crippling heart attack and died on the trolley on which he was being pushed unconscious and under the horror-stricken gaze of the hospital porter.

THE END
COMPLETED TYPING ON 21st APRIL 2016

Spring! (The Hawthorn!)

Fresh clean rain was falling upon fresh young leaves (just lately budded out) swelling the already heavy dewdrops, which adorned the tree like tiny sparkling stars. This sudden new weight of moisture forced them to tumble downwards causing a chain reaction of droplets from bough to bough and from leaf to leaf. A host of cascading silvery beads of liquid falling through the tree to the ground below. Amid the tiny shimmering droplets fleeting rainbows, almost too small to see with the naked eye, suddenly materialised and then vanished in the blink of an eye. For now, in this modern age of ours, nearly all human eyes had lost the ability to see such marvels and all its magic. Yet still the rain came down, persistently, clear and sweetly fresh. It rained with carefree abandon, unchecked and unhindered by wind or breeze. It rained steadily without being too strong to damage or bully the fresh young leaves onto which it fell joyously as it had always done, and with the love of life still to come.

The Hawthorn had been growing there longer than anybody, man or beast, could now remember. And moreover, hardly anyone knew it was there and even fewer had ever actually seen it in whatever season of the year it happened to be. How it came to be there, growing from shoot to maturity, now remained a great mystery. Indeed, it was the only tree growing in that particular spot and the only tree that had somehow managed to reach maturity. It had survived all the odds of nature, and it had miraculously survived man's intervention. It surely was a magic tree, a mystical tree, a tree that would outlive mankind no matter what happened with and around its roots. Those other specimens within eyesight were bent and twisted this way and that and were battered by the cruel winds that swept unremittingly across the moors and heath, and appeared to be hanging on perilously for dear life in the face of overwhelming odds. And furthermore, those trees, there or thereabouts, seemed to be constantly bullied by nature. Whereas the Hawthorn, it is true to say, was amidst the flourishing of life and thrived and grew ever stronger with every passing day. It was abundant and radiant with life and health. Its trunk was straight (for a hawthorn that is) but gnarled with very great age, and its canopy was full of healthy little green leaves and interspersed with tiny pink flowers. The pink hawthorn so much more beautiful than its white counterpart, I feel, don't you? It was all in all a very, very happy tree. Blessed one might say.

As I have already explained how it came to be where it stood, and where it still grows to this very day, it is impossible to say that it had been there for centuries, very possibly millennia; well that was easy to deduce. One had only to examine it closely and caress its lichen covered bark to establish its longevity of life. And right up until that very moment in time, all of the world's history, its peoples and all its events, had passed it by and left it alone in peace and solitude. Growing in humble and all but splendid isolation. However, that is not to say that it was a lonely tree and devoid of any other life. Far from it. Within its compass it was indeed the host to creatures both great and small, all of which depended upon it for almost everything, as they always had done and always would do as long as it remained standing, robust and seemingly indomitable. It was a life-giver and a life-bringer in every sense of the word.

The bees and the insects came first of all, followed soon after by the butterflies that came upon their delicate wings, floating and dancing in on the soft and gentle breeze that threaded the Hawthorn's twigs and branches. And then came the birds, tit and finch alike, cock-sure and eagle-eyed, to feast upon all, to sing and warble to their hearts content. All attracted to the Hawthorn as springtime broke free and the land thereabouts shook off its winter sleep and came back bursting into life once more. All attracted to its soporific fragrance, its powerfully hypnotic scent and its little pink flowers, resplendent, that festooned its thorny fingers. Generation after countless generations remained faithful to the Hawthorn and returned each season to pay homage to its bounty, and in return the tree gave them everything they needed. A myriad of twigs for elaborate silky webs, boughs for nests, leaves for shelter and nectar for honey. Even the bark upon its weathered trunk lent crevices and safe havens for even the tiniest of insects. All tucked away and safely hidden from view and the prying eye of opportunity. The mammals came next, the cows and the sheep. To these beasts of the field it bestowed succour when nature was out of sorts with itself. It offered and also gave them protection from nature's storms and from the harsh winter winds, and the summer sun's unremitting rays. And for all of this it neither desired, nor demanded, anything in return except their dumb reverence over the passage of time.

The Hawthorn was indeed a precious thing. The tree sent its roots deep down into the mother's earth. So deep in fact that when the air was frozen solid, by blasts of artic wind that swept the moors and heath, its roots touched upon the deep subterranean vein of heat that coursed the innermost depths of the planet and so gave it a favoured life. Where so many others withered and perished, and where those that somehow managed to survive, only just did so by the skin of their teeth, battered and twisted, they hung on to a precarious day-to-day existence. The Hawthorn had just happened to be in the right place at the right time. Or had it? Was it precious? Was it indeed special? Was it really a tree of life? A tiny hair upon the face of 'Mother Nature', as surely all trees are? Or is this just an old tale of stuff and nonsense? Well the wise old Brock didn't think so. Almost as old as the Hawthorn itself, his hoary jowls had brushed against its fathomless roots for time beyond counting. When above the earth, his wise old face had gazed into the depths of the night through its leafy canopy, understanding nothing but seeing everything, the moon and the scudding clouds glinting in his eyes. His secret set amid its roots a safe haven for generations of badgers. Many of which, it is sad to say, had not fared as well as he; when reaching their maturity, they had ventured forth into the realms of men and met their fate. But the wise old Brock had stayed put, always. He knew what was best for him and had fought and stood his ground, met adversity face to face and came through his trials and tribulations with a lifetime of scars. Thus he had grown very big, very old and wise with age. And so the two became inseparable, tree and beast. Friend and guardian. And even when the ancient track, that passed hard-by, had grown in importance and had eventually been metalled, and dry-stone walls on either side erected, the two remained safe and undisturbed. Very nearly invisible within their immediate surroundings. Almost that is! For one person, a woman, knew of their existence, knew of their very special place. And like them she appeared wise beyond measure and yet in years she was not beyond her middle age. Relatively, a young woman. Her face now weathered and withered by time and the continual worry of torment. Harried very nearly to the point of madness. And now unable to face the relentless persecution any longer she had fled and abandoned her cottage upon the outskirts of the village. Unable to withstand the growing physical pain from the attacks upon her body, and her magic spells now seemingly useless to protect her, the witch, if that is what she was, ran away in fear of her own life, in fear of torture and the flame! But she still had one last trick up her sleeve, a potion to defy them all. She'd show them indeed! They would never torment nor hurt her ever again. No they wouldn't! And in her near madness she tried to reason with herself. What had she done to deserve all this anguish? All she'd ever done was to help all those in their hour of need. She'd been a boon to the local community. A veritable rock on which to depend for help and advice. A fountain of wisdom. And in return for all of this she was hounded, molested, and accosted in the street in the broad daylight, treated like a pariah. Now she had been driven away from her spells and her beloved cauldron. Abandoned forever! But she knew that the ignorance and the intolerable hate, and the vituperation, would follow her like the plague and so she had fled, fled for her life. But like the plague, it would surely follow and dog her every step. Unless she was clever that is, cleverer than those who must surely come after her. She fled into a night that she knew would be well suited for escape, dark, cloudy, moonless, closing the front door behind her. There was no need to lock it as she would never be coming back. Well not in this lifetime anyway. She set off on wobbly legs, panting like a dog and at first unable to catch her second wind. Then she gained her composure and her stumbling escape became her motivated flight. She skipped around the 'Scammondan Water' in no time at all, nervously giggling and then softly wailing in turn, both subdued by the trials of her perilous journey. It was with a pounding heart that she fled across the 'Saddleworth Road', wraith-like, and made a beeline for the brilliantly lit motorway that stood out like a dazzling ribbon of light dead ahead of her, now not all that far away. She felt that she was 'safer' now, but after years of being a hounded young woman, her instincts were honed to perfection. At every sound, however faint, and with every shadow, however fleeting, she stopped and froze and listened with an acuteness that brought to her ears the whispers of mice, moles, and molluscs' in their shells, that were abroad in the night time of their relatively short lives. When she was satisfied that they meant her no harm, she ran on and continued into the night. She eventually came upon the entrance to the tunnel that would lead her under the motorway. She paused briefly looking back the way she'd travelled and turning her face into the growing wind she caught the scent of pursuit. She should have locked the front door! Too late now to think on that. They would soon be upon her if she didn't make all possible haste towards her ultimate sanctuary. She flew through the passageway, the muffled sounds of the traffic above her virtually lost in the echoing clatter of loose stones beneath her small booted feet. Then she crossed the fields and came by the weir at the 'Booth Dean Clough', gliding like a skimming stone across the water. Flying along the 'Oldham Road' until just hard by 'The Turnpike Inn' she suddenly stopped running and strode up the 'Pike End' panting like a dog, completely jiggered, then turned into the darkened tree-lined lane upon her left-hand side to relieve herself. Squatting down she succumbed to a few moments of respite in which to gather her thoughts and briefly rest a while. When done she left the road and cut across the fields and climbed the rising hill before her, on over the land running down to and across 'Blackwood Common', a strange name indeed, for there were no other trees in sight save for the Hawthorn in the distance, her ultimate destination. She suddenly saw the tree a little in the distance, straight ahead of her now. She smiled weakly and somehow staggered the remaining distance towards her goal dragging herself forwards. Her body was now very nearly a spent force. She had very little left. She stumbled the last few feet and fell exhausted against its aged trunk and hugged it for dear life, like a drowning man grasping at a straw. Then unable to control or contain her emotions any longer she burst into a flood of tears and wept her soul away and slumped to the ground as the Hawthorn's gnarled bark grazed her quivering chin as she fell. And there upon the ground the tree soothed and comforted her troubled heart, and very quickly, without her realising, her tears subsided and gave way to a deep, almost narcotic slumber. And the Hawthorn made quite sure that her peace wasn't disturbed. For, throughout the rest of that terrible night, her tormentors swarmed and threaded all about the place in frantic search of her. Backwards and forwards they came, torches ablaze. Motor cars came and went. In groups they searched. As individuals they searched. They listened in total silence. But all to no avail! Even though, on more than one occasion, they stood only mere feet away from her, she remained concealed and safe in sleep. Blissfully unaware of their presence. Not that the Hawthorn would have allowed her to come to any harm anyway, far from it. For the tree had enveloped her completely in its own magic, it had assimilated her physical form completely, and to all intents and purposes, she was utterly invisible. In the morning she awoke from her slumbers curled up in a ball at its base facing the dry-stone wall that had kept the chilly spring breeze from her face. She stretched the stiffness from her body and sat up propping herself against the Hawthorn's trunk and gazed all about her. It was the beginnings of what was going to be a truly beautiful day. A poet's day. A gardener's day. But ultimately, nature's day! She looked at the fields around her. The grass, emerald green, lush, a bovine feast for days to come. The distant and undulating hills carpeted with luxuriant heather and yellow furze, home to the numerous tiny creatures belonging to the moor and heath. And then she noticed that the grass all around the Hawthorn was a blanket of crocus and daffodil, and even some lingering snowdrop. Their heady scent already attracting the season's first foraging bees that were adventurous enough to venture out and brave the still somewhat chilly shade. And she also recognised the birdsong amidst the canopy above her head. The ebullient and cock-sure robin redbreast, the tiny but robust jenny wren and the occasional but gentle chatter of the tree sparrow. But then, what brought her back down to earth with a crash, to the world of men and her grave dilemma, was the sorrowful and haunting call of the distant curlew. She suddenly felt mournful and lost. Life was leaving her and the tree could no longer lend her aid or succour. She was forlorn and bereft of all hope. Now knowing that she was going to have to leave all this wondrous beauty behind her broke her already shattered heart still further. Tears came to her eyes and the old wise Brock, that unbeknown to her had emerged from his set, sat staring into her care-worn face and jaded eyes. She pulled a tiny ampoule from within a little embroidered pouch that hung around her neck, and holding it up to the light she tried in vain to see the sun through the opaque and milky-coloured liquid. There was no going back now. She could never go back now. That life was over and done with. No more spells, no more magic, no more fortune telling, and no more reading of cards and small bones or tea-leaves. And no more potions to those with swollen bellies desperate for the remedy to make things right again. All over with, finally, praise to be the forces unseen and all-powerful. She popped the phial into her mouth, pushing it with her tongue towards the teeth at the back. The old Brock crept slowly towards her and nestled gently at her side. Looking deep into his eyes she smiled and stroked his soft thick fur and for the briefest of moments they shared a common bond of love and respect. Surely the meaning of life? She had never ever thought that one day, and on a day such as this, her very existence could be so easily thrown away and extinguished. But hey-ho, no more fear and no more pain. She stared up into the bright blue sky that soared above her and clenched her teeth together. The Hawthorn's branches and its canopy were the last things she saw. From out of the ground one of its most ancient of roots slowly snaked itself around her waist piercing her clothes and gently, respectfully, penetrated her still warm flesh. And from out of her once troubled mind, body and soul, sucked the pain and the anguish out of very being until she was empty. All that was a shell, a husk that was once a living thing, now surrounded by peace and quietude. And that was the end of it all. The old Brock feeling that his presence was no longer desired withdrew and returned to his set to sleep the rest of the day away. But before his eyes had closed and slumber overcame him, her body had been drained and its human form had withered away to nothing, collapsing in a little heap of bone and leathery skin. And unless it had been examined closely, it would never have been guessed that this nondescript pile had once held a human form. Its work done, the Hawthorn resumed its peaceful existence, all around in peace and harmony, flora and fauna.

Her bones and leathery skin are still there to this very day. And if you ever happened to look down to the place where they now rest, you'd never have recognised them as such. Nature and time have covered them and concealed them from prying eyes. But they are still there I can assure you of that, for I have seen them and wondered. Moss and lichen have masked them, but I know where they are. Grass, weeds and sometimes flowers have threaded her bones at times, but still they are there, believe me. And what is left exposed now looks like earth and stone and commonplace. She is indeed lost but not forgotten. For robin, wren and finch still daily stand upon her to sing and warble and chatter, and wile the time away. The old Brock badger, who is still alive and well, emerges from his set in the dead of night and occasionally pads across to her place and noses and sniffs and softly grunts his respect. Whilst high up in the sky above them all, the unseen curlew issues its plaintive call in honour of a life that was, and had been, and was over.

THE END
COMPLETED TYPING ON 25th APRIL 2016

The Snowflake! (Winter!)

Standing alone in the 'Rat-field', known affectionately as the 'Ratty', he didn't dare move a muscle. Panting like his pet dog 'Ted' (the terrible terrier), his breath rose up in great steamy clouds up into a sky that had come down and seemed almost to touch the tops of the trees. He'd pelted like mad through the stringy winter grass all the way to the middle of the field and stopped dead in his tracks as though suddenly marooned in quicksand. He stood there, his little body a mere dot in the landscape, with his arms outstretched, pleadingly, begging the heavens above to release their bounty. With his eyes raised up to the skies, he whispered his first prayer that Christmas holiday day.

"Please, please let it snow, and I'll never do anything bad again! Please let it snow! I promise!"

But the snow didn't come that particular day although it seemed to be straining at the seams to do so, just for him, a poor little boy in a big old empty field. The big wide-open sky above him was indeed a heavy snow laden grey and promised much. The air, as still and as stodgy as cold Christmas pudding, was strangely silent. Altogether it forebode something that he couldn't quite put his finger on. But nonetheless, something fantastical was definitely going to happen. He knew that now. His father's voice suddenly rent the silence like a thunderclap and made him start.

"Jack! Get your backside in this house…now!"

He turned on a sixpence and flew like a rocket back over his tracks and scuttled back over the big old rickety garden fence. Yes! It was definitely going to be one of those days. As indeed it turned out to be.

Once over the fence he met his father who was stood like an indomitable oak looking up at the brooding sky above him and who was just finishing off his pipe. The youngster grabbed a hold of his huge hand and pestered him all the way back into the still un-curtained house which was blazing away with an orange light that indicated an inviting winter warmth.

"Well Dad what do you think? Will it snow? Will it? Will it snow tonight, come on Dad what do you think, will it snow then?"

He skipped alongside his father's grown-up strides gleefully swinging his arm in the fast fading light. His father suddenly stopped and without looking down at his son he cocked his leg and knocked out the remains of his spent pipe upon the heel of his boot.

"Aye lad, that it will. The winds picking up and it'll be a heavy'un that's for sure. You mark my words."

The boy released his hand and jigged around the garden, hopping from one foot to the other in sheer unbounded joy singing in his breathless broken voice in praise of the snow to come. On coming level with him the man grabbed the boy by his scruff of the neck and led him back into the house and to where a steaming dinner was already awaiting them upon the dining room table.

"Oi you, I'm talking to you!

His father whacked him hard on the head with the bowl of his spoon. The apple pie and custard that clung to it stuck to his hair like glue.

"That's your problem, you never bloody listen."

His father looked towards his fed-up looking and long-suffering wife.

"It's your fault he never listens to a word I say, you're too soft with him, that's your problem."

He turned back toward Jack with the spoon hovering like a snake ready to strike.

"Well are you listening to me?"

Jack nodded whilst still rubbing the front of his head where he felt a marble-like lump on the rise.

"Well think on then. Remember what I told you. No! The answer's no, and that's final! You're not going out again and that's that!"

The man shovelled still more dessert into an already dessert-full mouth. Jack was feeling brave indeed and was about to stand up for his juvenile freedom when his mother suddenly grabbed him by the collar and pulled him into her ample left bosom. The spongy sensation and the sudden unmistakeable sinking feeling into her sweet-smelling dress made his face turn blood red. He'd not felt so embarrassed for about a week at least. He tried to pull away in desperation and squirmed like a fish out of water, but she had arms wrapped around him like tentacles and he was in her power. His father roared with laughter at his young son's acute embarrassment until he got himself a great big belch stuck in the back of his throat just as another shovel full of apple and custard quivered on the end of his spoon. Jack's mother was distraught.

"Now look what you've gone and done to our Jack's hair! He looks like 'Tintin'."

She lifted his red face and rested his head between her cleavage.

"Come here my little man and let me smooth it down, there's a love." Jack shut his eyes very tight for he knew full well what was going to happen next. She spat a great dollop of motherly spit onto her hand and tried to flatten down his new 'Tintin' quiff, but she suddenly pulled her hand away as though she'd been bitten by a snake.

"Oh my god! It's all sticky and gooey, yuck! I'm afraid you're going to have to sort your own hair out, jack. I'm not messing with it now; I'm already late for my bingo as it is."

She got up quickly (surprisingly so for such a bonny woman) virtually dumping her son on the dining room carpet and vanished from the room in a whirl of movement. Thus freed from her heaving chest, Jack breathed a huge sigh of relief. He could put up with most things in life, including a sticky 'Tintin' hair-do, but definitely not his mother's heaving bosom, especially in public and for all the world to see! His father shouted after his dear departing wife.

"You're too soft with that one, I'm telling you! What he needs is a good old whack every now and again! Look at me. I mean…it never did me any harm, now did it?"

The front door slammed shut with a tremendous rattle that shook the mirror on the wall above the dining room table. His father winced and grimaced muttering something under his breath that the young boy couldn't quite make out. His parents had obviously had a blazing row probably over something that involved him somewhere along the line. It had been a row that he'd been completely oblivious to. Jack looked through the corner of his eye towards the place where his mother had been sitting and then back to where his father was still eagerly gobbling down his dessert, and he suddenly felt glum. He felt both sad and sorry because he'd been the cause of yet another argument between his 'loving' parents once again, or so he felt in his little heart of hearts. He just couldn't seem to do anything right at the moment. Everything that he did, he did wrong and badly. When he washed the pots to help his mum, he somehow managed to break one of the best dinner plates. When he washed and polished the car (which was hardly ever nowadays) he apparently scratched the paintwork, which subsequently earned him a good old thick ear, a real throbber, and no spends for a month! And, when he ran to the local shops on his errands, he always lost some of the money, either going there or coming back, and what he'd lost he had to pay back out of his money box, his holiday spends! But from now on, he contemplated to himself, he was determined to do better come what may, to try his very 'bestest' no matter what. He'd be the best son in all the world and someone his mum and dad would be proud of!

A little later on, bathed and pyjammed, teeth brushed and checked and fully prayered, he was packed off to bed with fingers crossed and with a little heart full of hope and wishful thinking, and with a night's slumber packed with all sorts of dreams full of everything but...snow! He smiled contentedly as he tucked himself up tight into a ball, like the frightened hedgehog that he'd seen on 'Blue Peter', and in a matter of moments he was as snug as a bedbug. He, very quickly, fell fast asleep and dreamed of goodness only knows what. He slept undisturbed and soundly, like a baby, all through the still and heavy winter's night. He came awake very, very early and very slowly, at first not quite knowing exactly where he was (something that never really leaves us), which seemed always to be the case with Jack anyway. When his panic was over, he pushed his feet, pointing his toes, into the bottom corners of the bed and felt the sleepy night's warmth still there and still inviting. His thoughts were all jumbled up, some of them belonging to a lingering dream he couldn't quite remember, some to his rumbling tummy and his breakfast, and some to the early birds that were chirping just outside of his bedroom window. Then all of a sudden, like a flash of summer lightning, he came instantly awake. He sat bolt upright in his bed and his heart began to race and pound against his ribcage. Was there any snow? Had it snowed during the night? With all his might he strained his ears to try and detect even the very slightest sound, whatever that might be, that would suggest it had fallen and come down to coat the earth all around where he lived. But all he heard were the muffled sounds of crockery coming from the kitchen directly below his bedroom, and at first he didn't dare get out of bed to peep through the curtains to discover the truth. Beneath him his mother was already hard at work, in her 'domain', making the family's breakfast. He glanced across to his alarm clock. It was already half past six on the clock and he'd missed his paper round—again, and that meant less spends at the weekend—again! Annoyed with himself he jumped straight out of bed and got himself dressed as fast as he could. He was in a mad, frantic rush. Opening his bedroom door he made his way downstairs giving the bathroom a miss. The stairs squeaked their usual creak as he went down them two at a time. He stumbled and very nearly fell head first as he reached the bottom, so he stood for a moment in the hallway, in silence, to catch his breath and gather his jumbled thoughts, bathed in the dust motes that his tramping down the stairs had just stirred up in the dull light that penetrated through the big glass window of the front door, listening to the blood pumping in his ears. His grandma's old clock (a present on her wedding day many years before he was born) suddenly shattered the silence and struck the three-quarter hour and chimed its ancient chime. Then all of a sudden the kitchen door flew open and his mother stood before him as bold as brass.

"And what are you up to standing there like that?"

He shrugged his shoulders.

"Nothing. I've just got up."

Then he blurted out.

"Has it snowed yet mum? I daren't look!"

She looked down at him tuttingly wagging her head.

"You've missed your paper round again, haven't you?"

She stood there like she might take on the whole world at any moment, blocking out the light from the kitchen, her hands upon her aproned hips.

"And that means less spends again, doesn't it my lad? Never mind, you'll learn eventually, it's no bother now. You're too young for a paper round anyway, all your father's silly idea if you ask me!"

She turned and made her way back into the kitchen.

"And no, for your information it hasn't snowed, not yet, (father and son had both been wrong for once) not that that really matters very much, horrible stuff that it is, good riddance to snow that's what I say!"

Her bossy and grown up matter-of-fact manner made him feel his age, young and stupidly silly. He'd felt himself go red in the face straight away, and he hadn't even been able to look her in the eyes, a sure sign of real boyish guilt that she had instantly picked up on, so he'd looked down at his feet and at the pattern in the hallway carpet instead. And he was still stood there, poking at the flowers with the toe of his shoe when she called after him.

"One of these days you're going to kill yourself coming down the stairs like that, aren't you? How many times do I have to tell you about that? Take your time in future. Now before you eat your breakfast, go and wash your face and hands please, and don't forget to brush your teeth. Now!"

He did as he was told, sulkily.

"And put a smile on that face of yours will you, for god sake. You look like a robber's dog!"

This was quickly followed less irritably with much softer and, with what seemed to Jack to be, much kinder, motherly words.

"Now do as you're told, there's a good boy, do you hear me?"

He turned around and smiled back towards his mum, his very best smile, and then he slowly re-climbed the stairs, one at a time this time, as though his feet were encased in lead boots.

"And don't be long, your breakfast's ready and I don't want it to grow cold. Do you hear me, Jack? Hurry up now!"

He paused briefly halfway up the stairs and leaning over the banister, he called out to her.

"Yes mum, I heard you!"

Then again.

"Yes mum, I heard you!"

And again.

"Yes mum, I heard you!"

And so the words echoed away. Many miles distant from the house that now housed Jack and which had been his home for as long as he could now remember. The sky above the hills had turned to a heavy leaden grey, which brooded, and cosseted the snow that was surely to come and blanket the land for many miles around. Ever ready to assist the gathering army of flakes, the wind was picking up its strength ready to blizzard the frozen moisture into every conceivable nook and cranny, and only awaited the necessary command to commence the onslaught upon the unsuspecting way, way down below. And then it began. The first flake fell through the clouds. It was instantly caught up by the wind and was sent as the vanguard upon its journey many, many miles hence from where it had been formed, to eventually fall down to the earth upon the 'Ratty', but more importantly, upon the excited little boy that was Jack who was awaiting its fall with trepidation. But how long would the little boy have to wait?

He had been sitting there for ages and ages. He hadn't moved at all. He hadn't wanted to. And because he'd been so quiet, they had decided to leave him on his own, it would be easier to do so, it was less bother and less trouble in the long run, and it had meant that they could all get on with something else. Jack was as quiet as a church mouse. He hadn't got the faintest idea what he'd been thinking about, if that is, he'd been thinking anything at all these last few hours. Indeed, his mind was a big, wide-open and empty sky. Then suddenly everything vanished and from out of the great blue yonder fresh new thoughts of snow and the pure whiteness that came with it hand-in-hand, covered his mind. And the thoughts of this snow were deep and crisp and even. They bounced around the insides of his head as he nibbled his toast in between sips of piping hot chicken soup. He glanced to his left and to his right only to find that he was the only member of his 'new' and enlarged family sat at the dining table as the light outside quickly began to fade away. And as he nibbled and sipped and dreamed his nose ran and dripped onto his cardigan, his new, brand spanking new cardigan at that. He sniffed up for all he was worth but he couldn't stop the seemingly endless flow of liquid mucus, which flowed like lave forever downwards. There seemed to be pints of the stuff! He smiled in amazement. Where does it all come from, he thought to himself? A growing, sparkling ball, dangled from the end of his nose and it shone and twinkled like a precious diamond. It wobbled and threatened to fall, and then it didn't, and it just sort of hung there threateningly. It hypnotised him. Like a snake on the prowl he waited for the right moment to strike back. As it grew and grew and quivered under its own weight, he suddenly pounced! He flicked out his tongue and licked the liquid ball off the end of his nose with all the speed of an executioner's axe and was justly pleased with himself. While outside, and beyond the big plate-glass windows, night had come at last.

Replete with soup, toast, milky tea and wind, Jack sat back in his chair and listened to the sounds of nothing in particular. Then from out of nowhere it came, like a bolt out of the blue. And so it was at that precise moment in time, in what was a rare moment of great clarity that he suddenly decided to go to the 'Ratty' one last time. He struggled and somewhat scrambled out of his chair and he made his way back upstairs to his room unaided, but more importantly, unseen! And once inside he quickly made up his preparations for his departure and what was to be his last great adventure. He duly removed his overcoat from out of the big wardrobe that seemingly stood to attention over in the corner of his room. Then sitting down on the end of his bed he tried desperately to decide whether to put on his outdoor shoes or to go out in his warm and comfy slippers instead! He pondered and deliberated over the decision for what seemed like an hour. Shoes or slippers, slippers or shoes, looking first at the shoes in his hands and then down at the slippers on his feet, and then back again. He wriggled his toes inside of his slippers and they felt as snug as a bug in a rug so to speak. Then with a smile and a nod of his head he came to his decision—slippers it was to be! He liked them best of all. He placed the shoes back on the little rack that was at the bottom of his wardrobe and closed the door behind them, then leaving his room, he made his way back downstairs passing through the brightly lit hallway, past the reception desk and suddenly, inexplicably, found himself outside of the front door in the freezing chill of the winter's night just a few days before the eve of Christmas.

He made his way silently and quite easily down the road and recognising a bus stop he planted himself besides it and waited patiently to see what would happen next. And what did in actual fact happen next? In no time at all the little purple community bus, lights ablaze, suddenly turned up out of nowhere, its doors opened and it sucked him inside its smelly, but inviting warmth, without further ado and carried him away to his destination which just happened to be the 'Ripponden' bus turning circle where the bus was to terminate anyway. But in all honesty it hadn't been quite as simple as that. The driver, in a mad rush to get back home, had repeatedly asked him for his destination and his pass, but all that he had received in return was Jack's vacant smile and the three stuttered syllables 'Rip...pon...den', followed by a desperately faint and hardly audible...please. Looking down and seeing the slippers upon his feet and the unshaved whiskers on his face, the driver shook his head and told Jack to go and sit down as he was running late already, and he had to be off and he couldn't waste any more time with the likes of him. And with that the bus was off, and nobody was any the wiser, or indeed missed him in the slightest. The bus driver was in a mad bad rush because the little vehicle sailed along the empty road 'over the tops' at an alarming rate of knots. Jack had plonked himself down right at the back and apart from himself, and the driver, the bus was completely empty. He sat at the rear of the bus bouncing around on the back seat laughing out loud at every dip in the road and at every rut and pothole that shuddered the vehicle's already dodgy suspension. He laughed until the tears sprung from his eyes and his ribs ached to splitting and gave him a whacking big stitch in his side. The bus driver feared that he had taken on board a raving lunatic. And that thought coupled with worried glances in his compartment mirror, made him drive all the faster, which in turn made Jack laugh all the more uproariously. In fact, he laughed so much that he very nearly wet himself and it was only down to the strength of his pelvic muscles, which took control of the situation that saved the day, and the depot cleaners an unenviable task. But what a joyous thing such carefree laughter is, but then, how fleeting and never to be regained, gone in the blink of an eye! The bus careered down the big old 'Ripponden Bank' at great speed, and through the front windscreen Jack saw the end of his journey coming towards him.

Once off the bus he knew exactly where to go. Turning to his left he walked as fast as his slippered feet would allow him to go up the 'Rochdale Road' and away from the village itself. He walked and walked, for how long he didn't know, or couldn't even begin to guess at. The wind, all the time growing stronger and gustier, slowed his progress, but on and on he went. Until that is, on the opposite side of the road he saw the entrance to the 'Ryland Park' estate, a relatively new housing development and which had all but consumed the numerous fields that had once been the 'Ratty' of his childhood and of the 'Ratty' that was indelibly linked to his most recent of day-dreams. The pavement took him down into the heart of the estate but he had no real idea where he was actually going or why really. Other than he was now being driven on and in the clutches of some invisible and irresistible force that he had no hope at all of denying. He drew level with number thirty-three and from goodness knows where or how, he knew instinctively that he'd reached his final destination. He shuffled up the driveway past the big slumbering high-performance motorcar, the all-important symbol of 'success' upon so many identical estates the length and breadth of the land. He somehow noticed the ugly scuff-mark that adorned its front end and smiled inwardly to himself as he passed through the gateway and made his way round to the back of the house. And as he passed under the rear bedroom windows two little faces were peeping down at him through chinks in the curtains and were watching his every shuffle. They watched him make his way to the old garden bench that was situated in an arbour way over in the corner of the garden. Until right now, that is, once their favourite place of secret play, away from the prying adult eyes of censure. Hard as they tried amid terrified whispers, they couldn't see the 'Bogie-man's' face, for that is who they now thought he was, come to watch over them throughout the long dark night, forever mindful of all their many, but innocent, misdemeanours. Shivering with cold and shaking to their bones with fear, they crept silently back to their respective beds and hid deep down under their duvets. Too stricken with fear to alert their parents down below lest they too be eaten alive. They'd already decided to best leave well alone and let the little baby 'Jesus', who was surely on his way with 'Father Christmas', guard and watch over them throughout the windy and shadowy night of their jumbled slumbers.

Down in the back garden, Jack sat and waited patiently. It was bitter freezing cold now, artic winds sweeping down from the north, but he felt himself to be as warm as hot buttered toast. The air inside his overcoat, and all around his body, seemed tropical, steamy almost, just what he imagined all the jungly islands to be like in all the lagoons dotted around the world. Nonetheless he couldn't stop himself from feeling incredibly tired and sleepy, and all he wanted to do now more than ever was to simply nod-off and have himself a good old doze. He then cast his gaze skywards and suddenly spotted the first falling flakes of snow. Through wide-open and mesmerised eyes, he followed the vanguard flake that had been in the forefront, for all of the way, for mile upon mile, as it not so much as fluttered as flopped down heavily, seemingly exhausted, quickly followed by all of its companions like falling blobs of cotton wool. And as that vanguard flake came down and gently rested upon the tip of his nose, he chuckled to himself and was, at long last, content and happy to be back home in the 'Ratty'. And whilst waiting for his father to shout him in for his tea he decided to have a little sleep. Which he did! And he slept for a very, very long time. And then, in the morning, as curtains and little eyes were opened and sticky sleep was rubbed away, the whiteness revealed its secrets, number thirty-three 'Rylands Park' discovered that Christmas-time had delivered them a snowman! Little slippered feet raced downstairs followed by excited screams of joy out and into the crisp and freezing air. Oh Christmas, lovely Christmas!

But in the end so many came to see him, and so very soon, that all the beautiful whiteness was spoilt and turned to brown mush, and as soon as he'd had his photograph taken, every which way, they took him away forever and he was never seen again, by anyone, and so it ruined that particular Christmas for one and all!

But little, if anything at all, did anyone really know what the future held in store for them, or, how quickly one's life could change and descend into utter chaos.

THE END
COMPLETED TYPING ON 5th MAY 2016

Summer! (A Favourite Place!)

On that particular morning I awoke ridiculously early and arose without any of the usual deliberation. I shaved and showered and then got dressed with a determination that belied my usual routine and manner before going down to breakfast. I opened the kitchen door and peeped outside. The night was beginning to fade and faced the inevitable retreat from the east, whilst the huge sky above and around me was framed with the indigo that heralded the warning that the sun was somewhere on the up, and that the blue-black ether would very soon be tinged with the first flickers of orange of the coming dawn. I had to make haste. I couldn't miss it, not on this particular day. I left the house in a hurry and was instantly tangled up in the crushing silence that hangs about just before it ushers in the dawning of a new day. As I breathed it all in (here and there) a few early morning birds were beginning to call and chirrup tentatively to one another, knowing full well that in a little while soon they'd be singing their tiny hearts out, and in full throat, in their chorus of dawn. The air I breathed into my lungs was fresh, clean and surprisingly sharp, and as I gazed up towards the changing light my breath rose up in great billowing clouds towards the few remaining bright stars that still showed their faces in the heavens above. I shivered violently. The chill air had taken me by surprise and the memory of a recently snug duvet was terribly enticing, but only for a split second that is. Shouldering my haversack, into which I'd packed a thermos flask of tea and a 'tupperware' box, containing some cheese and a few crackers, and a little polythene bag with a few digestives, and my little treat to myself, a slab of dark chocolate, I made tracks and headed off towards the 'Hollin Lane' which would lead me up to the 'Great House Road' and to my eventual destination. I still had plenty of time before the majesty of sunrise, for even in the mid-month of July, the flaming tongues of light wouldn't really begin to show themselves until after five of the morning, give or take a minute or two. There was no one else astir. I passed no motor-cars, nor saw any other human being, either near or afar. I was, or felt, quite alone upon this earth. A truly unique feeling. At moments like this it was a pleasure to be alive. A feeling of goodwill to all humanity (well to nearly all of it at least), and a feeling of pure exhilaration swept through my entire body as I tingled with almost childlike excitement. I had the feeling of being at one with nature, with my entire surroundings, at being enveloped by nature in all her goodness and innocence. Here I was, fit and healthy, in the prime of life (or so I hoped) and feeling once again happy to be alive and smiling from ear to ear like a simpleton simply because of it. I strode on. I had been dawdling and I certainly didn't want to miss the realisation of the new day simply because I'd been dragging my feet. And so, as I was about to put an end to my dilatoriness, and quicken my step, I was suddenly forced to pull up fast and turn, suddenly alarmed, upon my heel. Through the very slightest corner of my eye I had seen a shadow, a form, indistinct, but nevertheless there, just a short distance behind me. The fine hairs upon my body stood on end and I shivered to the very core of my being. I was being followed! I was certainly of it. My breath rose up before me. My breathing and pounding heart surely heard by all! I moved off once more, my stride double what it had just been. At every other step I turned and checked my back. Nothing! And then nothing again! And still nothing more! I calmed a little and slowed my pace somewhat. My near hysterical flight had shaken me and the tiny hairs on my skin still stood on end. I looked back one last time and saw nothing and felt that nothing was untoward. As I was now nearing my eventual destination, I allowed myself to chuckle at my unreasonable self-frightening. But the noise that emanated from out of my mouth was anything but convincing and certainly lacked confidence. And then, from God only knows where, I am absolutely sure that I felt something pull the haversack upon my back sharply and with some considerable force, and for a split second it slowed my pace forwards. I turned around, suddenly furious at my assailant, and to my horror I saw nothing! Nothing! Absolutely nothing at all! This was crazy! The whole situation now totally absurd, almost insane! I mean, not a mere five minutes before, all had been at peace with the world, everything had been positively harmonious. Now, from I know not where, I found myself in a terrified state of mind, and yet all around me was the same, nothing appeared to have changed at all. The expectation of the coming dawn that I had come to witness was just as it should be. The light was perceptibly changing. The birds were beginning to sing. Everything was as it should be. Normality. So then, this sudden situation was utterly ridiculous! Absurd even! And I wasn't having any more to do with it. So grasping the straps of my haversack I jogged on determinedly the short distance to my 'favourite place'. And so it was some few minutes later that I thankfully, and without further ado, reached my goal. I climbed the little grass verge and plonked myself down rather heavily, and with a huge sigh of relief, upon the wooden bench dedicated to two people that were unbeknown to me, and removed the haversack from my back. It was then that I realised my shirt was soaked through with perspiration. In my recent panic I had sweated heavily. This was not how I had expected to see in the new dawn. Uncomfortably damp, sat on, what now appeared to me to be, a decidedly uncomfortable bench. My 'favourite place' had suddenly lost its once magical qualities. Indeed, it would be 'favourite' for not much longer!

Satisfied that I was now safely out of harm's reach and that I had ample time to spare before the actual sunrise, I opened my haversack and took out the flask and the plastic container holding my early morning feast of cheese and crackers. I'd have my treat of chocolate and digestives on the walk back home with last dregs of my tea, and they would be treats that I now felt I fully deserved. They would be certainly relished and something to look forward to, I was sure! The food and the tea were reassuring and brought a much-needed sense of normality to the entire morning's proceedings so far. The coming of dawn would materialise any minute now and the expectation of its magnificence was very great on my part. I was now absolutely certain that this particular dawning would be something very special indeed. And so it was! As I sat there I suddenly felt completely drained, very nearly wiped out. I couldn't understand where this feeling of sudden listlessness had come from. And I could only put it down to my recent hoaxing. I mean OK, I may not be in the exact prime of my life anymore, but nor am I 'old' by any stretch of the imagination, in fact I consider myself to be a fit and healthy middle-aged man. Hopefully, with years of eventful life ahead of me, fingers crossed. But so suddenly dog-tired as I now was, I actually felt like having myself a little nap. No! Not now! Not right this minute, surely? I snapped myself out of my stupor and took a big gulp of my tea. It didn't really do the trick if I have to be honest with you all. It didn't work at all! The air all about me seemed heavy with a sweet seductive odour and it made me want to inhale it deeply into my body. I looked through a growing sort of haze towards the distant slopes of the 'Ryburn Valley' just as the first glow of orange illuminated the crests of the hills beyond. The sunrise was here at last. Oblivious, as I now was, I was in a soporific kind of trance, and now unable to move a single muscle. The Beatles' 'Here Comes The Sun' began to reverberate around the insides of my head, and I was now so sort of heavy that I felt completely numb of body and mind. The tea tumbled out of my hand, the little flask cup bounced off my leg and rolled down the little grass verge directly in front of me. It rolled and rolled—it rolled beyond my bleary field of vision—and I was unable to focus on anything beyond the nose upon my face. Before and above me the sky was blitzed and ablaze with a fire of brilliant orange sunrise, but I saw none of it. All I now saw, just moments before I sank into unconsciousness, were the indistinct forms of what I thought were two small shapes, surely female, moving all about and behind me, but I couldn't really tell if they were female or not. They were doing something, or so I thought, to my arms and hands, but being near paralysed I could offer no resistance, and whatever 'they' were doing 'they' did freely and without hindrance from me. And that was all I saw and felt. I disappeared without a trace into the white mist that completely fogged my brain and was thus rendered lost to the world.

I don't know how long I remained unconscious. I have absolutely no idea. Seconds, minutes, hours maybe, I know not. When I did slowly and inevitably come around the sunrise was long over, the sky was bright blue and here and there fringed with white fluffy clouds, like cotton wool, and the new day was no longer new and well into itself. The first thing I was acutely aware of was that I was absolutely perished and shivering with cold, and secondly, that I was as naked as the day I was born into this god-awful world! And worse, much, much worse in fact, I was tied to the bench securely and was subsequently unable to move a single muscle! My poor head pounded like never before and made me wince in pain. But more terrible than any physical pain I might then be suffering was the self-realisation that I could not indeed escape from my new found and dreadful predicament. I was 'bollock' naked! I was tied, indeed lashed, to the bench and on display for the whole world to see, lily-white and shimmering in the light of day in all my glory!

At first I called for help in a rather subdued and half-hearted 'British' sort of way, politely, with little obvious result, except

95

from the sheep in the field below me who had gathered together to stare at me, and whose confounded gaze just made the whole situation a great deal worse than it already was. Then I yelled for help, again with no result at all. Then I screamed and begged and pleaded for all I was worth, and was, at long last, rewarded with the sudden sardonic presence of the white-haired lady who owned the farm across the way from where I was lashed in bondage.

"Well I'll be blowed! What in God's name have you been up to then?"

I tried to explain. I stammered and stuttered from the very beginning, but no matter how I started it nothing came out right. Unable to convince her of my sincere innocence I grew hot under the collar and irritable, and I fear I must have said more than just a few objectionable words, most probably mingled here and there, with a smattering of choice expletives, which only resulted in her turning abruptly on her heels with much wagging of her head and tut-tut-tutting as she went. And her *coup de grâce*, in a clearly discernable Yorkshire accent, that the police would very soon get to the top and bottom of my little capers, she marked my words! And where are the 'bloody' police when you need them most, I ask you? For after what appeared to be an interminable age the 'Woman in blue' (it just had to be a woman, didn't it) eventually turned up. Her opening salutation, after a good long and hard look at me, was textbook police vocabulary and made me shrink still further.

"Well, well, well, and what have we got here then! What have you been up to then, you naughty boy!"

And this was spoken with a wry smile upon her stern and officious visage. After having had me 'checked out' over her police radio, and once the W.P.C. was utterly satisfied that I was 'kosher' and sound of body and mind, I was untied and relieved of my human bondage and gratefully accepted a blanket to hide my shrinking dignity and another to place around my shoulders so as to offer me some additional warmth. Once safely ensconced on the rear seat of the patrol car, the police lady gathered up my belongings and put them back into my haversack—after that is, having given it a thoroughly good 'going over' first. Back inside the motor car the W.P.C. contacted the police 'control' over her radio with regards her intended movement, namely taking me home, and was about to thankfully move off when there was a sudden sharp knuckle-rapping on the side window next to where I was sat. I ducked down instinctively, expecting nothing good to come of it all, especially after my recent ordeal. But the police officer reassured my cowering form that it was only the old lady from the farm over the way. The window was duly lowered and the silver-haired and grimacing face was somewhat rudely thrust into mine, followed by her sneering, scowling, rendition of an explanation. Her breath was rancid, almost over-powering, and seemed to fill the motor car in an instant.

"You do know where you been sitting, eh lad?"

I shook my head vacuously. Her grubby little hands grasped hold of the windows edge and in a voice renewed with glee, she added this.

"Well that be the 'Tinker's' that be!"

I was none the wiser for that.

"Nellie and Nora. Tinkers by birth, tinkers in life, and sure as anything, as eggs is eggs, tinkers in their death!"

I gazed stupidly into her wizened and weathered face, and all I could muster by way of reply was a somewhat pathetic retort.

"But it's my favourite place!"

She sneeringly replied.

"Then it's high time you found your'sen another'un in'it lad! You see they don't like the looks of yous do they now!"

And with a thoroughly rotten smile she was gone in a flash, completely disappeared. And so the window was closed and we were gone from there. Shortly afterwards I was deposited outside my front door. The W.P.C. kindly retrieving my spare front door key from underneath the flowerpot held the rear door open for me as I awkwardly made my way onto the pavement, and after an embarrassing bow and a grovelling thank-you, I was once more secure and safe inside my own home. And that was it really, nothing else occurred, and there was nothing else untoward. It all seemed rather silly on reflection. All returned to humdrum normality except for the occasional re-enactment of the incident in the odd dream or two, thus necessitating a change of the bedding the next morning as a result of my mumbling and thrashing perspiration! However, nothing was ever said to anyone. I told no one of my ordeal. It was buried, lost to all knowledge, like an 'Egyptian mummy', and I left my 'favourite place' well alone for nigh on a year. Until, that is, one wild winter's night close to the eve of Christmas. Having had more than my fill of festive ale and wine in the 'Beehive', I decided, in my swaggering boldness, to pay my 'favourite place' a rare visit. To show the world, and especially myself, that I was no longer intimidated by it, and its memory could frighten me no more. I reached it without incident and stood before it swaying, belched rather loudly, and put two fingers up to it in bold defiance, and much less bravely and more warily, urinated upon the grass verge directly to one side of it. Smugly satisfied with myself I carried on with my wayward journey back home, my fears vanquished. However, I had not taken more than a dozen steps or so when I felt a sudden great thwack right in the middle of my back, smack between the shoulder blades. Being already somewhat unsteady upon my feet I dropped like a stone to the ground and rolled upon my back so as to see my assailant. I saw nothing, but instead heard the angry hissings and unintelligible whisperings and then something roughly brushed the side of my face and nipped the flesh of my cheek, a something that smelt dreadful. I was up in an instant, suddenly completely and utterly sober, and was off like a sprinter. I ran like the wind! I gave it my best legs. And I hadn't ran as fast since my school-boy days. And for nearly all of the way I could hear their barely audible voices behind me, and once or twice, their terrible mocking laughter. By the time I reached the bottom of the 'Hollin Lane' I knew that I was free of them at long last. I slowed my frantic, heart-attack, pace but didn't stop actually running until I reached my front door. For a long time afterwards, I remained jittery and on edge, peeping out through a chink in the curtains, making absolutely sure that the coast was clear, and that I had not been followed right back to the front door of the house. And so with the assistance of a good single malt whisky, I eventually calmed down and settled down before a roaring log fire, my definitely new 'favourite place'!

Postscript.

I have not ventured anywhere near that spot since, nor do I intend to 'tinker' anywhere near it ever again. I have since found myself a new 'favourite place' and it alone is my secret!

THE END
COMPLETED TYPING ON 9th MAY 2016

Stony Lane! (Molly!)

"Oh Molly, Molly, Molly! Oh how could you!"

Both women chuckled mischievously. The younger suddenly blushing to the roots of her straight brown hair.

"How could you make me take such a wicked old book?"

All this was spoken in barely a whisper, even though the library was empty save for the speaker herself, and the diminutive librarian facing her. She leant even closer over the counter with a wicked glint flickering in her eyes.

"And the sensations! Well, well, well, I never did!"

The older woman pinched the tiny librarian's cheek playfully.

"You naughty little thing, you!"

The speaker looked all about her as though expecting somebody to be listening to their secret conversation before she resumed, stooping down, her eyes glistening with conspiracy. They were very nearly nose-to-nose.

"Now what do you recommend for me this week? You naughty little minx, you!"

Molly smiled back up into the hungry, demanding eyes, smiling her thoroughly disarming smile. And so the two women conspired in sibilant whispers. Molly then withdrew a book out from under the counter and almost thrust it into the eager outstretched hands of the older woman, who quickly and deftly plunged it into the depths of her handbag and left the library without another word or another glance in the librarian's direction. The book, an old out of date, and out of print, somewhat racy 'Victorian' romance, was harmless enough. Its words very nearly obsolete, its plots bordering upon the inane, and its characters shallowing out to flat. But when all put together as a whole package, and after numerous glasses of sweet sherry, and read by that lascivious part of the brain that often lies dormant, it suddenly became a very different kettle of fish altogether. Add to this a good dose of auto-suggestion and mixed with a little bit of boredom and loneliness, and then with more than a hint of sexual repression, when all of this spewed forth why it had all the explosive power of an 'atomic bomb'! Its rhetoric and sub-plots and barely hidden innuendo locked bathroom doors and stirred the loins in the dead of night! And what's more, books of its ilk had the power to keep one's brooding middle-age at bay and occupied for a few hours at least.

There had only been the two of them in the small, flat-roofed, annex sort of building that comprised the 'Ripponden' library. And in actual fact the library was about to close for the day. It served the local community on four days of the week. Monday, Thursday, and Friday afternoons, and on Saturday morning. All in all, a sum total of thirty hours per week. It was very well used and very well loved by the local people in the surrounding areas that used it on a regular basis, and it would be sorely missed by all if the dreaded 'Council' somehow managed to close it down and shunt its services elsewhere. This was very much a perceived threat and the local inhabitants were indeed ready to bear arms in its defence if need be. And if this threat ever came to any sort of realisation then the 'Ripponden' Parish Council had promised, one and all, to fight to the bitter end, and that they would indeed go down with this political ship rather than see its continuance ultimately severed. It could very well become a very hot political potato indeed! But all of this passed over the head of the tiny, almost miniscule librarian, who was revered (by adults) and feared (mostly by children) alike.

"What will be will be."

She very often thought to herself. And this being her standard form of reply to the voiced fears and grumbling of her most staunch and regular users. All the same this nonchalance was in reality a mask. She was a dreadful and secret worrier at heart, and in the quiet moments, when away from enquiring and prying eyes, her deep-seated fears and worries for the library's future very nearly consumed her equilibrium. So much so that each and every Sunday morning, when she attended St Bartholomew's, she earnestly prayed with all her might for the library's continual existence, for its salvation from the clutches of 'Hell' and oblivion. Her prayers were so deep and so prolonged that she was seemingly lost in an evangelical trance and appeared almost divinely spiritual to those seated around her. So intense were they that they completely wore her out, body and mind. In contrast, the parish's new young vicar, on witnessing her 'strange departures' from the pulpit, thought her to be surely epileptic, and what he believed to be her repeated petit mals, would inevitably be leading up to a catastrophic seizure. The imminent fear of which churned his delicate stomach and made him sweat profusely whenever he happened to glance in her direction. When in actual fact the reality and the truth of the matter was that Molly was simply fast and sound asleep.

By nearly half past six, the library had been very well used. Books had come in and books had gone out. All the computer terminals (of which there were two for adult use and two for children) had been in constant demand, and had only just ceased being used. And now, the library, with under a half an hour to go, would soon be getting ready to close, and involved a routine that Molly followed quite methodically. And then with just a little over twenty minutes to go, the library door suddenly opened and in came two more customers. Molly sighed heavily and followed them into the building with her keen eyes. A child, a young girl in matter of fact, already much taller than Molly herself, approached the library counter tentatively, her mother a little distance behind issuing whispered instructions. Molly smiled and removed her round-rimmed spectacles, the child suddenly abashed by this action seemed to cower before her eyes. The child's now awkward mother nudged her daughter towards the counter's edge. The young girl's mouth appeared to be formulating the words that played about the corners of her lips. Molly, the peaceable smile still radiating kindness and her little eyes oozing warmth and understanding, edged closer to her side of the counter and so to the young girl on the other side. In response the child seemed to waver but then suddenly rallied and just in the nick of time blurted out.

"Please miss, are you a real midget?"

The mother aghast, her mouth agape, pulled her daughter away from the counter and reproved her severely. The child burst into a flood of tears. Tears of shame. She positively wailed. The mother instantly contrite, and submissively placatory, hugged the sobbing child into her body for all she was worth. Whispering soothing benedictions into her daughter's ears. Molly replaced the spectacles on her face and with her foot she dragged towards the counter the little plastic stool upon which she stood in moments of crisis, situations of acute embarrassment, such as the one now confronting her. The mother and child hunched before her now looked on. And now elevated by a good twelve inches Molly took possession and command of the situation in her own indomitable, yet magnanimous, manner. After all she'd heard it all before, so many, many times before. From the very earliest times that she

101

could indeed remember she had heard that word used to describe her in one-way or the other. That word! That horrible word! Midget! The ridicule, the derision, and at rare times the actual bullying. Hurtful and very nasty! But most upsetting of all was the being spat at and the indescribable things that were flung, hurled and thrown in her direction. But thank all the gods the latter had ceased to happen, for some inexplicable reason unbeknown to her, once she had reached the end of junior school. Secondary school and her five years of study at 'Ryburn High' were completely (and strangely enough) incident free, and Molly was left free to grow, sadly not in stature, and be educated and to contemplate her future life. And all of this was achieved whilst being enveloped by the love given to her by her parents, and in her own great love of books and music, which kept the bouts of depression and worry at bay. She had recently acquired a great love of cycling, which gave her a greater independence, and a growing sense of freedom with which to explore the environment around where she lived. These things were crowned by Molly's deep love of the beautiful countryside (which she felt herself to be an integral part of), and which was just dying to be explored and enjoyed to the very fullest from amidst the loving safe haven of her family home. And as she grew and matured, Molly knew that she had never been quite so happy and contented. But she also knew that she was very different indeed from other people her own age. However, she was, at long last, at peace with herself and with everything and everyone around her. And that, for the most part, is how it had remained, right up until that very moment in time, except for the occasional blip on the radar and the odd word said in jest. All quickly brushed aside and equally quickly forgotten. And today's little incident, which had occurred only moments before, was just such a blip, a minor irritation, and something said if not in jest then something said in pure and child-like innocence. But now suddenly, quite unexpectedly, the hated word had unexpectedly been used again. And used by one with her in mind. Used in all innocence, and used in ignorance, unaware of its devastating meaning, but used all the same and now once used it had to be confronted and dealt with. Midget! What a silly old word it was. What an ugly little word it sounded when voiced. And what a horrid word it was when used with people in mind. People like her! Molly! She felt the butterflies in her tummy as she stood upon her little stool smiling serenely before the still clearly embarrassed mother and her shrinking violet of a daughter who tried desperately to hide herself away in the folds of her mother's floppy coat. She now looked towards them both as the word 'midget' receded in her mind. The mother was about to say something, something that Molly suddenly felt would only make matters much worse so she intervened quickly and precisely.

"Please! Please don't worry. It doesn't matter, honestly. It doesn't bother me at all, really it doesn't!"

Molly laughed as if to vindicate her words. Her laugh was reassuring and it was also a pleasant one at that, neither forced nor fake. Its happy tones calmed the child who emerged from the folds of her mother's coat with a blotchy face and a runny nose and wet eyes. Molly smiled beautifully towards her and reaching forward proffered a delicately scented paper handkerchief, which the child hesitatingly accepted. In one simple action, accompanied by a smile, Molly had won the little girl over and gained her complete trust. The mother was suddenly in awe and consequently Molly had gained another diehard follower, and the library another adherent to the cause. In the next fifteen or twenty minutes or so Molly explained, without ever being condescending or patronising, and without being, or drifting into, the pompous, why she was what she was. She explained in a gentle manner, which she possessed and in such a way as the little girl clearly and fully understood, the medical condition from which she suffered and what would be the eventual outcome of her condition. All politically correct and acceptable! The child was soon returning her smile and before leaving the library she held out her small chubby hand for Molly to hold, an innocent gesture of friendship and kindness. The mother looked into Molly's eyes and whispered a genuine and heartfelt.

"Thank you."

To which Molly once again simply replied to by giving them both her peaceful and radiant smile. Once outside the library both mother and daughter burst into tears and hugged one another in one of those rare and special moments, and which both of them would remember and never ever forget. And that was the end of that little episode. Over and done with. As the library door closed behind them, and mother and child were swallowed up by the dark and cold of the winter's evening, Molly prepared to close the library for another day. Her little heavenly place of peace and tranquillity. Her little place of sanctuary. Her bolt-hole from the hustle bustle of the wider world beyond the library's doors. Not that one could, or would for that matter, call 'Ripponden' (and its surrounding districts) 'wild' in any sense of the word. A place of far reaching vistas, rolling, peaceful hills, yes. 'Wild'? Certainly not!

She stepped off the little stool upon which she was still standing, then folding it up, she placed it neatly away upon its shelf and made her way round the library counter towards the front door, which she locked carefully but with a definite flourish. It was so very nearly home time at last! She then turned to face her little domain, her 'queendom', with hands on hips and wearing a wispy smile upon her freckly little face. She walked towards the right-angle of her smallish librarian's counter so as to be able to take in all of the library that now lay before her and she savoured what she saw and nodded her head in appreciation. Delight surged throughout her little body. She then closed her eyes tightly and edged slowly forwards. She knew every square inch of the building inside and out. At first, the fingers of her out-stretched left hand, touching, tickling, the spines of the books that resided in the 'romantic' fiction (the library's most popular section), the collection of which had been assiduously built up under Molly's personal supervision. She felt a sudden tingle, a shiver, that made the tiny hairs that lived upon her skin stand proudly on end, and she giggled out aloud in wicked delight. She gently wagged her head from side to side and tutted, softly whispering,

"Naughty, naughty, naughty! You bad, bad people!"

She then instinctively turned to her right at the corner window, and as she glided along, as if floating on air, her finger tips touched the spines of 'crime' and 'murder' most foul. And in mock warning she hissed ever so softly.

"The devil's awaiting you all! Each and every one of you. You mark my words!"

At the end of their shelves she turned still blind and slowly retraced her steps, and still with fingers out-stretched, they lightly skimmed across the key-boards of the library's computers.

"The 'world-wide web' at my finger tips, and all of it mine to do with as I please!"

Once again, she shivered with delight and then stopped with a sudden frown upon her face at the 'non-fiction'.

"Cold hard facts! Heartless! Forlorn and forsaken! Loveless!"

The spines of these she flicked with her finger's tips and passed them by all too quickly as though to show her displeasure. Turning sharply towards her right she knew that she had reached the 'children's' section, and here she opened her eyes and viewed the scatter of books upon the kneeling rug. She shook a reproving finger but remained silent. Squatting down on her haunches she gathered them all up and replaced some in the trough of books close to her little body, the others she returned diligently to their respective slots upon their shelves. When all was tidy and as it should be, she unlocked the library storeroom and wheeled out her bicycle, 'Ripponden's' two-wheeled wonder, back past the computer terminals and lovingly leant it up against the library counter. Back inside the storeroom she turned off all the library's main lights and retrieved her coat, crash helmet, gloves and muffler, and after carefully closing the door behind her she crossed the floor once more towards her bicycle, gently caressing its saddle and whispered,

"My trusty steed. My 'Champion the Wonder Horse.' Carry me home safely!"

When she had fastidiously donned her coat, crash helmet, gloves and muffler, and was suitably satisfied and attired, Molly switched off the library's remaining light and stood in the doorway looking into the winter darkness, her vision momentarily diffused. She blinked repeatedly until her eyes became accustomed to the early evening gloom. Scanning the library's shelves and the barely discernable spines of the countless books, she smiled and waved.

"Goodnight my loves. Sweet dreams until the morrow."

And with that heartfelt sentiment, as though saying goodnight to a dear and molly-coddled child, she blew her charges a loving kiss. Then turning her back upon the library and with her bicycle in hand, she left the building carefully locking the front door behind her. Checking that it was indeed secure at least three times before she moved away to begin her journey back homeward. Once outside she turned sharply to her right and wheeled her bicycle along the pavement, past the bus stop towards the 'Royd Lane.' At the 'Conservative Club' Molly crossed the road and began the steep ascent up the mighty hill. Immediately past the 'Club's' car park she suddenly caught sight of something moving in the deep dark shadows cast by the towering trees that staggered up what was left of the hill up to the 'Coach Road' above. The flickering light captivatingly revealed two lovers in the throes of their intimacy. She was shocked, appalled, (but without doubt mesmerised by what she saw) and her righteous indignation rose up like a volcano and she stamped her tiny foot in anger and called out!

"Stop it! Stop it at once! Do you hear me? You're very rude, and very naughty!"

The sudden urgent movements that seemed at first to be disjointed, awkward, and in utter confusion, suddenly became a movement of uniformity as the coupling was achieved. Molly couldn't move. She was rooted to the spot. Her tiny feet glued to the pavement. Her heart pounded. She perspired profusely under her layered insulation. She trembled and her trembling passed through the frame of her bicycle right through to the rubber tyres and into the cold tarmacadam beneath them. Her eyes were like saucers! This was never in any romantic novel that she had ever read! Animal passion replete! Fornification! She tutted loudly out of sheer displeasure. This wasn't right! It was wholly wrong! It was downright improper! The couple, whoever they were, however old they were, (and one would hope that they were young, or would one?) were suddenly rumbled and they stumbled at their detection. Aggression: their only defence.

"What are you looking at? Go away! Go on clear off!"

(Or words very similar to that effect!) Shouted the female in pure consternation. Her pleasure now thwarted for the next hour or so at least. Molly couldn't answer back at all, but only smiled her lovely sweet smile in any sort of reply. Not that they were able to see it from where they were concealed.

"I said what are you looking at, you freak! You weirdo!"

Then Molly clearly saw the female trying desperately to restrain her 'beau', but seemingly to no avail. Molly heard the distinct sound of crashing, snapping and thrashing of foliage coming towards her and fled accordingly without waiting to find out whom the bodily form belonged to. The little bell on her handlebars tinkling out aloud under the vibrations as she ran away as best and fast as she could. She scuttled up the 'Royd Lane' as fast as her little legs could carry her. In her muffled ears she heard the disgruntled and refractory lover calling out to her fast vanishing form. His words ringing out in the cold night air.

"Get lost! Get lost, you freak!"

On up the 'Royd Lane' she scooted and when she very quickly reached the 'Stony Lane' upon her right-hand side, she briefly paused to catch her breath, turning back to see whether she was pursued. Satisfied that she wasn't she wagged her finger and tutted softly in their direction then admonished them under her breath.

"Naughty, wicked things! I hope they've taken precautions?"

And with that she made her way slowly up the 'Stony Lane' and followed its steep hill of repentance.

Stopping after a little so as to get her second wind back, Molly decided that it was high time that she got herself a little battery-powered engine for her beloved bicycle. It was her aunt who had first broached the subject on a cold, wet and gusty autumnal night, and not that very since. She'd decided to talk to her niece about it after watching her trying to 'flog a dead horse' on up the murderous hill that eventually led to their peaceful little cottage. And, after getting Molly to see the sense in such a positive practicality, she'd agreed in the end, and they'd both gone to see 'Mr. Bob' the bicycle man in 'Halifax' town centre. Once there they had been bamboozled with ratios, outputs, horse-power and speed. After that visit she'd wavered and 'ummed and ahhed' one way and the other. But now, after a hard day's work in the library, and the daunting up-hill climb still to come, and with the wind smarting her eyes to tears and stinging her tiny face, (not to mention her little untimely upsets!) Molly definitely saw the advantage of a little battery-powered engine for her bicycle. As long that is, and she was absolutely adamant on this point, that it wouldn't mean that she had to purchase a new bicycle. For, she adored her 'precious' friend with a passion. Nor would it, in any way, damage her bicycle in any way whatsoever, and if need be the battery-engine could be removed at the drop of a hat if, or when required. Mr. Bob would have to agree to these things, she said to herself, before she'd agree to anything! Now halfway up, she turned and looked back down in the direction that she'd just travelled. One day very soon she was going to go flying down that hill aboard her trusty bicycle free-wheeling at top speed, the wind rushing through her thick and wavy hair, and not applying the brakes until she reached the 'Conservative Club' car park. One day!!

Nearly home now she stopped at the wooden bench and rested for a short while and softly sang and hummed her favourite song off the 'Beatles' 'Abbey Road' album, 'Golden Slumbers'. Her voice was high-pitched (some would say squeaky, but that was really unfair) but melodic and perfectly in tune. She held and steadied the bicycle by holding its little padded saddle. It was a strange looking contraption altogether. Unique, in actual fact. One of a kind! It was, to all intents and purposes, a lady's bicycle which incorporated a strange looking frame, low-slung, and which appeared to have no pleasing symmetry at all. And furthermore, it had a saddle so low that it seemed almost impossible to sit upon, let alone ride upon comfortably. And then to cap it all the handle-bars of the bicycle appeared to be somewhere between those of 'cow-horns' and 'choppers', altogether too high, and only added to the bicycle's overall bizarre appearance. But that Molly loved this ungainly machine with all her tiny heart was beyond question. She loved it with every inch of all her might! And it was further embellished with old-fashioned front and rear battery-powered lights, a rather copious brown leather saddle-bag (for whatever was needed whenever), a traditional 'tinkle-tinkle' bell on the handle-bars, and finally, a chain-guard to protect Molly's tiny ankles. And all of this technological and mechanical wonderment was spray-painted her favourite colour, bright, and shocking pink. You certainly couldn't have missed her in the daytime! But finally, the 'pièce de résistance', was the actual bicyclist herself. Attired in her black round-topped cycle helmet that looked far too big for her very small head, and gave one the impression of a miniature whizzing (for she always rode too fast wherever she went!) madman! A human torpedo, too dangerous by far for the public thoroughfare at large!

Well anyway, after singing her song, and fully rested, she shortly afterwards gained the crest of the hill and made her way directly to her aunt's cottage that lay just on the outskirts of the tiny hamlet that comprised the 'Soyland Town'. After carefully locking her bicycle away safely in the adjoining lean-to-cum conservatory, Molly made her way back round to the front of Auntie's cottage, a place where she'd now lived for some considerable time, and let herself in through the front door by the specially adapted bottom lock. The insides of the cottage smelt truly delicious. Her aunty was sat listening to the radio softly humming some unknown tune and casually reading a book by the light of a table-side lamp. The whole lounge gave off an orange glow that was both warm and snugly-cosy and awash with the scents of rose petal and lavender oil. Molly had had no trouble whatsoever in falling in love with her auntie's cottage (almost instantly in fact) after she'd been forced to move in and take refuge there when both of her parents had died, within two months of one another. They had indeed died from the same degenerative disease that they'd unwittingly and tragically passed on to their beloved and only child. Still, that a child was born alive at all was indeed itself a miracle. The money raised from the subsequent sale of the family home was bequeathed to her as her legacy for when the time eventually came around (and it would!) when she would undoubtedly need it to ease, and cushion, the time of her own passing away. But what of that now, I ask you? That was still, hopefully, a long day away as yet! She flopped down into her favourite armchair and smiled tenderly at her aunt, a loving, and benign silver-haired spinster now in her mid-sixties.

"Well Aunty, you just won't believe the type of day I've had! It was a real topper, it really was! And you just won't believe what I've just seen at the bottom of 'Royd Lane', you know, in that little bit of land just past the car park, in the trees!"

The Aunt smiled back and closed her book and patted it affectionately. She spoke softly and her eyes twinkled mischievously.

"Well now my love, why don't you go up and have yourself a nice hot bath? I've bought some new scented bath oils, you'll love them, and then you can tell me all about it when you come down."

Molly shuffled her bottom out of the armchair.

"And when I hear you pull the plug, I'll make you a delicious cheese and tomato 'toasty' and a nice hot mug of 'Ovaltine', how's that my love?"

Molly nodded and smiled and rubbed her tiny hands with glee and off she went to have her nightly bath and so make herself ready for bed. Being a tiny young woman, she tired easily and very often her days were very much shorter than those of others. Halfway up the stairs she stopped as she heard her aunt calling after her.

"And don't forget your rubber ring if you have a deep one! And be careful Molly my love, those new oils are really slippery!"

Molly hesitated on the stairs for a moment longer for she instinctively knew that there was still a little bit more to come.

"But don't be too long my love, don't keep me waiting for ages; I can't wait to hear your news!"

There were no secrets between them and they shared everything, always, together. She smiled in return. She loved her aunt dearly and with a passion. She was indeed her surrogate mother, her rock upon which to run aground. Her very best friend.

"Alright I will, and I promise I won't be too long, and I'll be extra careful as always! I really promise!"

She closed the bathroom door and began to run her bath. Steam billowed into the room quickly filling it completely from floor to ceiling. She added the new scented oils that her aunt had bought especially and breathed in the aromas and then commenced to undress herself, carefully folding her clothes and placing them upon the bathroom chair, putting her little boots very neatly side by side underneath. Then, with a bath flannel in her tiny hand, she quickly wiped the condensation off the bottom half of the big mirror that was fixed to the inside of the bathroom door. Now completely naked she stood before the full-length mirror and looked diligently (her head to one side) at every inch of her tiny reflected image in turn. Her entire body was indeed perfect in every detail, only in miniature, as the gods had intended it to be. Satisfied with what she saw she turned her back upon herself and stepped towards the bath. Then donning her rubber ring she climbed into the bath, after first testing the water's temperature with one of her tiny feet, and submerged herself into the liquid bliss, and she was so well pleased with herself that she was soon bobbing about the big roomy bath tub completely camouflaged by the clouds of rising bubbles that she wittingly loved to create by twirling and thrashing her hands in the water by her sides. Heaven indeed. And emanating from out of those scented bubbles came the 'Beatles' back catalogue of number one hit singles (in no particular order) replete with sound effects. And thus, Molly's bath time was complete.

They talked until very nearly ten o' clock, until, that is, Molly suddenly grew terribly sleepy. Full of 'Ovaltine' and toasted sandwich, and under the insistence of her aunt, she reluctantly retired to her bed. Molly embraced the older woman lovingly and kissed her warmly, and with deep feeling, upon the lips and with a sleepy goodnight she dragged her little body off up the stairs to her warm and snuggery bed, her safe nest of dreams. They had talked for nearly three hours. For long periods the aunt mainly listening, as Molly went through her day's adventures. And at certain key moments Molly, her tiny knees tucked up right under her chin, listened attentively to the older woman's answers and advice, nodding her head in complete agreement. Of what had happened to her that day not much, if anything at all, had really bothered her. Not the couple caught in the act of copulation, nor the somewhat embarrassing encounter with the mother and child in the library just before closing. These she had taken in her stride. Especially the visual image of the crude, vulgar, yet striking sexual act, the image of which had remained in the foremost part of her mind, so far, all night long. The act of intercourse had been a prominent and constant thought within her mind as of late. It fascinated her and she linked it indelibly to her notion of romantic love and ultimately to how she believed a man and a woman should behave towards one another. The ultimate coming together as well as the bonding of two souls forever. That it actually really wasn't like this at all; she adamantly refused to accept. And the near animal urgency of the act that she had witnessed she cleverly blocked from her mind completely. That she herself would never make love, or have love made to her in any shape or form, was beyond any reasonable doubt, and she accepted that fact at face value. It didn't really bother her anymore, or so she believed. It had done, terribly! But now, having reached her early twenties, she had come to accept and resigned herself to the fact of being a barren young woman. And this was how it should, must, remain. Her aunt was incredulous and urged her, pleaded with her, and importuned her, to abandon such drastic and devastating thoughts most vehemently. But on this particular question she was unsuccessful. Her pleas had fallen upon deaf ears. Molly wouldn't be swayed. Her niece wouldn't budge an inch and couldn't be persuaded at all to even contemplate the matter again, let alone change her mind. On this issue Molly was implacable, and she had accepted that all aspects of physical love-making were now already beyond her. But what still remained, marooned and unshakeable, and deeply seated within her mind was the romantic ideal of love, which she justly regarded as fine, decent, and noble, and which she guarded zealously with her very being. And that was why the vision of the young couple in the shadowy trees on the 'Royd Lane' had appalled her and yet more disturbingly for Molly, had mesmerised her also, she was enthralled with what she knew she could never and would never have. But hey ho not to worry, for all of this was very soon dealt with and pushed away to one side and, for the time being at least, quickly forgotten. But what had really troubled her was a word thrown back at her in haste and surely (hopefully!) in pure anger. And the word that had stung and cut her to the quick was 'freak'! She had always known that she was different from other children, and subsequently from other people as she grew up. But she had never, never at all, not even for one single moment, thought of herself as 'odd'! Her aunt had pulled out all the stops and used all her guile in the arts of persuasion to calm, soothe and pacify her niece. She had beckoned for her to come over and sit before her which Molly duly and willingly did, resting her troubled head upon her aunt's knees, as her older woman gently stroked her hair and tenderly caressed her forehead, thus easing, and eventually banishing, the thoughts of torment that had confounded her innocent mind. The Aunt further persuaded her niece that the 'word' had been spoken in a sense of frustrated disappointment. It had been impetuous and would undoubtedly be greatly regretted in the clear light of day. Thus Molly's anxiety was assuaged and all her doubts and inner fears dispelled, but only for the time being that is. They would arise again very soon and they would play a significant part in the ultimate decision that would eventually decide her fate. The word 'freak' was a seed that had been planted in her innocent mind and it had shaken her, and shaken her little body. But for the moment, tired and placated, Molly made her way back up the stairs to her bed, and as soon as her head touched the pillow she fell fast and soundly asleep. Her dreams that night were untroubled and unremembered. She had slept well and soundly all night long, and in the morning she awoke to calm, and found herself to be as fresh as a daisy. Molly rose with the larks and breakfasted on a pot of leaf tea, granary toast and 'Dundee' marmalade, as well as a bowl of her favourite cereal, and rounded it all off with a chapter from her current romantic novel, 'When Love Came A Calling!'. Then, when she could contain her itchy feet no longer, she got to her feet and made a move to leave the cottage. Then with an apple and a banana, a flask of camomile tea (if it was good enough for 'Peter Rabbit' then it was certainly good enough for her!) and a handful of mixed nuts and raisins, all for her saddle-bag, along with her book and a very small pair of binoculars, she retrieved her bicycle from the conservatory come lean-to and made ready for her morning foray into the surrounding hills and countryside. As always, diligently locking the back door behind her, she crept along the gravely garden path careful to avoid making any real noise as she went so as not to wake her aunt who softly snored upstairs in her room. Or so she thought. For had she looked up towards her aunt's bedroom window, she would have seen the clearly discernable chink in the older woman's bedroom curtains and a little beyond that, she'd have caught the tiniest glimpse of that woman's smiling face and dishevelled hair. But she didn't look up. She never did. Outside of the garden gate Molly mounted her bicycle and rode away as the maternal and satisfied Aunt climbed back into her warm inviting bed and snuggled up to her still sleeping lover. Whose sweet-smelling hair appeared to have exploded upon her pillow, and with her free hand the aunt caressed the big and beautiful sagging belly that she loved so much, then she too fell fast asleep, blissfully unaware of what was about to befall her niece later that very same morning.

Having bicycled very nearly all of the way over the 'tops', passing through 'Hubberton Green' and peddling her little heart out on through 'Boulder Clough' and down into 'Luddenden Foot' where she dismounted, thoroughly jiggered, and sat down and had herself her flask and a good old rest. Walking back along the main 'Burnley Road' Molly stopped at the green roadside cabin and asked for a fresh flask of 'Earl Grey' tea to see her back on the homeward journey. She and the jovial café owner had a lively little chat about the latest romantic novel that had blipped on their radar, with Molly giving away tiny hints, miniscule titbits, of mouth-watering delights to whet the other woman's appetite. Without giving too much in the way of detail away. And then with a wave of her tiny hand she was gone. Riding along the pavement as much as possible before turning to her right and crossing the 'River Calder'. She crossed by the bridge close to the weir and made her way along a very bumpy road that every now and again bounced her clean out of the saddle and made her scream then giggle uncontrollably. She made her way back up to the hilltop lanes and then back the way she'd already travelled. She was indeed a marvel to behold as she whizzed by, her little legs a blur of motion.

The day was cold, (the wind gathering strength all the time) but thankfully dry. The air was crystal clear and stung the back of her throat and she could see for miles and miles all around her. On hillsides many, many miles distant, she could quite easily make out the grazing sheep and cattle and just about discern their step-by-step movements as they crossed their fields of pasture. She made a quick mental note that these would be ideal areas to explore in the not too distant future. On sunny days perhaps, when the air was still and full of warmth and the lanes were tar-bubbled and dusty. On past 'Hubberton Green' again. But no stopping this time for tea and day dreaming as the flying Molly disappeared and completely vanished from sight below the dry-stone walls that littered and obscured the spectacular view. Twice Molly very nearly came off her bicycle coming down the hill towards 'St Mary's' church at 'Cotton Stones'. Once, when her cycle helmet dropped down over the top of her eyes forcing her to raise her head up high in order to see where she was going. But the dazzling blue of the sky and the brilliant white of the clouds suddenly made her very dizzy and disorientated. She almost passed through the open churchyard gate, but at the very last moment she somehow managed to swerve and regain the road proper. And it was with a palpitating heart that she was able to push her cycle helmet back into place and peddled on tremblingly. Her second near mishap came shortly afterwards and was, for her, potentially much more dangerous. All in all it was a silly little incident, and if anyone had witnessed it they would surely have found it more comical. Molly hit the bottom of 'Salt Drake' with her tiny heart still fluttering from the scare of only moments before. She was travelling at a fair old speed now and just as she was about to cross the small stone bridge when, from out of the dense hedge upon her right-hand side, a huge bull's head suddenly thrust itself out into the open and bellowed out loud for what it was worth. Startled she veered sharply to her left without time to correct her balance and hit the bridge's parapet with a thump and a clatter amid the sounds of metal scrapping against stone. Her beloved bicycle! Within a split second she was catapulted over the handle bars and ended up flat upon her back on the bridge's capping stones, semi-conscious and utterly dazed, her bicycle resting peaceably against the stonework by her side. It had all the trappings of the bizarre. Very slowly the blue of the sky above her gradually filtered into her brain, and the still bellowing bull, brought her back down to earth with a start. She began to cry for no apparent reason at all for she wasn't really hurt or in any real distress, except that she cried out of the pure unexpected shock of it all. Still sobbing out loud she plopped herself down off the parapet and proceeded to check over her faithful machine. And apart from some superficial scratches on the mudguard and on one of the pedals as well as some missing spots of paint here and there, there was no real harm done. However, on immediate reflection, it was a jolly good thing that she'd been wearing a good solid cycle helmet, otherwise the back of her skull would undoubtedly have been caved in! She patted the helmet reverently. And after shaking her tiny fist at the somewhat bemused old bull and gave him something of a lecture before she took hold of the bicycle and walked shakily the rest of the way up the 'Salt Drake', past 'The Alma Inn', with the machine free-wheeling at her side. With her heart still beating excitedly against her ribcage, and with an odd sob rising every now and again to her throat, Molly continued to walk for quite a way before she felt sufficiently settled and had calmed down enough for her tiny mittened hands to have finally stopped shaking. She eventually reached and turned right into 'Gough Lane' and now felt herself to be composed enough to mount her bicycle once more and peddled off (albeit slowly) down towards the 'Ripponden Woods'. She passed alongside fields of pasture and their grazing sheep and cows inhaling the sweet fresh smell of manure as she went. (Good old muck!) She pulled it deeply into her little body filling her tiny lungs to bursting. It made her feel good to be alive and living in the countryside. Away from the over-crowded towns and cities, (where she wouldn't fit in at all) all full of noise and pollution and annoying people! At the end of the lane, which in truth, had now dwindled down to nothing more than a mere track, Molly dismounted and manoeuvred herself and the bicycle onto the steep downward path that was hemmed in on both sides by tall conifers and deathly silence. This was the path that would lead her down to the old water mill that was situated at the bottom of the small village of 'Mill Bank'. And this old building marked the beginnings of her most very favourite place of all, in all her world. The ancient 'Ripponden Woods'! Untouched and unspoilt for many and many a year. After quickly crossing the narrow 'Foxen Lane' she passed by the side of the old mill itself (like so many of the old buildings converted into very desirable living accommodation) with the cascading stream directly upon her left-hand side. Molly followed the winding and increasingly precipitous track up into the woods themselves. In places the track was decidedly muddy, not that she really minded at all for she was wearing her sturdy little boots and was well prepared for any eventuality—save one!

The big wheels of her bicycle were now grown cumbersome and were bouncing awkwardly at every dip, hollow, stone and rock that littered her path. But what caused her the most bother were the many ancient and often-tangled tree roots that, more often than not, lay concealed beneath the heaps of dry and crunchy leaves. These hidden obstacles seemingly brought the bicycle to life, and on more than one occasion it almost bounced itself out of her tiny hands. Pity that it didn't do so! For that would have been the disaster that just might have saved her life! After a little more than fifteen minutes she reached her secret spot. It was her most favourite place of all. An ancient rooty beech tree. Its gnarled trunk rose straight up and towered mightily above her miniscule body. She leant her trusty bicycle against its massive bole and patted it respectfully; then she unpacked her saddlebag and made herself ready. It was here that she could talk, out aloud, and without fear of being over-heard or interruption. It was here that the many strands of her complicated little life coalesced and danced before her mind's eye. Her inner most thoughts, her words, spoken and those inside her head, her wishes and her desires, her many concerns and worries, here, they all came together and paraded themselves before her. Here she sang her love songs and wept and cried out the tears of her troubled life. Here was the very place of her magic, the fairy dust of life's great wonders. But more important of all, this was the place where Molly came to dream! And the dreams that she'd left behind the last time awaited her coming and enveloped her once more and warmed her little body and soul like a close-fitting and comfy coat. She perched herself like a tiny tree sparrow upon the tree's biggest root and looked up through the leafless winter branches out and over towards 'Mill Bank', and then waited for her special friend to come. There, upon the tree roots that burst out of the ground like octopus's tentacles, Molly was soon deep in reverie. Instantly detached from the world all around her, lost to her innermost dreams and desires that only she would ever know of. She looked up, as though in a trance, into the branches and twigs of the tree that towered way, way above her, and they danced and sang in the winds playing so far above her tiny frame and hypnotised her still further. And then suddenly she was there, standing serenely before her. Her fairy witch. Bathed in light and warmth. Indeed, the ancient spirit of the 'Ripponden Wood'. And for all but too short a period, Molly melted into the vision that now stood before her very eyes. And for a brief time she became one with her alter ego, her secret soulmate. Her very special friend!

"This has to stop, Molly. You cannot go like this. It has to stop. Now!"

She stamped her slender foot down into the cold earth causing a little flurry of dry beech leaves and dust to rise and cling to the hem of her plain and faded gown.

"Do you hear me? Molly, are you listening to me?"

Molly had bowed her head and her face was buried in her tiny mittened hands as the tresses of her hair hung down and fluttered in the breeze. The woman's voice was both forceful and yet endearing.

"You must find love. It is your only salvation. Molly, you have to find love or else you will perish. You will wither in an everlasting autumn all the rest of your life, and so you will die a lonely woman and remain forever unfulfilled, my love."

Molly, her face still hidden in her hands and flowing hair, wept genuine tears of anguish. Then suddenly raising her head towards the apparition, her face wet and shining with her distress, she fell to her knees, her voice begging and full of pleading.

"But what can I do, oh, what can I do? Oh please, please, please tell me what I must do!"

There was only a moment before the reply came, crystal clear and emphatic.

"Well, first of all my love you have to let go of your fear. If you don't, it will ruin your life. You do know that, don't you? It will feed upon your great loneliness and like a monster it will devour you completely!"

The apparition glided silently across the crisp and crunchy leaves as silently as a woodland deer, up towards the still kneeling Molly, and grasped her outstretched hands within her own and pulled the tiny young woman gently, yet firmly, to her feet and pierced her sparkling green eyes with those of her own.

"You have to banish and exile it from your mind! You have to live your life to fullest beat of your heart. You simply must Molly my darling girl, you simply must!"

The spirit swept the younger woman off her feet and held her tightly, lovingly to her breast, her words were imploring and so deeply heart-felt.

"And it is so very imperative that you do so, and soon my love, very soon!"

She held out the tiny woman in her outstretched arms, their eyes locked in each other's burning gaze.

"Love is out there somewhere, and somewhere not very far away from you, waiting for you, waiting for your touch."

Her voice had now risen in earnest. Her words were firm and forthright and trimmed with conviction. And her words revealed the urgency of her thoughts as she returned Molly to the ground.

"You must find love for your heart, my dear. Please, I beg it of you upon my bended knees, for both our sakes. Find love Molly, find love for your heart!"

The power of the voice seemed to be fading away into a distant place as the apparition began to slowly melt into the surrounding light and began to perceptibly slip away. The tiny woman launched herself towards the image that was fast fading before her trying desperately to stop the vision from leaving her. She screamed hysterically at its shimmering outline.

"Stop! Please! Don't go just yet, please don't leave me!"

She'd flung herself forwards seemingly grabbing the apparition about her waist but only to find that she'd taken a hold of nothing more than the fresh air itself. She fell to her knees totally devastated and wept, uncontrollably. She was utterly wretched. She lifted up her face and stretching out her tiny arms as if reaching out to heavens themselves. Molly implored salvation.

"But how can I ever hope to find the love you speak of, and all the kind of love you've given? Tell me! Help me!"

She collapsed to the cold earth beneath her knees, prostrate in abject misery and sheer helplessness.

"I mean look at me!"

She'd almost screamed her voice away and all that was left was a hoarse plaintive cry for help.

"It's hopeless, and I'm nothing but a freak!"

The apparition fluttered back to life and stooped down and gently squeezed the tiny hands that she now held in hers and her soothing words came one last time to Molly's ears.

"That's nonsense Molly, my dear sweet girl. You're a beautiful young woman, remember that, a beautiful young woman!"

The spirit flitted and seemed about to disappear but then it wavered and came back strongly and distinctly once more, but it was obvious that it could not last for very much longer. Molly's little heart pounded against her ribcage and the blood raced inside her veins. The apparition bent towards her upturned face.

"You have to believe that, Molly, my love. Find your love Molly, banish your fears and keep the lonely monster away from your heart. I beg you, Molly, for both our sakes. Find love and let go of your fear go… let go of your fear… let…. your fear."

And then as it had come upon her it was indeed gone from her. And she was quite suddenly all alone with the wind and the cold and her trusty bicycle, and a flask of tea that had grown stone cold. And although she didn't know it right then that would be the very last time that she would ever see her fairy witch, the spirit of the ancient 'Ripponden Wood'.

Molly, now back upon her feet again, stamped her tiny foot in utter frustration. She felt that she had been robbed of the all-important answer to what she considered to be her unbearable anguish. But her peevishness passed like a flash of summer lightning, as it always did. For she could never remain angry with her special friend for very long, she loved her far too much for that to happen. She hunched her tiny shoulders and sighed and it was a long deep sigh of resignation that escaped into the surrounding air about her.

"She's gone too soon again! She always goes too soon! Well never mind, it can't be helped. I expect she's got far more important things to do with her time at the moment?"

Molly quickly straightened her clothing and her hair, brushing away the dried dead leaves and the bits of twig and grass that clung to her.

"But never mind. I must get on, I must get home at once and put all that she said in my diary, straight away. I mustn't forget a single word of what she said to me, I simply mustn't!"

She spoke these final words in deadly earnest and to no one but herself as always, or to anything else that just might happen to be listening out in the ancient stillness as she gathered all her things together and diligently replaced them in her saddlebag. Then, when satisfied that she had forgotten nothing, she quickly retraced her steps and made her way back towards the old water mill and the 'Foxen Lane' without as much as stopping once to daydream or to catch her second wind.

At the bottom of the lane, and just over to her right-hand side, there lay the still and oft forgotten pond, and across its water and over by the far secluded bank, two swans were engaged in their ancient ritual courtship. Heads bobbing up and down and sometimes their long and slender necks entwined. In Molly's eyes they appeared to be kissing and it was obvious that they were very much in love with one another. If the truth were known they were indeed life-long mates and had been coming back to this, their special backwater, for many and many a year. And they couldn't care a hoot or a hiss who witnessed their intimate courtship. Their dance was gentle and full of tenderness and over-flowed with mutual respect and admiration for each other. The obvious love they bore one another suddenly sparked something deep within Molly's soul and so her resolve was irreversibly set. For if they could find such everlasting love in a world so very big and open, then so could she. She would heed the advice that she'd been given! She would banish her fears. She would venture forth out into the open, out from behind her cloak of invisibility. She would, from that day forth, become Molly the brave! She would find love no matter what, wherever it might be, and she would do whatever it would take to grab a hold of it by the scruff of its neck. She would indeed be loved. Molly stamped her tiny foot. She was adamant! She would be loved even if it killed her!

She ascended the rest of the unremitting lane that stretched upwards before her in a thoroughly determined manner. Onwards and upwards she trudged. On and on and on she went, pushing her bicycle up the lazy snake of the 'Foxen Lane. A lane, that at times for those who hadn't shook its hand, was never ending, but very pretty, nonetheless, to climb. And so, at long last Molly reached the last bend in its tarmacadam and stopped to catch her puff by leaning against the dry-stone wall that fronted the final dwelling before the top. After wiping away the perspiration from off her tiny brow, Molly resumed the last bit of the climb, come slog, with a renewed sense of vigour now that the end was clearly in sight. And so with that she achieved her goal and reached the top of the 'Foxen Lane', and without wasting any more time she turned a sharp left onto the 'Lane Head Road', her road, and the road that eventually led to her aunt's cottage and to the place that she'd come to call home with great love and affection.

She crested the small rise in the road that lay before her, and with legs suitably rested, she prepared to mount her bicycle once again for the short cycle ride back to the 'Soyland Town' hamlet and her aunt's house. She was full to the brim with an almost overwhelming feeling of emotion. She felt positively light-headed. All stemming from her new-found resolve and the determination to go out into the world and find herself some real 'loving' come what may. She was going to grab it by the throat and throttle it for all it was worth! Suddenly how free she felt. Unbelievably light. How completely unrestrained, and unrestricted she now felt. Like a dreadful weight had been lifted from her tiny shoulders. She simply couldn't wait to get back home and tell her aunt the good news. She would be so pleased. And her very special friend, hidden deep within the ancient 'Ripponden Wood', would be very, very proud of her at long last.

On legs that were still a little shaky after the arduous ascent of the 'Foxen Lane', Molly climbed aboard her trusty bicycle and wobbled away on up the lane towards home. She had not travelled more than a few dozen yards or so when she noticed a shiny black motor-car tucked hard into the dry-stone wall a little distance in front of her. She thought nothing remotely unusual about this or the vehicle and sailed past it at a leisurely pace with nothing but child-like happiness in her mind. But just as she drew level the motor-car's bumper she distinctly heard the unmistakeable sneering bark just before the engine was started.

"Bloody freak!!"

Then a young female voice resounded clearly in her ears.

"It's that freaky midget again!!!"

Before she knew anything about it the motorcar flew past her, almost knocking her clear off her beloved bicycle. Its wheels spinning furiously amid the acrid stench of burning rubber and the flying loose chippings that rebounded off her helmet, and which could easily have knocked her eye out! That word again! It hit her like a thunderbolt straight out of the blue. It was the one word that she least expected to hear again so soon, if ever at all, and it blew her composure to atoms. It shattered her fragile sanity and like the flick of a switch, it ended all sense of reason that she had somehow managed to maintain throughout her relatively short life. But above all, it struck her tender heart as surely as though a dagger had fatally pierced its delicate flesh. Her demeanour changed in an instant. The happiness she had radiated and that twinkled in her eyes vanished like the sun behind a thunderous cloud. 'That word' had obliterated the smile upon her face, a face which now bore the expression of one possessed as if by a demon! Tears of rage and of loathing streamed down her cheeks and clouded the image of the motor-car now fast disappearing in front of her. Her enemy! She wouldn't, she couldn't, let them get away with this, not a second time. She couldn't let them get away from her! She'd show them a thing or two. She'd soon show them what a 'freaky midget' could really do when she put her mind to it. Molly now stood on the pedals of her bicycle, and coupled with the new found strength of a full-sized maniac, she powered up her machine and was soon burning up the road beneath her wheels. Flying along with an alarming and an ever-increasing turn of speed. She'd show them all right! She'd catch them up at the bottom of the hill and she'd give them what's for, straight to their miserable faces! She'd show them 'freak'; she'd give them 'freaky midget'! She'd teach them both a lesson that they'd never forget. Her little legs, her tiny feet, and the pedals of the bicycle, became as one and whirled round and round as if in a world of their own, as if somehow detached from machine and body. She flashed like lightning past her aunt's cottage, her lovely home, just as the two sleepy women were turning to face one another. A little later they both claimed to have heard the strange sound of what seemed to be a cross between the humming and spinning of a child's old-fashioned top, zipping past on the road outside. This, the police later explained to them, was undoubtedly Molly and her bicycle zooming by the cottage, at what they reckoned to be was, at the very least, forty miles per hour, maybe more! And with what they were to discover a little later on both women would shiver right down to the marrow in

121

their bones, and become almost physically sick whenever they were unlucky enough to recall this recollection to mind.

By now, and travelling at such a phenomenal speed, Molly had very quickly reached the top of the 'Stony Lane'. And with her head bowed down low, just above the bracket of her handle-bars, she all but flew downwards like the very devil himself, mixing her roaring and uncontrollable laughter with a high-pitched scream, which grew into a wail of the banshee! Her tiny feet could now no longer keep up with the spinning pedals, and with a sense of almost childish glee, she flung her legs outwards like the tiny wings of an aeroplane. She was indeed now streamlined to the extreme. And at the subsequent inquest, the coroner was emphatically informed that had she been able to muster up a further fifteen, to twenty miles per hour, she would undoubtedly have taken off!!

The bicycle, obviously not manufactured for such ridiculous speeds, was smoking and beginning to break-up under the tremendous strains placed directly upon its construction. First, her beloved little bell, and then her saddle-bag, detached themselves and flew through the air, quickly followed by the front and rear lights. However, the jettisoning of this equipment only encouraged the machine to fly that little bit faster! Not that Molly minded a jot. She was neither scared nor alarmed. On the contrary, she was having the time of her life. She was really living now. And the exhilaration absolutely thrilled her to bits! She was loving every single second of this unbelievable adventure. However, this particular adventure's end was now sadly in sight. She suddenly saw the bottom of the 'Stony Lane' fast approaching. And she knew that her only option was to somehow chance steering, guiding, the bicycle round to the left and onto the 'Royd Lane', and with a little bit of luck, hopefully, slow the machine down to a stop by the 'Conservative Club' at the bottom. But what Molly couldn't have known at that precise moment were the physical laws of momentum. She was going too fast! Far, far too fast to stop! And her bicycle couldn't be slowed down in time to save her. She was indeed already a goner! She gingerly applied both the rear and the front brakes only to hear them 'ping' off high up into the air. And then she suddenly realised that it was all over. Her last waking thoughts were of her aunt, and how very sorry she was that she would never be able to see or speak to her ever again. And her tiny heart broke in two just as she slammed into the garden wall with a sickening thud, a sickening thud that was accompanied by scarcely any real noise or reverberation of sound, a wall belonging to the house that lay at the junction of the above-mentioned lanes. The impact killed her instantly, I think, I hope! The force of which catapulted her ignominiously, like a black-topped bullet, through the kitchen window (slowing her down tremendously) and then crashing through the connecting doors to the dining room (slowing her down still further) before depositing her, dead as a door-nail, upon her back, her arms pinned to her sides upon the dining room table and as lifeless as a lukewarm entrée waiting to be served.

And there poor Molly lay undiscovered and undisturbed for well over an hour, until around one o' clock in the early afternoon. Until, that is, an inquisitive and hapless motorist spotted her crumpled bicycle hard by against the wall, and following the trail of destruction, discovered her lifeless corpse and telephoned for the police. And that, as they say, was the end of that!

Postscript.

Just for the reader's information. It was, quite rightly, decided that 'Ripponden's' little library should close for a period of three days in Molly's honour, and as a mark of the great respect and very high esteem in which she was held within the community. She would have been amazed, and I think just more than a little pleased with herself!

THE END
COMPLETED TYPING ON 26th MAY 2016

Sticky Fingers! (Norbert Ramage!)

Norbert Ramage was a born liar! Born into a long and distinguished line of illustrious liars, who throughout the various periods of history had found themselves tortured and imprisoned, hung upon the nation's many gibbets, and transported to the far-flung antipodes upon more than one occasion. But now, as the twentieth-century progressed, society had calmed itself somewhat and found itself a conscience, the young Ramage was safe from expulsion, being flogged, inhuman penal servitude, and the rigours of capital punishment! Indeed, he grew and he became a pillar of society himself, and one of the many 'long arms' of the law used by the 'great' and the 'good' to ultimately teach people, like him, a lesson. Above all, the growing Ramage prided himself upon the trusted adage of 'where there's muck there's brass'! And by all the gods Norbert Ramage had a very long neck indeed, made of the very finest and purest of brass that the 'United Kingdom' of 'Great Britain' and 'Northern Ireland' could ever have hoped to manufacture even at the very pinnacle of its 'Industrial Revolution'!

And so as the young Norbert Ramage matured, he decided to join the police constabulary, not because he was at all concerned, or even interested, in any aspect of law and order, or, wishing to see justice done—the innocent upheld and the guilty subsequently punished and upbraided. No! He joined out of sheer filial obedience, parental coercion. He joined simply because his father had desired it of him and what he desired came to pass. Ramage senior was, at best, a bully, a tyrant, a man of many shades, either at sunrise or sunset. He knew the weaknesses of the 'high and mighty'. He knew, at first hand, of the intimate failings of the 'Chief Medical Officer' currently residing over the 'West Riding of Yorkshire', and more importantly, this particular human being owed him a very, very big favour indeed. In other words, in plain speaking, he knew that he could be bribed! Easily! And bribed he duly was! The young Ramage, like his beloved pater, turned out to be as honest as the day was long, and his motto to, all and sundry, never changed, it was, 'you can always rely on me'!

Ramage junior stood a mere five foot and nine inches, and that was in his special shoes, in his stocking feet he was considerably shorter. But with cleverly concealed foot supports he could top six feet and so make the necessary entry requirements a formality. Which indeed they were. And so was everything else along the way, all smoothly rubber-stamped. He sailed through 'Police College' without a care in the world. He had the wind favourably at his back all the way, without the slightest murmur of discontent, and without a breath of trouble or challenge. After passing out of 'Police College' (with flying colours) rookie Ramage was at first stationed in small rural town down in the heart of the country where, after a little more than twelve months he was, with great relief, transferred to a much bigger, and more nondescript, constabulary in a big and bustling city back up in the north. And it was there that he really learnt the finer arts of corrupt policing and subsequently flourished as a 'bent' but clever copper. And from that moment onwards his star was in its ascendancy, and clearly recognising this, he quickly put himself forward for his 'sergeant's exam', which he passed easily without any real trouble and with top marks all round. Once again, with the keen and timely assistance of Ramage senior who pulled all the necessary strings of all the necessary puppets who'd been caught red-handed, at some time or other, with their grubby little fingers in a whole assortment of juicy, dirty, and unwholesome pies! And so, it was that Sergeant Norbert Ramage somehow made his way back to 'Rishworth' and 'Ripponden' district as station sergeant and the leader of his obsequious and subservient little band of 'bobbies', which totalled four in all (one part time) including himself. And so at long last his little empire had been established and he was its 'Caesar', and oh dear me how it thrived!

He was indeed the long and the short arm of the law. And at the end of those sinuous and dangling arms were two hands whose fingers found their ways into every conceivable pie imaginable. They were greedy and took everything they could, and they were very, very clever indeed and never left behind any trace of their inveterate pilfering. Nonetheless, however large or small a particular wrong-doing might have been, its contents stuck to his sticky fingers like glue, and dogged his every step wherever he went, however long or short his journey might happen to be. (The consequences of his many misdemeanours would get him one day!) That was the cross he had to bear throughout his life, but like so many, it was a cross he had no idea that he was carrying. So he blundered on regardless with little or no idea of the harm or damage he was causing himself or to those around him.

He was also, when pounding the beat, ever eagle-eyed, ready to swoop down upon the very smallest of opportunities. He would saunter along the pavement in his haughty and arrogant manner, swinging his trusty weapon by its leather strap, (an old and decorated Victorian truncheon purloined from an elderly and frail neighbour) round and round with the deft skill of one who revelled in his unquestionable authority. He could sniff out profit and gain at a thousand paces. The little hairs on the back of his neck suddenly standing proud and so alerting him that hidden opportunities were about to reveal themselves. And nine times out of ten they did!

His very first day on the beat in 'Ripponden', (his new patch) as he was approaching to where the 'Villa Margarita' stands today, he spotted a little sour-faced boy picking his nose and staring at him insolently. The law straightened his back and squared his shoulders and made a beeline towards the 'culprit' swinging his truncheon with a captivating flamboyance, whilst whistling nonchalantly and loud. As he passed the child, who had already stepped off the curb and onto the road to get out of his way, the truncheon's leather strap suddenly got itself caught in between his fingers and unexpectedly flung the wooden cudgel outwards, where it spun round and walloped the youngster smartly upon the top of his head with a loud crack that even made Ramage junior wince. The victim dropped like a stone, as though he'd been shot, and screamed blue murder. Through the corner of his eye the sergeant of police saw frantic movement on the other side of the greengrocer's big shop window, and in a flash he stooped down and whipped the child to its feet and commenced to dust it off amid a series of authoritative, yet conciliatory platitudes. The mother, snatching away her 'darling boy', smothered it amongst a host of 'there there's' and 'what's wrong now' and with lots of little kisses, so many in fact that they appeared to be fired from a machine gun. She was then duly explained to, in the very best official manner, which would surely have done the 'Police Manual' proud indeed, what had actually just taken place. She was informed, in no uncertain terms, that her child (her sole responsibility in fact!) had fallen off the curb, whilst larking about, and banged its head, and as a result it was now going to be the proud owner of a consummate lump that would require a good half-pound of best margarine to take the swelling out of it. And it was a good job that she was already at the grocer's shop, now wasn't it! And what's more, if he, station 'Sergeant Ramage', hadn't have happened to be on patrol and in the right place at the right time, to timely save the young rascal, it might well have easily had its skull crushed by any passing vehicle and killed dead outright. In other words, he'd saved the youngster's life, no thanks to her. And furthermore, if he ever saw the child alone again, unattended, he'd personally have her summoned before the local magistrate and fined heavily for undue care and attention! So let that be a lesson to her! At this point, she joined her son in floods of tears and vows of eternal gratitude and heart-felt and sincere apologies, too numerous to count. Among which were the usual: 'It'll never happen again' and 'I'm so sorry' followed by, 'I thought he was by my side, honestly, I did'. (Contrition itself before the beady eyes of the law!) With his eyes screwed up tight he returned his note-book to his tunic pocket and amid his many conciliatory remarks, like 'never mind madam', and 'no lasting harm done' followed by, 'the little devil's head must be made of wood', he asked her (very adroitly) whether she'd care to make a small donation to the 'police benevolent fund'? Which she did hastily, showing her appreciation, and grateful thanks, in the shape and form of a crisp, brand new, five-pound note! Then amidst the many little bows and 'cheerio's' on both sides, and beaming smiles, the little drama was ended and the actors parted company and went their separate ways. Less than twenty paces further down the road, Ramage junior removed the note from his tunic pocket and placed the gratuity safely in his trouser pocket. Later on that same day the little boy duly told his father how he really got his lump and what had actually happened. Horrified by the tale the father had soundly thrashed his son to within an inch of his life for telling and making up such vile and heinous lies. Whilst the boy's mother, quaking in her slippers, mentioned absolutely nothing about the five-pound contribution to the Sergeant Ramage 'police fund', and even though it was still only Monday, she willingly consented towards her husband's tentative advances later on that night, out of pure guilty contrition. A little later still, when he'd completed his day's duty, Ramage junior thoroughly enjoyed his hard-earned reward in 'The Junction' public house, and afterwards made his way back homewards with a paper of chips, and more pleasurably still, with change jangling in his pocket.

For the next twenty odd years, especially after the sudden death of his parental mentor, namely Ramage senior, Ramage junior grew, by degree, increasingly negative, pessimistic and above all, sour! His veins ran green with envy and spite and he harboured a malicious intent toward every living creature. Except that is, towards his dear lady wife, a prison officer in 'Leeds', who, from the very earliest days of their courtship, had the exact measure of him, inside and out. She always knew what he was thinking and she could read him like a book! Ramage junior was keenly aware of this and he truly hated her for it. In other words, and much more importantly, she always knew what he was up to, at all times! But he couldn't get rid of her no matter how hard he tried. He couldn't shake her off no matter what! He was stuck with her come what may, 'for better or for worse, till death do us part'. And she clung to him, and to his 'police pension', like a drowning woman clings to any semblance of hope throughout life's roughest of seas. Thus, awash with the 'selfless' love for one another, they went along in their separate ways, and were yet, indissolubly entwined. And without his father being around to advise, cajole and guide him, (and show him a way out of his predicament) Ramage junior soldiered on, patrolling and policing, trapped and ensnared and turning more caustic with every step of his beat. And with consummate skill he took his spiteful revenge out upon his patch of 'Rishworth' and 'Ripponden', as well as their outlying areas. And on his patch there were certain individuals, as well as a number of commercial concerns, that he despised and detested. And whenever, or wherever he could, he went out of his way to do them harm or mischief, but always very cleverly, keeping his 'sticky fingers' clean and his reputation (if not always above muted suspicion) above reproach. For there were always numerous others to blame, (village simpletons and village drunks, those with something to hide and something to lose) and 'stitch-up' for his meddling, and there were always those he could lean on with a little monetary persuasion, or if necessary, arm-breaking. And so, like the halcyon days as a student at the 'Police College', he sailed on and with a fair wind at his back, unscathed and untouchable!

He blocked, or buried, almost everything that came his way that needed or required the obvious or tacit approval of the 'area constabulary'. He personally advised the 'parish council' and where necessary, he rendered it misleading advise to suit his own needs and ambitions. He purposefully misinformed all the political parties with regards to their constituents' hopes, fears and very real necessities whilst portraying a jovial optimism amidst a fawning, cringing subservience. And so, to many, he came to be revered as a dependable pillar within the community. While to a growing band of others he became a fearful figure of contempt and festering hatred. But nonetheless he remained 'squeaky-clean' as nothing stuck to him or to the uniform he represented. He remained unsullied. For anything that might have been deemed 'hard' or 'reliable' evidence against him, quietly and quickly disappeared from sight, and any complaint, voiced or written, fell upon decidedly deaf ears! Norbert Ramage played a mean and clever game at all times. Here's an example. He thought the newly appointed vicar of St Bartholomew's a right southern half-wit even before he'd had a proper introduction, let alone a chat with the man in question. A plum that was right and ripe for the picking. But after a sudden and hastily arranged meeting with him at 'The Bridge Inn' to discuss the disappearance and misappropriation of church funds just after the children's 'duck race' on the nearby 'River Ryburn' (which he, Ramage junior, had personally overseen and supervised) he very quickly changed his opinion of the 'lily-livered' young clergyman who now sat sweating and trembling before him, thoroughly agitated and utterly dejected. He now estimated him to be nothing more than a cretinous imbecile. A dullard! Right for the taking! But a potentially dangerous dullard nonetheless. Someone who needed to be watched like a hawk. And so, he took charge of the promised investigation personally. He displayed verve and vigour and a good dose of vim, and subsequently buried it deep within a proverbial empty grave carefully wiping the procedural spade clean of any residual sticky clay. At a parish council meeting, not long afterwards, he declared that the culprit was more than likely from outside of the surrounding area, and was certainly by now, well beyond his 'station's' meagre reach and that he'd passed on the investigation to the detectives at 'Division', who had the resources necessary to apprehend the felon in question, wherever he might show his ugly face. Done and dusted! After that particular incident, he never went anywhere near the church ever again. He'd had his fill and his cup had truly runneth-over! He couldn't stomach the thought of having to listen to any more of the monotonous blather emanating from the mouths of idiots, but more importantly, out of the mouths of people he thoroughly and absolutely detested. The snobby and

129

moneyed people that got right up his nose! And the 'ten-bob' millionaires, so many of whom he'd had the pleasure of taking for a ride! They were so-called 'shining lights' within the community and he hated every one of them. So in the end he took his chances outside of the love of Christ, and so gave the church and all church matters a very wide berth indeed, and assigned them to a junior constable instead. But all the same he kept his eyes peeled and his ears pricked just in case. One could never be too sure or too careful in his line of work. And so he continued to reign supreme with a rod of iron firmly within his grasp. But his 'dog-days' were fast drawing to their inevitable end, as they surely must, only he was blind to the truth, now utterly corrupted. His dear lady wife clearly saw that they were nearly over, (only he didn't!) and she delighted herself with the prospect daily, but she kept it to herself and didn't warn him of its coming!

As he grew older, he became increasingly bitter and twisted and his thoughts on just about every subject under the sun turned from a dark unpalatable grey, to an indisputable shade of hellish black. He tried his damndest to block any of the community's planned events and celebrations by raising all manner of objections regarding 'health and safety', and concerns regarding the ultimate 'well-being' of those citizens directly under his charge and protection. Moreover, his misgivings were, he stressed, wholly laudable and genuinely heart-felt and he vehemently reiterated them time and time again at the various planning meetings, there would be no calamities anywhere on his patch. And so his 'presence' soon became a domineering dark cloud, forbidding, doom-ridden and negative. The law (specifically Sergeant Norbert Ramage that is) became a major hurdle to overcome, and the said 'community's' events and celebrations dwindled and very nearly disappeared altogether for a significant period of time. Until, that is, the police (namely he) were despairingly invited onto the actual planning committees, and where he became intricately and intrinsically involved. His especial attributes being his extensive knowledge of all things appertaining to 'law and order', and the invaluable jewel-in-his-crown, his 'integrity'!! It was a winning combination. Events, festivals, carnivals, and all sorts of celebrations flourished like never before. Indeed, 'Ripponden' and 'Rishworth' became the very bywords of community success. Unquestionably, they were seen as paragons of carefree, joyous and integrated community involvement. People from all over the region, as well as the other three envious 'Ridings', flocked to see 'their way' of doing things, and how to put on a 'jolly good show'. Every month without fail they were featured in some magazine or other, every article outlining their enviable methods of success. People were interviewed, formulae scrutinised and demanded to be shown and revealed for all to see. The 'regions', both near and far, begged for the recipes of their success. Photographs in their abundance showed countless happy smiling people. A myriad of faces of all ages, bright-eyed and wide beaming smiles, face upon face, some instantly recognisable, but none (not one single image) of Sergeant Norbert Ramage was anywhere to be seen. He kept himself far removed from any of the 'limelight'. The gleeful celebrations were most definitely not his thing. He avoided (like the very plague) all kinds of publicity. He doggedly stayed away from all the 'slap-on-the-back-time' sorts of parties. He left those to the fawning hangers-on. He stayed in the shade allowing the shadows to engulf him, and there he stayed, like a dog licking its wounds, but the wounds he licked were pleasurable, rewarding and above all, financial! But when all the self-congratulations abated somewhat, and the glow of success had waned, no one could quite understand why each particular event failed to live up to its projected financial expectations. In other words, why they made such a profound loss! Where had so much money gone? Why had it disappeared? Who was to blame? Who indeed! And so the law was used to find the dastardly culprit. A 'who' who was supposedly suspected and found, but a 'who' who always, somehow or other, alluded capture and always managed to avoid provable detection!

But every dog has its day as the saying goes, and 'his' was fast drawing near, unbeknown to him. And his ultimate dénouement was something that even he would be unable to avoid whatever words, lies, and excuses he summoned up from his extensive arsenal. However expertly he boxed-clever, his time was up, as the day of his retirement from the police force was looming near. The 'powers' that be had finally decided that it was time for him to go, only they had not told him as yet, it was to be 'their' surprise! He had, in actual fact, not long since put in to 'Division' a special request to extend his length of service. An earnest plea to the 'Chief Constable' himself. A plea for more time in which to complete his 'mission', to be able, at long last, to rid his little part of the 'Calder Valley' of all things criminal. This was emphatically rebuffed and systematically rejected. Retirement was inescapable. New blood was needed in the 'Force'! Young recruits were being sought at that very moment. Their employment was imperative! He was to be put out to grass, at long last. He was finished! And so was the physical presence of the local force. For on the day earmarked of his impending retirement, the two remaining constables were to be transferred up the valley to 'Sowerby Bridge', whose much bigger Police Station was purpose built and relatively modern in comparison. And it was from here that 'Rishworth' and 'Ripponden' were to be subsequently policed. The 'station house' in 'Ripponden' had already been sold off, unbeknown to Ramage, and only awaited the day of his reckoning to be transformed. And again, unbeknown to him, in certain quarters celebrations were being planned to mark his passing as a bright new future was believed to be dawning for both 'Ripponden' and 'Rishworth', and there were more than just a few in the district who were now breathing a huge sigh of relief as the news of his demise spread like wildfire! But still further, in one or two quarters, debts of honour were being whispered and secretly bandied about and discussed in dark corners, and in a few instances grubby 'marked cards' were removed from out of dark places and brought out into the light of day, once more to be contemplated and twirled around in long-memoried and unforgiving fingers. But that was still to come about. It still lay in the future, or did it! For Sergeant Norbert Ramage, tomorrow was still another day. And that day was his official retirement and his big 'sending off' party, arranged and organised, by his now in the ascendant and, dear lady wife. In his turn, he dreaded the 'momentous' day, he dreaded the very idea of his retirement party, and above all, he dreaded his wife and her rising dominance over him as his power and importance suddenly diminished!

The retirement party was to be held in the 'Ripponden Conservative Club', upstairs above, in the newly refurbished 'Victoria Hall'. It could hold well over two hundred people and comprised of a stage, fringed with fine old theatre curtains, a whole host of nondescript round and oblong tables and various sized chairs, toilets and cloakroom, and a newly acquired bar, a very grand item indeed, rescued and lovingly rebuilt, and which they had got for a very reasonable price from a closed pub in 'West Vale', over the hill away. But the piece de resistance was the huge sparkly ball that dangled precariously from the ceiling and which, when the lights were duly dimmed, fired diamonds of light throughout the entire room and lent a dream like effect to even the most mundane of occasions. But sadly, even on the occasion of Sergeant Norbert Ramage's retirement party, the big sparkly ball was unable to weave its magic spell. And though it shot forth its diamonds of light all over the place, they fell flat on their face and their sparkle was immediately doused in the sombre atmosphere that pervaded the entire proceedings from the beginning to nearly their very end.

Mrs. Wendy Ramage had sent out nigh on two hundred R.S.V.P. invitations, and by the first post on the morning of her husband's retirement, she had received less than thirty replies back. Twenty-three definite and grateful acceptances, the rest a mixture of 'sorry but we can't make it because...' or 'we'd love to but only we're...' and a few 'if only we'd known sooner, we...' the rest outright declines. She was in her element, and her near ecstasy threatened to overwhelm her completely, she was obviously over the moon, as pleased as punch! Her husband's retirement party, so carefully planned by her, right down to the minutest detail, including all the special balloons, was going to be an abject failure, an unmitigated disaster! She was so happy and couldn't wait to see the forlorn look of misery upon his sad, jowly face. And what's more, the literal icing upon the cake was, he was going to have to pay for it all! And to rub the veritable salt in his wound, she had already agreed to volunteer to work a late shift at the 'H.M. Prison' where she had just lately been promoted to a position of seniority and which had galled him even more. In other words, she would be leaving him to wallow in his own spiteful venom. And this marked the very beginnings of her 'payback time' and she was going to adore every glorious millisecond of it! And just when he couldn't stand it, or her, anymore, she would reveal her own dénouement. Her coup de grâce would be final and devastating, of that she had no doubt.

When Mrs. Wendy Ramage returned from the ladies' toilet she strode back into the room to find her husband's retirement party in full swing. He was exactly where she'd left him only a few minutes before she went away to relieve herself of a little bit of excitement. He was sat in exactly the same position, with exactly the same grimace upon his face. In reality only twenty-three people out of the 'hundreds' his wife had supposedly invited actually turned up to wish him well and share in his grand finale, his celebratory 'send off'. Indeed, 'Victoria Hall' echoed and sounded even more empty than usual, and the various guests that were dotted around inside looked more like the survivors of some dreadful disaster rather than the revellers at a party in full swing!

Worse still, the buffet was already beginning to 'turn'. The telltale signs being that some of the delicately cut sandwiches were already curling at their edges, and a couple of the huge trifles, adorned with tiny cones of freshly whipped cream, were looking decidedly flat and dejected. Their hordes of 'hundreds and thousands' already sinking below the surface like colourful armies in fields of quicksand. And what's more, the 'D.J' had twice dropped-off and actually stumbled onto his precious equipment causing everybody near to him to jump clean out of their skins as the stylus shot across the vinyl record it was playing. Moreover, the bar staff, promised and expecting much, grew increasingly impatient and fractious with everyone, including themselves, at the obvious lack of 'tips' that now loomed on their horizon. And at times they displayed their bravado as they openly refused to serve and continued in their private conversations with one another. And Mrs. Wendy Ramage took it all in and enjoyed every minute of it all. Her husband's every wince, and his gradual sinking, like a doomed ship, into his chair, as well as his obvious 'hating' to be there expressions, were pure bliss to her poor aching heart. Indeed she positively revelled in the entire atmosphere's debacle.

However, in reality, she was a very different woman altogether. Not bitter at all. In fact she was a very amiable and jolly human being, positive, and a woman who saw the good side in everyone she happened to meet. She had always given all and sundry the benefit of the doubt. The complete antithesis of her mordant husband. And it was especially these, (amongst other things) her positive qualities, that gained her an enviable reputation as well as promotions within the prison service. She was noticed and she was admired! Sadly, for her, she'd never had any children, and even more sadly for her, she had resigned herself to her fate. Ramage had adamantly refused to let her conceive. Children were a waste of time and money, a millstone around one's neck and a definite block to any future promotion, for either of them! And so, when and where copulation did take place, conception was utterly thwarted. And thus the 'Ramage' household remained puritanically barren. And all of this she bore stoically and unbegrudgingly and carried on with her life as happily as she could, under the circumstances, regardless of her husband. But through her contacts within the prison service she made plans, and with the help of others, an eventual master plan was drawn up and eventually it came to fruition. So through her work she found a greater degree of happiness than she had known for a very long time and she was content with her lot, for the time being that is, and with what was inevitably to come. But all of this belongs to yet another story and it doesn't behove to be told at this particular time or place.

At exactly nine o' clock she rose to her feet ready to leave for work. She looked down at Ramage who was staring at the wall beyond the buffet table as though his eyes could penetrate through the stone and brick and see through to the other side.

"Righto then, I'll be off to work now. Have a lovely time, and I'll be seeing you sometime tomorrow then, alright."

And with that she turned upon her heels and made her way across the room leaving him alone, in despair, a sinking ship, behind her. As she neared the door that would take her down the stairs to where a car had already pulled up and was awaiting her; she suddenly burst out laughing, unable to contain her mirth any longer. While his acerbic gaze followed her retiring form until she'd gone from his sight, and so left the hall to himself and to all his jovial guests. Goodness only knows after how many double scotches later he decided to call it a day. He couldn't take any more of it any longer.

On his way out he was stopped and questioned with regards his 'retirement cake', he merely scowled and grunted something inaudibly under his breath, but on immediate reflection sounded just more than a little like this.

"You can shove it up your arse for all I care!"

And with those fragrant words he too left the 'Victoria Hall' and made his way down the stairs and out into the night and onto the 'Halifax Road' to await the taxi that he had called to take him back home. What he failed to notice was the motor-car, across the way, near to the doctor's surgery, suddenly move off in his direction, with all its lights switched off. When he did eventually spot it, his 'copper's instincts' were immediately aroused, but by then it was too late for it had already drawn level with him as he stood on the pavement smoking his last cigarette. His taxi had indeed arrived!

A little later on, but not all that very long really after the above-mentioned incident had been played out, the 'Club's' stewardess announced to everyone in the downstairs bars that there was food, oodles of it, and a party to be finished off upstairs in the 'Victoria Hall', and so there was, and they were all quite welcome to it! And so downstairs decamped en masse to upstairs and an uproarious party suddenly exploded into life, and as for everyone involved, it was the best night's party that had ever been held in the 'Victoria Hall' that anyone could remember for a very, very long time!

THE END
COMPLETED TYPING ON 9th JUNE 2016

Dust to Dust! (Maggie Habergam!)

That she considered herself totally to blame for her niece's sudden and unexpected death was beyond all reasonable doubt in her mind. Even the 'grief councillor', a liaison officer provided by the police could not change her aching and troubled mind otherwise. She could not forgive herself, never, ever! Lurid visions of that horrendous morning still plagued her, both night and day. Whilst she had been enveloped in sexual intercourse that fateful morning, Molly had passed by the cottage, on her way to her death, and she had been completely oblivious to the fact. Whilst she had sated her urges and cravings, Molly had crashed her bicycle and she had died. Bitter sweet orgasms indeed! Utterly unreasonable though this flawed logic undoubtedly was nothing and nobody could sway her reasoning brain to the contrary. She, Maggie Habergam, had been irresponsibly involved in fornification and that question was beyond all reasonable doubt. And in her deeply troubled mind it was that sexual act, that she had so wantonly committed, that had killed her little beautiful Molly, her only remaining family, stone dead! The grief and worry of it all had very nearly killed her. The despair that she had felt, especially leading up to her niece's funeral, had almost driven her to utter and complete madness itself. But like so many others, in similar situations before her, she'd somehow got over it, she had survived, but only to a degree. The entire 'Molly episode' had been nothing short of dreadful. Catastrophic! It had scarred her irreparably.

But now, at long last, Molly, may the gods rest her soul, had been scattered to the four corners of 'her' world. One portion in the cottage's back garden in 'Soyland Town', another in the ancient Ripponden Wood, one more in her beloved 'Pickering' in the 'North Riding', and this last and final one, on Molly's secret path atop of the 'Great Orme' in 'Llandudno' in 'North Wales'. And so Maggie Habergam's job was now done, Molly was now disposed of and she hoped and prayed that she was finally at peace, and hopefully there would be no more ghosts to plague her waking and sleeping hours. But this she knew, for the time being at least, was impossible!

Maggie had waited well over a year before deciding to scatter her niece's remains, and hadn't done so until she felt that she was strong enough, and confident enough to go through with it all, and she'd gone through with it all on her own. It had to be so. To her it had been obvious. She felt that under the circumstances of Molly's sudden and unexpected death that she didn't deserve any support, and that she alone had to go through the ordeal on her own. And anyway, it is what Molly would have wanted herself, she was absolutely sure of that. Now it was all over; she hoped that she could resume some aspects of her life and get back to some degree of normality. But deep down she knew that her life would never ever be quite the same again, no matter what. How could it be? But now back in her room, in 'The Empire Hotel', situated at the junction of the 'Church Walks' and the 'Upper Mostyn Street', she took off her walking boots, removed her socks, and let her hot tired feet and toes get some well-deserved cool air. She poured herself a big glass of red wine and collapsed into one of the comfy armchairs, which were placed over by the windows within her room, and relaxed for a little while before taking a good soak in a long hot bath. She had already drawn the net curtain across the window so that she could spy but not be seen, and she casually stared down at the holidaymakers on the road and pavement below without looking at anything or anyone in particular. The third floor of the hotel gave her a perfect vantage point to spy upon the oblivious and unsuspecting down beneath her. Once more she mused on the day's events and once again she was terribly glad that it was all over and done with at long last. It was over! It had ended! But then again, who on earth was she fooling? It would be never ended. With a huge and heavy sigh she finished her wine and disappeared into the adjoining bathroom and ran the big bath full to the overflow.

After soaking in the bath for very close on an hour Maggie's mind was quite suddenly and finally made up. She had made her decision. And the decision that she had come to, as well as the deal that she had struck with herself, went some way to placating her troubled mind for the present moment. She pulled the plug with her toes and watched the water level disappear until she was finally marooned in nothing but clouds of soapsuds. Then she climbed carefully out of the bath and towelled her still firm and shapely legs then shaved them clean of the faint hairs that had irritated her over the edge of the bath. When satisfied that they were smooth enough, she got into the shower and washed herself totally clean of the old Maggie Habergam, and she emerged transformed and somewhat reinvented and felt amazed that it had been as easy as all that. From that very moment on she had taken the decision to become an inactive gay woman. Not so much obsolete, no not at all, more de-commissioned, mothballed, indefinitely. Abstinence personified. Those days were now well and truly behind her. And this new person, an active lesbian no longer, would be true to her word in honour of her niece's memory. This was how she would make it up to her lovely, precious, Molly. And now that she had reached this drastic conclusion, the re-shaping of the rest of her life would hopefully present fewer obstacles. Maybe her demons would leave her in peace now? She suddenly felt be-calmed, and at long last, at some kind of inner peace with herself, and with the world at large.

She took her time in getting dressed and dressed herself very carefully. And then, when suitably attired, she went down to her evening meal in the renowned 'Watkin's' restaurant. When she entered the restaurant it was still quite early and relatively empty. She was guided towards a prominent table but she suddenly stopped the waiter and asked him for a table over against the wall, altogether less conspicuous to other guests coming to dine. An out of the way table so to speak. Those who entered the restaurant after her were now of little or no interest to her and they received from Maggie nothing more than a cursory glance in their direction. And so, overall, dinner was a very dull affair and offered her precious little by the way of distraction. Even her choice of food, as splendid as it always was, was unable to excite her usually excitable and rapacious taste buds, and she was very soon bloated with ennui and so decided to leave the table without taking her dessert, or her coffee in the lounge, and made her way directly back upstairs to her room. Once inside her room she quickly removed all her evening clothes and, naked, poured herself a glass of red wine which she placed on the little table over by the window. She then slumped into one of the small armchairs and drawing aside the fine net curtain she bathed her nakedness in the diffused orange light that found its way into her room from the main street down below, and casually sipping her wine she allowed her bloatedness to slowly subside. And there she sat for goodness knows how long. Thinking about what she had been and what she was now about to become in the time still left to her, until all the wine had been drunk, and the goose-bumps covered her skin in the early morning chill and the main street below, inert and as quiet, and as still as the proverbial grave. Still naked she climbed, a little wobbly, into bed, her hard, erect nipples chafing against the duvet cover and which felt decidedly uncomfortable, so much so, that she rolled onto her tummy and fell instantly fast and sound to sleep. And that particular night she slept soundly, not waking at all, not even to relieve herself. Her dreams were peaceful and undisturbed and without the hint of death and past horrors. And when she awoke, shortly after six o' clock, her body felt warm and soft to the gentle searching caress of her fingers. The bed around her stirring body, dry and warm, and deliciously free of the fretful and anxious sleep-ridden perspiration. Up with the lark she showered and dressed and made her way down to an early breakfast with a decided spring to her step. And as she was making her way downstairs, she definitely felt that she had turned over a new leaf, turned a blind corner, that this was in actual fact the first day in a new way of life for her.

After eating a somewhat rushed, yet hearty breakfast, she paid the balance of her bill and went, this time, up in the lift to her room where she hurriedly packed away her things, but very carefully taking her time over tucking away a little jam jar of what was left of Molly. Then leaving the room she went back downstairs to foyer and finally checked herself out of 'The Empire Hotel'. She took a moment to look up at its elegant façade; she looked up towards the room in which she had stayed and thought to herself,

"I'll stay here again because I love it all so very much. But next time, it'll be a new me, and I'll be happy!"

And with that she made her way round to the back of the building to her motor-car and prepared herself for the long drive back home to 'Soyland Town'.

The drive to 'Llandudno' had always been a joy to her. And she had flown along the A55 expressway like a veritable wind. Only breaking heavily, and slowing the motor car right down, when she came to the downward slope that led into the wide-open plain through to 'St Aseph' and the seaside beyond. The sheer beauty of hills and mountains that dominated the background made her heavy heart skip a beat, and like an elixir it had lightened her soul. The drive home to 'Soyland Town' on the other hand was a different matter altogether. It was long, arduous and tedious in the extreme, and completely devoid of any real or perceived kind of pleasure. The traffic was challenging all the way, and when, after joining the M6 motorway, very often chaotic and she thoroughly detested every minute of it. (Next time, she resolved, she'd travel by train!) Moreover, the thought of the now empty cottage, looming ever nearer, frightened her no end. She simply couldn't get used to all the emptiness; the voids of silence swallowed her up whole. And the thought of having to sleep in her big empty bed again, the bed where, in her mind at least, the fateful sexual act had taken place at the very moment that Molly had been killed, now physically repulsed her. She vowed right there and then, out loud in her motor-car, that she would never sleep in that bed again, no matter what. She had indeed already decided that she would now sleep and use Molly's old room, for the time being at least, that is until she decided what to do with the cottage itself. But that decision was also fast becoming clearer in her mind with each passing day.

When she eventually arrived back home, she was utterly exhausted, mentally and physically, completely drained. She brought her travelling bags into the cottage, secured all the doors and went up to her niece's old room and straight to bed. She knew that the following day was going to be momentous and difficult to face, but face it she must, and in order to do that she would need a good night's sleep and above all, a clear head upon her shoulders.

Having awoken late and well into the morning, and having had a good long lie-in, after at long last an untroubled night's sleep, Maggie Habergam got up and dressed herself lightly in shorts and a t-shirt, and immediately set herself to work without washing or having breakfast. By the time she'd finished she'd filled close on twenty black bin bags of Molly's clothes and shoes, and a whole assortment of other paraphernalia, such as teddies, cuddly toys, hundreds of nick-knacks, films by the score, and her precious collection of the music that had been ever so special to her throughout her short life. All the flotsam and jetsam of a short life ended all too soon. All now packed away and ready for disposal. Her books, the dearly beloved 'children of her life', had been already packed away by Maggie willy-nilly into cardboard boxes and would be taken to the local council tip on the second or third trip there later that same day. Nothing, absolutely nothing, was going to be sent to the charity shops that were dotted around the area. The very thought of seeing someone dressed in Molly's clothes or shoes, of accidentally spotting any of her belongings in a shop window or on a shelf, was utterly repellent and abhorrent in the extreme. Therefore, everything that she had owned and held most dear must be disposed of, completely destroyed, and obliterated from the face of the earth and out of Maggie's living memory, if at all possible. She was seeing to it personally and she would make sure that absolutely nothing at all remained intact to remind her of her beloved niece. That was the mission for her to fulfil. She would deal with the lingering and irritable memories when everything else was done and dusted!

By late afternoon, thoroughly jiggered, she'd made the two successful trips to the council tip at 'Sowerby Bridge' and returned back home dusty and be-grimed with sticky sweat. Realising that she'd not yet washed and that she smelt decidedly sweaty, she took a good, extra-long, shower and washed the day's protracted tasks away with lashings of warm water, soap and shampoo (heavily applied) which acted like a paint-stripper as she felt another layer of her old way of life peeling off her body and disappearing down the drain, forever gone. Once done, dried and liberally moisturised, she went straight to bed. No snack and definitely no wine to comfort her. All she now needed was a good night's rest. Again, like the night before, she slept soundly and peacefully all through the night, and awoke bright and early with nothing untoward upon her mind, save the completion of yesterday's task and the disposing of the last remnants of her niece's belongings. Namely, Molly's shoes and some other curios which were already bagged and ready to go to the tip, and were by the cottage's front door, waiting patiently.

Over a leisurely breakfast she telephoned the main estate agent in the village and arranged to have the cottage valued and put on the market as soon as possible, if not sooner! Once her repast was complete, she had a quick wash to freshen up, pulled a brush through her hair, dressed, and left the cottage with a bulging rubbish bag full of the past, and drove the long way around down into the 'Ripponden' village. She would never travel down either the 'Stony Lane' or the 'Royd Lane' ever again. Knowing full well that they remained and were there, very close, was terrible enough, and she could just about stomach their close proximity, that was all. That the cottage would soon be on the market and sold, hopefully very quickly, and that in the very near future she would be away from there forever, was the only immediate succour that she could draw on at the moment. She pulled up just before the village shops and not very far from the traffic lights and walked the short distance to the 'Post Office'. She needed to buy a sheet of first-class stamps. For even after a year there were still a great many letters that still needed to be written. She couldn't put them off any longer. She had been woefully neglectful, and she needed to get them out of the way as soon as possible. Out of sight was out of mind! As she came out of the shop a smallish, yet brilliantly coloured poster, which had been placed in the shop's window caught her eye and her attention. It was advertising the 'Ripponden Bowling Club'. Its vivid red and green colours and its striking words drew her to it. It stated that practice sessions for beginners were now being held each and every Saturday morning, from ten to twelve o' clock. All were welcome. She walked slowly back towards her motor-car mulling the poster's words over and over in her mind. She was absolutely certain (although she couldn't swear on it for sure) that she still had her mother's old wooden bowls somewhere tucked away in the loft. She would have a jolly good look for them as soon as she got back home to the cottage. Maggie turned the idea over and over in her mind. Taking up crown green bowling just might well be the kind of distraction that she needed to enhance the new life that was beginning to take shape in front of her. In actual fact she had played the game before, (never thankfully with Molly) but not for very many years now, not since she was in her early forties, and that all but briefly and never ever really taken seriously. Now at the age of sixty-two, or maybe three, not old by anyone's standards, especially hers, (or bowling's) she felt that it just might suit her current frame of mind and changing circumstances. Yes! She made up her mind right there and then. She would give it a go. She would find her mother's old woods (if they were indeed still up in the loft) and she'd go down on Saturday morning, at ten, and give it a whirl. And guess what she pondered, she just might well enjoy it and hopefully meet some new friends into the bargain. Maggie made her way back to her motor-car feeling somewhat elated having made, what turned out to be, a very positive decision in her life. So there it was then. Bowls it was to be! As soon as she got back to the cottage, she went straight up into the loft ready for a good rummage. However, Maggie Habergam found what she was looking for almost straight away. In a dark and cobwebby corner, almost hidden away over against the chimney-breast, there they were. The bag, covered in years of grime, but still proudly sporting her mother's initials in tarnished gold leaf and yet still clearly discernible to the naked eye. With the bag in her hand she scanned the piles of clutter that lay all about her feet. She decided that she was touching none of it. It could all go to the devil as far as she was concerned, it was of no interest to her now. She climbed down the ladder onto the landing and closed the hatchway forever. What remained up there would be the junk or the treasure for the cottage's new and future owner. She wanted none of it any more. It had felt like closing a tomb and it was all over and done with, thank heavens.

Down in the kitchen she unbuckled the straps and opened the bag which then gave up its prize. And what was revealed to her gaze were a pair of light-coloured wooden bowls which were in remarkably good condition considering the length of time they had been abandoned and forgotten, untouched, in that dark and dusty exile in the loft. And now here they were, ready to be used and rolled in anger once more. They carried the usual scratches and scraps, and the odd patches of varnish missing here and there, but these were the scars and trophies of games long since forgotten. Battles won and lost. And she admired them all the more for that. She caressed them lovingly and proceeded to rub them vigorously with a damp cloth and tried the best as she could to conjure up as much of a shine as their old lacquer could muster. The bag took much longer to clean. It required a lot of polish and elbow grease before it reached her meticulous standards. But by lunch time the task was complete and she was suddenly the proud owner of two vintage crown green bowls and an old leather bag.

The rest of the day was taken up with the estate agent and the organising of the viewings of the cottage, of which she wanted absolutely nothing to do with it at all. This was finally arranged after much haggling by both parties concerned, and once done she went out for a drive in order to clear her mind and to forget about it all and she ended up, before she knew where she was, at the 'Beehive' where she ordered something to eat and a bottle of the best wine.

Saturday morning soon came around. With the bowls bag in her hand she locked the cottage front door and drove the long way around to the 'Mill Fold', and the 'Ripponden Park Bowling Club'. She made sure that she was early, and was in fact, the first to arrive. It was a beautiful morning and couldn't have been better for bowling. The 'Club Secretary' introduced her to the other early arrivals and the 'Treasurer' eagerly accepted her membership fee, and with that done she was off and running so to speak. Moreover, once it was known that she'd played the game before, she was very quickly absorbed into a ladies' four-some and away she went. It soon came back to her. She was amazed just how easily she found it all. And nobody really believed her when she told them that it was well over twenty years since she had last played the game. The two hours that Maggie was there absolutely flew by! By twelve o' clock she left the green and made way into the old wooden pavilion to retrieve her bowls bag and on coming back outside she quite literally walked slap-bang into Stewart Utterthwaite. They both jumped backwards as though stung by electricity. Both utterly shocked and dumbfounded. Both unable to speak or to find the appropriate words to use for this sudden and quite unexpected encounter. Somehow or other Maggie had completely overlooked that he was a long-standing member of the bowling club, and that it was indeed highly likely that she just might happen to bump into him. Furthermore, it was very highly a distinct probability! What a complete idiot not to have foreseen this happening. And why such a thing hadn't crossed her mind she couldn't begin to understand. On the other hand, and in all honesty, she was the very last person ever that he had ever dreamed of seeing coming out of the 'Club's' pavilion. They both stared awkwardly at one another. He smiled his silly smile as always, (it was just as she had remembered it) something for him to hide behind. And in response Maggie held out her hand towards him in a polite, conciliatory gesture, a gesture of future peace. He took hold of her outstretched hand in his, and, for some ridiculous and inexplicable reason, he bowed down obsequiously as though he were greeting some royal personage or other. Still shaking hands, each not knowing how to let the other's go, Maggie suddenly felt that she had to say something, something to break the thin but awkward ice so to speak otherwise in all probability they'd have been there all day.

"I've joined you know, this morning. I've joined the club. I've taken up bowling!"

Thus said, they were able to let go of each other's hands without further ado. Stewart simply nodded his understanding of what she had just told him. He then wished her well. And said that he was sure that she would surely enjoy it, being a member, and that the club was really fantastic, and that all the women were great, a lovely bunch and all very warm and friendly to get on with. As was everyone else he further added, all very welcoming. And he was sure they'd all (including himself) make her feel right at home. He then realised what he'd been saying to her and blushed from ear to ear, from pink to puce. He inadvertently pushed past her and went into the clubhouse and up to the team notice board pretending to check on team selections for the following week, his mind awash with panic and confusion. Whilst she, turning her gaze away, waited patiently for him to come back outside. Which he didn't! She waited a little while longer then left to go home, waving goodbye to everyone she passed on the green somewhat embarrassed, all the time looking back over her shoulder, and leaving Stewart to look at the team-sheets, names and team selections for the one-thousandth time. She felt his acute embarrassment and awkwardness and she sympathised with him. But she knew right there and then that they would meet again, probably many, many times. And that is how they met again. The first time after so many, many years.

It was a beautiful summer's day, late afternoon to be exact, late on in August, the day of 'The President's Cup' competition. They were sat together, across from the 'Club's' pavilion, on a wooden bench almost directly opposite the spot upon which Stewart Utterthwaite's tale had woven its magic spell and then vanished into the twilight and the coming storm. They were bathed in glorious summer sunshine. Both dressed in shorts, his ill-fitting and bought on the cheap from a charity shop in 'Sowerby Bridge', hers faded pink but still fashionable, and showing off the shapely spheres of her bottom. Both wearing floppy-rimmed hats, his full of badges, hers full of embroidered flowers. Maggie Habergam and Stewart Utterthwaite were now the very best of friends. They had wound their respective clocks back over fifty years. They had rediscovered themselves, and each other, in the few short months since their first meeting already mentioned. They were in fact now firmly established as platonic lovers. Indeed, they were now inseparable, joined at the hip so to speak. In a ridiculously short space of time they had become reliant upon one another, each drawing on strengths from hidden depths to help the other. Drawing on strengths from a past friendship, a friendship that had been so incredibly important to each party concerned. And now here they were, these two damaged ships now sailing on be-calmed and peaceful seas and utterly dependent upon each other for almost everything. They knew each other inside and out once more, and each had laid their respective cards upon the table. There were no real secrets anymore, and there were no lies. The air had been cleared between them. Their many doubts and fears had been assuaged to a degree that surprised them both, and they now found happiness in one another's companionship, much to the very great relief of the other. And to those who knew them, it was abundantly clear that they had grown to be soulmates and they were in actual fact like a married couple. Indeed they breathed much easier these days as the weight of invisible burden dropped away from their weary shoulders and the light returned to their eyes once again. But in order to achieve this there had been a great deal of soul searching and more than one lengthy 'air-clearing' talks, talks that stretched far into the night and the early hours of the morning. But now all that was over and done with. The slates had been wiped clean. And their lives, both separately and together, could begin again. And at long last, as summer was beginning to line-up its parting shots, Stewart's poky little terraced cottage had been spruced up and cleaned from top to bottom and given a fair lick of paint and was finally up for sale. It had been decided once and for all that as soon as it was sold, he was to live with Maggie as her life-sharing companion. Before he had agreed to all of this, Maggie had sat him down and explained to him, in the minutest of detail, the situation that he was soon to find himself an integral part of. She explained to him the rules of engagement. She made absolutely sure that he, Stewart Utterthwaite, understood clearly and unequivocally, the absolute and unbending rules of their co-habitation. These he accepted unconditionally! He capitulated completely and most willingly without the slightest murmur of protest or complaint. And from that moment onwards contentedness reigned supreme. Stewart fully understood that Maggie was, and always would be, a lesbian woman. Maggie had made it quite clear to him that as a gay woman, and she would be a gay woman until the very day she died, there would never be, and could never ever be, any question of, or the remotest possibility of, sexual intercourse between them however informal. If there had ever been a semblance of hope within his mind then that hope was well and truly extinguished forever, beyond any shadow of a doubt! She promised him that since her niece's sudden death that she had become a celibate woman and would now always remain so. She fervently assured him that he would never ever see her again with another woman, intimately. Yes, she would always remain friends with other gay women, and that at times these women might well contact her, but they would never be allowed to call at their apartment uninvited. Well not in the foreseeable future at least. Not until their platonic relationship was firmly and unshakeably established. She even hinted that there was a strong possibility that at times she would want to attend a few meetings of the gay women's support group she'd been a part of for so long over in 'Hebdan Bridge', and that she would in all probability, stay over with friends. But she re-affirmed most adamantly that there would never be any question that she would be at all involved in any form of sexual activity. That was over with! Like a born-again preacher she protested her celibacy and declared her sexual inactivity absolute! Likewise, she expected that if Stewart wasn't able to master his sexual urges, and if these urges got the better of him, then these were to be satisfied somewhere away from home. And she wanted absolutely nothing to do with them. She could not and would not tolerate him bringing a woman home so as to engage in any act of sexual gratification, even though they slept separately, at all times, and in their own rooms! There was to be no question of 'hanky-panky' on either part, ever. That was clearly understood. It was then that Stewart divulged his last remaining secret to her, that he was and always had been a virgin. That he had never been close to anyone else but her. And after the day of their 'fateful' encounter he had never been able to get remotely close to any other girl again. He had tried, but not succeeded, and that none had ever really approached him and so he'd left it at that and just got on with his life. And that life had been small and self-contained. He was a virgin still, and at close on sixty-five, he certainly wasn't interested in having sex at his age, nor did it interest him in any shape or form, not any more. He had grown and matured to become a completely asexual human being, and he had accepted it willingly as an integral part of his life. He didn't need it and he didn't want it and was very happy without it, thank you very much. When Maggie had listened to this last and most intimate (and most painful) of confessions she immediately burst into a flood of tears, and for a long time she couldn't be consoled at all. She flung her arms about his neck and sobbed her heart out onto his shoulder. Stewart, for his part, felt decidedly awkward and didn't have a clue what to do with his great flapping hands or indeed even where to look. Maggie, very, very, very rarely ever thought about 'that day', now so very long ago, and so very far away. It had sunk down into near oblivion for her. Whereas for Stewart, she now fully realised, it was still of importance, it was still there. He still remembered. And probably always would. True the wound had healed and scarred over, but that scar was still proud and sensitive and painful to the touch. It was best left hidden and unseen by the light of day. Maggie now saw that as her life had marched on and flourished and been subjected to every conceivable experience, running the entire length of the alphabet, Stewart's had stalled and reached a dead-end. His life had sunk into insignificance and shrunk away to almost nothing at all. As she peered into his sensitive and wholly innocent eyes, she vowed to herself that she would never hurt this man ever, ever again, no matter what might happen to her, or to either of them. And moreover, she knew in her heart of hearts, that is exactly how Molly would have wanted her to behave. And right up until this very day I can confirm that they have remained true to their word and their vows to one another. They are the very best of friends. Not all that long afterwards Stewart's old cottage was sold and he moved, the very same day, into Maggie's apartment, 'their' apartment now, down at 'Spinner's Hollow', and he felt contented for the first time in his life for as long as he could remember.

After they had eaten their 'competition tea ', and were finishing off the last licks of their ice creams, Stewart turned towards her and asked what was on her mind. In a relatively short space of time together he had got to know her so deeply, her every look and action. He was so finely attuned to her wants and needs that he was able to read her face and her moods like a book. As he looked into her eyes, he saw her face cloud over and so continued to press Maggie for an answer. The explanation, when it was eventually teased from her, was, in actual fact, the last little confession to him, the last little secret from a past that had now been cleared of the litter and the bits-and-bobs of her once cluttered life. Stewart was already fully aware of where her niece's remains had been scattered. Indeed, they had already planned a pilgrimage to visit Molly's favourite places for the coming September, before the light nights completely disappeared, and it grew too cold to stroll arm in arm. He hadn't been aware; however, that one tiny jar of dusty ashes still remained to be disposed of. She explained to him why she'd kept it until the last, and why it had been so very difficult to let them go. At the time she'd desperately needed a little bit of Molly to keep to herself. That way she would never quite let her go; she'd always be by her side so to speak. When she held the tiny jam jar in her hand, she was able to talk to her intimately, tell her personally how very sorry she was for not being there, in her hour of need, when she died. When she held the tiny jar she prayed for forgiveness with all her might and begged Molly not to hate her forever! But, that since meeting Stewart again, the force of this contrition had abated somewhat and now she felt that it was the time to let her niece go and find her eternal peace wherever she was want to. Then one night, quite recently in fact, she had had a whole series of turbid and turbulent dreams, all of them involving Molly and the dreadful incident that had caused her sudden and unexpected death. She had dreamt of the last conversations they'd had together concerning Molly's quest for true love, and her very great fears of lasting loneliness, of dreaded abandonment if she, Maggie, passed away before her. The tears and the sobbing of it all had caused Maggie to instantly awake and sit up in bed, trembling, bathed in perspiration. She was so disturbed that she had to go to the kitchen to make herself a cup of camomile tea. On the way to the kitchen, through the beginnings of dawn in the hallway, she peeped into Stewart's bedroom (he always slept with it ajar so the ghosts could get out!) he was fast asleep and gently snoring. She didn't disturb him. Although this was a night that she really could have done with him there to talk to for she was clearly agitated. To discuss the dreams that had really shaken her and what he thought they might mean. But despite her anxiety she let him be, although she was sure that he would have loved a mug of cocoa and a chocolate biscuit had she woken him. So she drank her camomile tea alone, and when she felt she was sufficiently calm enough, she switched off the kitchen light and went back to bed to sleep-in fits and starts. Of these dreams she had told Stewart nothing, nothing at all. He was completely oblivious and suspected nothing untoward. She had hid them away very well indeed. And so it was two, or maybe three days later, that Maggie had the same terrible dreams again. This time they were more full of angst and uneasiness than before. In fact this time there was an overriding sense of fear and panic inter-mingled with the dreams and once more they awoke her. But this time, much to her horror, she awoke telling Molly, in no uncertain terms, to get away from her, to leave her alone! She sat up in bed panting and trying to catch her breath back. She was certain that Stewart surely must have heard the uproar, but all was still and silent and there wasn't a sound to be heard anywhere in the whole apartment, save only that coming from her pounding heart. But then something quite extraordinarily strange occurred. There came against her bedroom window a light, gentle, but persistent tapping against the window-pane. She felt forced to answer its pleas and getting out of bed, not at all scared in the slightest now, she made her way over to the window and drew up the decorative blind, and there standing proud, as bold as brass, was a little 'cock robin'. And it was he who had tap, tap, tapped upon Maggie's bedroom window, rousing her from her bed. On seeing her roused he trilled his cocky-song loud and clear, standing high and proud as punch upon his spindly legs, and then when done he up and flew away and she followed his dipping flight and peered out across the car-park over towards the bushes, shrubs and trees that bordered the 'Oldham Road'. And there, over by the wall, straight away she saw her, tiny little Molly, with her cycle helmet upon her head, obviously holding her bicycle below the parapet of the wall. There she was as clear as day, waving vigorously, the biggest smile upon her face and then suddenly mouthing the silent but clearly discernible words,

"I love you! I love you very, very much!"

With tears streaming from her eyes Maggie began to wave back and answered her niece's silent words with the simple ones of her own,

"Forgive me, please!"

And then the tears swamped her eyes so much that she was forced to wipe them away and when she blinked and glanced back Molly was gone. She had gone forever! Maggie finally, at long last, knew that to be the case now. It was over!

All of this had remained her secret, until now that is. Telling Stewart, finally, unburdened her soul and removed the dreadful weight that had been pressing down unremittingly upon her weary shoulders for so long, and she now felt a huge sense of relief. With a frightened look upon her face she showed him what was in her hand-bag and briefly explained to him what she now intended to do. Stewart, in his quiet and gentle manner, took her by the hand and walked her slowly round the bowling green, stopping her every now and again by a particular shrub, bush, plant or flower, that he felt she might feel suitable for the task she now had in mind. Where to empty the little jar of what remained of Molly's ashes. It would be completely up to her to decide where this was going to be. It was up to him to remain absolutely silent on this one. They had walked around the green twice before Maggie tugged on his arm and stopped him. She had indeed stopped before an unusual shaped plant, the type of which she had never come across before. Maggie looked to Stewart for enlightenment and asked him if he knew what the plant was called. He shook his head and said he hadn't got a clue what on earth it was. But he agreed that it was a very good spot all the same. He especially liked the little clump of silver birch trees, five in all, just on the other side of the privet hedge, and he said that he was sure that Molly would be grateful for the shade on a hot summer's afternoon. Maggie whole-heartedly agreed with him, and so the spot was chosen then. This would be where the last little portion of Molly's dust would lie. And here her dust would mingle with the dust of nature and the dust of life in general until all such dust was irrelevant and time itself was lost and of little consequence. From out of her hand-bag Maggie pulled out the little jam jar that contained what was left of her niece's ashes and clasped it tightly to her heart and closed her eyes as if in prayer. Stewart, as perceptive as ever as to her state of mind, and fully aware of her acute agitation, placed a reassuring arm about her waist to support her gently shaking body. Then with contemplation done and with eyes wide open she removed the lid of the jar and bending down, together with Stewart, she emptied Molly onto the soil beneath the unknown plant and wished her well with all the love that she could muster. And it was done. However, the tension of the moment and the unexpected squatting down upon his haunches, had taken its toll on Stewart, who was now unable to shift his weight quickly enough. He looked into Maggie's eyes and the only word that he could manage was, "Sorry!" as his body crumpled to the ground, and unable to remove his arm from about her waist he pulled her down on top of him. Her sudden dead-weight forced the air out of his body, and he exhaled a wheeze so loud that it was even heard across the green by the 'Club's' pavilion. At the exact same time that he wheezed he uncontrollably passed wind, and his body, now seemingly unsupported by any form of air, almost completely deflated. Maggie suddenly burst into roars of laughter and couldn't stop herself as Stewart's face turned bright crimson, and as the last of the air escaped his body, he looked up into Maggie's face wearing his trademark smile like some speechless ventriloquist's dummy. If she could have laughed any more then it surely would have killed her outright there and then. She rolled off him and lay by his side as her laughter subsided and took his hand in hers. Just as people, suspecting the very worst, rushed across the green to lend their assistance to the stricken couple. She looked deeply and smilingly into his purely innocent and yet caring eyes.

"Thank you, Stewart, thank you for everything!"

As they were helped to their feet and dusted off and were making their way arm in arm back across the green, a tiny speck of a thing, unseen, and just below the height of the privet hedge, whizzed by and past the clump of silver birches. The noise of something, something like the whirling of chain and wheels, suddenly sounded familiar to Maggie's ears. She turned and looked back and caught the very merest of something (travelling like the very wind) through the very smallest of gaps in the privet hedge. And then, whatever it was, it was lost in the confusing light that was merging everything together with sky and the trees over by the 'River Ryburn's' banks. And just in the split second, as she turned her gaze away, she heard clearly the words spoken by someone close by and yet very, very far away.

"Goodbye Maggie!"

And so from that day to this that particular corner of the bowling green is commonly known as 'Molly's End', and very probably it always will be.

Postscript.

For those of you who perhaps might still wonder about the well-being of Maggie Habergam and Stewart Utterthawaite, well I am pleased to say that they are fit and well and very happy in one another's company. Albeit, to all intents and purposes, living their separate lives whilst being indubitably joined together at the hip in every other sense of the word. And, moreover, they can still be found down at the 'Ripponden Park Bowling Club' most weekends, between April and September, holidays and weather permitting of course.

THE END
COMPLETED TYPING ON 21st JUNE 2016

The Weights of Space! ('Great Man's Head Hill'!)

It had been a good three months since her husband's ill fated, ill attended, and utterly miserable 'retirement party'. It was now mid-August and summer was thrashing the land with a vengeance, no mercy in any quarter, day or night. The days and nights were stiflingly hot, oppressively so. The three months had veritably flown by and Mrs. Wendy Ramage had enjoyed each and every moment of her liberation so far. She had grown in confidence daily and flowered immeasurably. To all intents and purposes, she was a new and completely different woman. Her shackles shattered to smithereens and the bonds of her servitude cut to ribbons. No further proof of this was needed other than to locate her in the exact spot where this meagre narrative now finds her. Meandering her way slowly, almost idly, across the tussocky moor of 'Great Man's Head Hill' very close upon the hour of midnight. Replete with great amounts of gin and tonic, cheese and tomato teacakes, and freshly baked scones, which she smothered in raspberry jam and fresh, full-fat cream. She was all alone in the dead of the night. But she wasn't at all afraid, and knew exactly where she was going. She knew instinctively, even in the dark, what little paths she had to follow in order to get her back onto the 'Coal Gate Road'. Which was still some distance way ahead and below of where we now find her slightly staggering, humming something or other to herself, and most definitely more than just a little bit tipsy, but blissfully happy, with herself, with the world at large, and with all living things. Indeed, in the three months since the 'retirement party' she had achieved a level of inner peace and contentment that is very rarely achieved by many human beings, transcendental beyond doubt, and grasped only fleetingly by just a few. But Mrs. Wendy Ramage had somehow managed to grab it by the scruff of its near invisible neck and keep a firm hold upon it for very nearly three months. And now, walking across the barren heath in the deep dark dead of the night, when evil and all things bad should be abroad, she found herself to be cocooned within this inner feeling of peace and tranquillity, a oneness with everything. She positively glowed with it. It was a little bit like 'sainthood', or so I was told!

They hadn't really intended to picnic upon the moor but necessity had rendered it so. All of the members in their little group, male and female alike, had suddenly needed to spend a penny, or two, and this urgency had meant that they stayed upon the heath for much longer than they had at first anticipated until that is they had adequately relieved themselves, and all their respective bladders had been completely drained dry. They had originally intended to meander their ways down to 'Mytholroyd', and there to take the train to 'Hebdan Bridge', where they had hoped to picnic in the park by the canal and then to finally visit their favoured 'watering holes' to round off a perfect day. But now, for obvious reasons, that plan had had to be changed. So instead they had all flopped themselves down overlooking the 'Turvin Road' and broke out their bounteous provisions and partied alfresco upon the 'Great Man's Head Hill'. Out of their knapsacks came all sorts of stuff, such as copious amounts of gin and tonic, wine and even well chilled beer. And they positively feasted upon good wholesome sandwiches and teacakes, cold pies and quiche, and all manner of pastes and spreads as well as pates. Then there were the biscuits, cakes and chocolate, (of all description) and even some tiny cooled fruit jellies and trifles! It was a veritable summer feast to die for! And out of this 'bacchanalian' banquet came forth joyous laughter and all manner of carefree chitchat. It was seemingly apparent that they hadn't a care in the world. Their minds were as empty of worry and strife as the deep blue sky above their heads. It was the sort of beautiful day that one always remembers and never ever lets go of. The memories of which linger in the mind's eye for a very long time afterwards, memories so poignant, that when recalled, one could almost taste them whole. What a day indeed!

All stuffed to bursting they'd lolled and lay around and chatted in the drowsily, lazy way, that can only come about at the end of a very hot summer's day. When everyone is thoroughly worn out with the heat, utterly lethargic, and unable to proffer even the slightest protest about absolutely anything. When everyone seems to be in perfect harmony with one another and in love with everything that is near and dear to them. And so they chatted, patted, and softly stroked one another in the mildly flirtatious way that only age-old friends can do. For between them all there appeared to be no hidden agendas that could have raised even the remotest barrier of hostility. They were old friends and as such they had shared so much together, all their good and the bad, and some of that was very good indeed and when very bad it had certainly tested their bonds, but nonetheless they would remain friends until they all, one by one, went the way of the world.

When their little soiree was almost over, and the sun had sunk down low leaving behind a rich pomegranate sky, they decided to decamp back down to the village and take their last drinks down at the 'Bridge Inn', their favourite watering hole. All except, that is, for Mrs. Wendy Ramage. Her lover had not been able to make their planned excursion due to work commitments over at 'HM. Prison Leeds'. But had promised her that, come what may, he'd make it over to her place as soon as his shift had been completed. The expectation of the night still to come thrilled Mrs. Wendy Ramage no end. She positively tingled with latent excitement and could hardly contain the sexual spores that seemed to be oozing from the pores on her skin. Thus she made up her mind to make her own way down from the hill, past the plantation, and along the lanes to her new home. Her little cottage of love, as she fondly referred to it. At first no one would countenance her walking across the moor on her own. They simply wouldn't hear of it. Couldn't allow it. Especially now. In the near pitch-black of night. But Wendy Ramage simply laughed at them all and threw their protests back into their bemused faces and insisted. And as usual she got her own way and popped all their arguments against such a venture in her very best authoritative manner. (Although it was with a voice often slurred and stumbling flagrantly here and there.) Nonetheless it was just such a manner that had got her noticed in the service and had gained her promotion after promotion. Besides, she further argued back, she knew the entire area of moor and heath like the back of her own hand. So there was absolutely nothing to be afraid of for her sake. Now was there? She'd be fine, completely and utterly fine. And as ludicrous as it must surely sound, she got her own way amid much tipsy protestations and group hugging, and with numerous kisses of goodbye and good luck, they parted company and went their separate ways: Wendy Ramage across the heath and into darkness, the others back-tracking and down the other side of the 'Great Man's Head Hill', towards the 'Baitings Dam' car park, until they too were swallowed by the night. And so, the ancient hill was silent once again. No one would have guessed that they had ever been there at all had one not been able to see the clearly flattened tussocky grass, and the shallow indentations where their bodies had lain. And even these had but disappeared when the sun once more bathed the moor in light the following day.

Mrs. Wendy Ramage strode purposefully into the night. Her only objective now was to get home, and to get home as quickly as she could and to prepare herself for her expectant lover. The over excitement deep within her, fuelled by lust and alcohol, fizzed through her body. And for a woman in her mid-fifties and still surprisingly sprite of step, she almost floated down across the moor as the plantation, the secret witch's wood, suddenly loomed ahead of her, darker, much darker than the night itself! She was fairly flying across the ground now. When, for some inexplicable reason, she decided to remove the rucksack off her back in mid-stride. It was making her perspire and her top was uncomfortably stuck to the skin on her back. As she pulled it off she suddenly lost her balance and fell to the ground with an almighty thump. She fell as a dead weight as though she'd been shot, clutching the rucksack to her belly as though it were her little baby. When she fell, she fell upon her stomach and the rucksack, which had her walking boots inside, amongst other sundry things, rammed itself into the soft skin of her tummy driving the breath completely from her body. She groaned in agony as she rolled onto her back utterly dazed and bewildered, liquid vomit pouring from her open, gasping mouth. The sudden shock of it all must have caused her to momentarily pass out because she distinctly remembered coming to as her eyes tried desperately to focus upon that which was before them. And for a number of moments, what was indeed before them, she couldn't quite make out or clearly comprehend. In fact, for those interminable seconds she had completely no idea whatsoever where on earth she was. It was like that early morning panic, when one suddenly awakens from a deep, deep sleep, totally disorientated and unable to recognise one's surroundings, that primeval and childlike fear completely strangles all our senses and we suddenly feel like screaming or calling out for help! This was exactly how Mrs. Wendy Ramage felt as she looked up into absolutely nothing that she recognised or was indeed able to identify. Her body suddenly convulsed and in her panic she tried to raise herself up into a sitting position. But in reality she was barely able to lift her head and shoulders off the ground at one end, and her feet at the other. Still winded, her sails hanging limp, the heavy dead weight of her body took control of her limbs and she could do nothing but lie there, prostrate, and let nature take its course. But strangely enough she was now fully aware that she was neither afraid nor scared of the dark, in fact she was decidedly calm considering the panic that had gripped her so desperately only moments before and which had now completely subsided. There she now lay, beached and becalmed, limply still, a tiny speck upon a vast open moor in nowhere in particular. Very slowly getting her breath back as she clutched the rucksack to her stomach, and as her eyes slowly revealed the great chasm of space above and beyond her utterly insignificant form to her slowly comprehending brain. It suddenly dawned on Mrs. Wendy Ramage that she had been as sick as a dog. Now, as all her senses began to return to her, she could taste the pungent remnants of vomit in her mouth. She could still smell it on her breath. In fact she could smell it all around her, and intermingled with its smell was the unmistakeable aroma of rancid gin, and it was this smell alone that made her retch, again and again. But still unable to move yet properly, or fully take control of her body, she had to put up with it for a little while longer. She felt as though she were glued to the moor itself. And so for the time being at least, she was its captive.

She gazed up into the huge black abyss above her, and as she tried (in vain) to focus on its endless depths, it almost seemed to come down and touch the very tip of her nose. Like an awe-struck innocent child, she suddenly became aware of the vastness of space for the very first time in her life. Like so many countless tens of millions before her, she had taken space and the night sky and everything it stood for completely for granted. It was just there and that was that. But now here it was and it was big, very big, and it spellbound her. It was big and black and twinkly, and that is how it was and how it had always been, and how it always would be even after she was dead and gone. Even after hundreds of years after she had breathed her very last breath, it would still be there, and still be exactly the same as it was at that exact moment in time. It was as simple as that after all. As simple as a pimple. It surely couldn't be simpler, or could it? But now tonight, this very night, as she lay prostrate upon the still warmly breathing heath, clutching the rucksack to her belly, it was different and it would never be the same again, ever. She would never be able to look at it again in the same indifferent, blasé manner. From that moment on it taught her a lesson, it taught her about humanity, her humanity. It completely and utterly levelled her playing field. It taught her things about herself, things that she had never ever considered before and she was shocked. It touched the very core of her being and existence. She peered into its depths and saw its great dimensional beauty. It was like looking at a familiar painting and yet seeing it again for the very first time. Mrs. Wendy Ramage saw things very near and things very, very far away, and things that had lay hidden for so very long. She tried to gauge its depths, its limitless distances and they shocked and frightened her, causing her to catch her breath. She saw but was unable to comprehend, its hidden meanings, meanings that surely someone understood, people, beings, far more knowledgeable than she. This cosmic phantasmagoria that had always been above and beyond her, and now enveloped her, was both spellbinding and bewilderingly beautiful. Altogether, the most beautiful thing that she had ever seen. This sudden consciousness of the weights of space that completely surrounded her entire life upon the earth was truly awesome! Without being able to identify them, or let alone recognise them, she saw the stars in all their glory. She stared intently upon the familiar zodiacal groupings and then, for the very first time in her life, she caught the flickering glimpses of distant galaxies and solar systems, tiny clumps of misty cloud, so very, very far away from her. And because, by some unknown miracle to her, she was somehow able to place them in some form of dimensional distance from one another, she was able (albeit but briefly) to gauge their unfathomable distance from the very point where she now lay. She saw the cosmos not in black or white or silver, but in vivid breath-taking colour, and its indefinable and ineffable beauty (if beauty it could in fact be called) made her weep with almost childlike joy. A joy she'd never experienced or felt as an adult. Or so it appeared at that specific moment in time. Surely, her reality was distorted? Surely she was seeing things through rose tinted spectacles? Had she somehow hoodwinked herself as well as her mind's eye? Was someone playing a cruel trick upon her innocent and naïve state of mind? Or was she still simply drunk?

If the truth be known, this sudden indiscreet show of unbridled emotion, was most certainly the last fling of the huge amounts of the gin and tonic that she had earlier consumed. And the tears that she now wept were the last throws of the dice of her drunkenness and the results of its fast waning influence upon her mind. As her sobs subsided, and her bosom heaved less and less, she continued to stare up into the heavens, but her thoughts, once of awesome bliss and wonderment, were very quickly replaced by fear and panic, now brought on by what was really registering before her eyes and the resulting images that were now being sent to her fully conscious brain. And they shot across her sky like the most dazzling of shooting stars!

Her entire life, from the very earliest of her memories, travelled past her wide and staring eyes. She suddenly became startlingly aware of just how meaningless her actual life really was. In reality, how meaningless all of life actually was that now existed upon the earth! The earth, which for the very first time in her ordinary little life, she now saw as an actual planet, a mere blob of rock, endlessly spinning round and round like a stupid ball in space, space that was vast upon vast, so very, very empty and so very, very cold! Meaningless! Pointless! And as for all the 'brain-boxes', discovering all those meaningless things that things that lay millions and millions of miles away from her, what use was it all to her? To anyone in fact! Clots the lot of them. That's what they were, absurd clots clogging up the great vein of her infinitesimal little life! And what's more she pondered, what was her life all for if the truth be known? What was its point? Indeed, what was the point of anybody's life come to think of it! It suddenly all seemed ridiculously silly and somewhat worthless, and what was it all for anyway, for whose benefit?

Looking up into so much blackness, void of any form of life that she, in her limited way, could possibly think of, she saw the lives of countless millions spread out before her eyes. The constant struggles for existence from the very outset, from birth to death. The striving and the strife. And if one was lucky, very lucky, one had a few meagre years of carefree happiness and contentment. And if one was even luckier one might live a long life! Long life? What on earth was a long life any way, what did that actually mean? A life of mere years, meaningless time, she thought to herself looking up into the very maw of time itself. A maw that now gaped and yawned and enveloped her insignificant form laid upon the moor. She saw her own tiny little life pricking the emptiness above and beyond her. And her soul ached. The years of schooling, learning nothing in particular. The hours of fruitless study. Then college and even more wasted years. All of this interspersed with the pain and embarrassment as she grew and her body changed from that of a girl, to a young, and finally into that of a mature woman. The fumblings and the disappointments. Here and there, a dot, a microcosm, of pleasure and happiness to make it all seem worth the while. Then came her career. A profession that constantly bombarded her with all the negatives that life and society could throw at her. At first she had accepted it all, then she grew to hate and despise it, especially the human beings that surrounded her day-to-day. Then it slipped into her body, unseen and effortlessly, and she learnt to live with it. She learnt to live with a husband whom she had cuckolded from the very outset of their union, she learnt to live with the guilt and then quickly felt no guilt at all as she gratefully accepted the fleeting pleasures of illicit coitus. Living a life of acceptance, pointless, fruitless, and above all, meaningless. Right here and now, as she lay peering up into the incomprehensible, everything that she could remember seemed totally irrelevant in the extreme. And now as she lay there exhausted by the weights of space, gazing up into what had always existed, she felt the very truth of her life numbing her body, and the numbness overwhelmed her so completely that only the brain inside her head seemed to be functioning properly. And so the ultimate question begged an answer. Why was she alive? Why did she exist in so much empty vastness? Now when everything appeared so meaningless and all so very stupid. What was the point of it all? Surely there must be a point? What was it all for? Why? Questions! Questions she knew full well that she could never answer. Questions she knew full well that no one could ever answer for her, ever, until the very end of time itself!

She breathed a heavy sigh of consternation the noise of which shattered the deathly silence that clung to her. She attempted to raise herself up on her elbow, but the severe winding had left her still too weak to move as yet, and she flopped back down with another less heavy sigh, this time of resignation. She again stared up into the vast black depths of space above her body. And then she knew that she would have to accept it for what it really was. Something that she could never, and would never, understand at all. No matter how hard she tried. And as she stared up into the vast depths above her, she suddenly realised that she had wet herself, and that where she had wet herself now felt decidedly cold and uncomfortable. She grew exasperated with it all. How ridiculously stupid, I ask you! Peeing your pants, at her age! Well I never indeed. With a new-found determination Mrs. Wendy Ramage rolled onto her side like a beached whale. She struggled to her feet wincing with the pain from her badly bruised stomach and the dehydrated thumping inside her aching head. And so up on shaky legs, at first tottering from side to side, up and off the moor she went, occasionally staggering every now and again but nonetheless growing more sure-footed with every step. All thoughts of her expectant lover were now clearly gone from her head. She was in a foul mood and a vicious frame of mind, and she'd have easily felled a bull (with her bare hands!) if only one had happened to come near her. She eventually reached the end of the track. And, with very great difficulty, eased her body over the style puffing and panting, and groaning herself onto the 'Coal Gate Road', just as the first great dollop of rain fell down from the sky. It fell through all that space above her under its own weight and landed squarely and flatly upon the top of her head with a great fat splat! And as she turned her head skywards, once more towards the great black hole of space, its majesty now masked by dense and heavy black clouds, the heavens opened and duly drenched her right down to the underwear beneath her clothes. But rather than having a salutary effect upon her (far from it!) it served only to drive her mood deeper into an abyss of resentful contempt towards all mankind. And so the rest of her walk home was riven with a whole host of foul-mouthed obscenities, blasphemies and tears of self-pity. She eventually arrived home at her cottage more drowned than alive, thoroughly wet through, and most thoroughly fed up! She went immediately upstairs and ran the shower. What an utterly rotten day it all had been. What an absolutely horrid picnic it was. All that fancy talk about nothing in particular, and worst of all with people whom she didn't actually like at all come to think of it. All that syrupy cooing and petting, it made her sick to the stomach. Well, there you are then, she'd never go on another one that was for certain.

Naked she climbed tentatively into the bath and drew the shower curtain across, and reaching for her favourite soap to wash with, it was only then that she first saw the full extent of the bruising to her stomach. It was huge. It was an angry bruise, blue, black, and purple, the size and shape of a rugby ball surely, and it covered her skin from just below her ribs to well below her belly button. And when she tried to run the bar of soap across it, she felt the dreadful pain of it all for the first time and she subsequently cried like a little baby all through her shower. And she was still softly whimpering as she ever so gently towelled her body and her hair as dry as she could. Back down in the cottage's kitchen, hair dishevelled and still damp, and bath-robed up as though it were a winter's day, she heard the soft, yet somewhat urgent, knocking at her front door. Her lover had arrived, eager and expectant. But very soon that self-same lover was unceremoniously plonked down in an armchair accompanied by a mug of hot sweet tea and very quickly rendered dismayed, disheartened, and dejected! For there was most definitely to be no love-making, or any other form of amorous pursuits, beneath the starry skies, that particular night, nor for many nights and mornings to come for that matter. And certainly no impromptu couplings whatsoever! A little later on that same early morning, even after consuming pain-killing tablets, the weight of space that formed the slender cushion of air between the duvet-cover and her skin was excruciating agony. And Mrs. Wendy Ramage couldn't even bear the very thoughts of fornication let alone stand the pressures of being touched, however gently. And it was during this prolonged period of inactivity that she gave a great deal of thought to how she had lived her life and what to actually do with the remainder of it. The decision that she very quickly arrived at was indeed portentous.

From that momentous day on she became a fully-fledged devotee of a new god, whom she worshipped most willingly and happily, within or without the walls of their temple. And the god she now showed obeisance to was 'Bacchus'. From that moment on she lived her life to the very fullest and would let absolutely nothing come between her and the pleasures she was seeking, enjoying each and every moment of their savouring. So she explored everything from the beginning to the ends of the alphabet. And even the occasional illness could do nothing to thwart her vigour and enthusiasm. She became a willing disciple to all the principles of pleasure and embraced them whole-heartedly. The weights of space that had hindered her vision for so long had now been lifted from off her eyes, and the millstone from around her neck had gone at long last! She had found herself a new reason for living, a new freedom of sorts and she revelled, nay wallowed, deep within its sensual depths, tasting all its myriad flavours for the rest of her natural life.

THE END
COMPLETED TYPING ON 1st JULY 2016

And Hopes Sprang External! (The 531!)

He got to the bus stop early, but he needn't have bothered really because the bus came bang on time. It was neither late nor early, for once, and that put him in a perfect frame of mind for the journey ahead and indeed, for the whole day itself. The 531 reached the bottom of the 'Royd Lane' and turned a very sharp left, and then left again, into the 'Ripponden' bus turning circle, where it came to a sudden halt and allowed him, and the few other passengers hanging about the bus shelter, to board the little bus. He paid his fare and took a seat on the right-hand side, towards the back, his favourite spot. And as the vehicle started its return journey back to town, he took note of his fellow passengers aboard the bus.

There were four other people as well as himself, and because his seat was the one just before the rear row, the other passengers were easily accessible to his scrutiny without his being noticed at all. Three of the four he'd instantly recognised as fellow 'Ripponden' residents. And although not at all his friends, or even really strictly speaking, acquaintances, he'd nodded to them all the same and wished them a cordial good morning as they'd boarded and taken their seats. The fourth, a woman, with natural red hair, peppered with strands of silvery grey, (which meant his determining her age was extremely difficult) he didn't recognise at all and she was completely unknown to him. He then suddenly realised that he hadn't noticed her waiting for the bus to turn up, so he (quite rightly) deduced that she must have been already sitting on the bus when he'd got on it. For a brief moment she intrigued him and he gazed at her without being at all able to define her facial features. However, his attention very quickly waned and he paid little or no more attention to her whatsoever. For the time being that is. The little bus groaned its weary way back up the very steep incline that was the 'Stony Lane', eventually reaching the summit, and changing into a more pleasing gear, thus relieving the engine of its whining and diesel fumed protests. Looking out of his window he noticed the newly planted 'For Sale' sign outside of the front garden of his most favourite of cottages in all of 'Calderdale'. He made a quick mental note of the estate agent and telephone number and promised himself to make urgent enquiries about it as soon as he got back home. In all honesty he was shocked. He never ever thought for one moment that it would ever come up for sale, well not in his lifetime at least. Now, it suddenly being up for sale, flustered him considerably. His extreme agitation made him feel very hot and considerably uncomfortable and he felt an acute sensation of heat upon his brow and under his arms causing him to perspire profusely. He had always wanted that cottage for his very own. It was his dream house. And he had always longed to live there, a seemingly unattainable desire. A 'what if' kind of place, or more appropriately, an 'if only' sort of daydream! It was a place in which, once settled, he could surely find lasting happiness and peace of mind. Contentment. And now, suddenly, here it was, up for sale! Thank the heavens that he'd never squandered or even touched his inheritance. He felt he had to have it! Surely, now it would be his? He quickly contemplated getting off the bus and immediately making his way back down into the village so as to arrange a quick viewing. To strike while the iron was hot so to speak? No. No need to do that! He'd give them what they wanted, the full asking price, and maybe a little bit more if necessary, to secure its purchase and its subsequent removal from off the market. No! He changed his mind again. He decided to stay on the bus. To keep calm. Wait until he reached town and he could no doubt sort it out there and then. He'd strike whilst the iron was hot, red-hot! By the time that he had reached this decision the little bus had just passed the junction with the 'Blue Ball Road' and was heading down the hill at a fair old rate of knots. And as it reached the bottom of the narrow road, just at the point where it crossed the battered stone bridge which traversed the fast flowing waters that would eventually tumble their way down to the ancient 'Ripponden Woods', the driver suddenly applied the brakes, taking all the passengers completely unawares, so as to slow the vehicle right down in order to get it across the bridge. Everybody lunged forwards out of their seats. Someone (and it might even have been him) gave a little cry of shock horror just as they were flung backwards with an almighty jolt as the accelerator was depressed and power surged through the forward gears once again. The driver, obviously enjoying himself, gave a wry smile and a cocky wink in the bus's rear view mirror, as the vehicle passed the bridge and roared up the hill on the other side. In the very few seconds in which all of this had taken place, and in the very merest blink of an eye, he had shot a fleeting glance towards the unknown woman passenger, and what he saw in that quick-as-a-flash glance changed his life forever! As her body had been thrust back into the seat, as the rubber of the tyres bit hard into the tarmac sending the bus screaming up the hill, her right arm suddenly dropped to her side and he caught sight of her ample right breast just as the taut fabric of her blouse outlined its full and weighty form. And as the vehicle had lurched forwards the force and momentum of its movement had caused the heavy flesh to bounce, twice, and it was deliciously erotic beyond belief. In the mere blink of an eye he had been captured, his heart ensnared, his lust enslaved. And from that moment on he couldn't take his eyes off her. And so intense was his gaze that once or maybe even twice, she shot him a look, which he instantly deflected by cleverly averting his eyes back to what was beyond the bus's windows. Thus he remained, for the time being at least, that is, undetected and innocent of rudely ogling her. He kept his head turned away but craftily espied her reflection in the bus's window whenever he could, and patiently waited for the bus to reach the downward part of its journey into 'Mill Bank'. For here, if his guess was right, and with the aid of the reckless driver, he would be able to ambush her bosom once more, hopefully undetected. And as it turned out his little scheme worked like a dream and he saw exactly what he longed to see, and more, much more!

As he suspected he was indeed right about the bus. After turning right at the 'Alma Inn' they shot past the pub's car park and then came almost to an abrupt halt at the treacherously tricky bend in the narrow road that bridged the gushing stream below. Once again everyone involuntary lurched forwards, and this time including the driver himself. Before being flung backwards he somehow managed to shoot another quick glance in her direction, and he was just in time to catch sight of her right breast as it wobbled like a jelly. His eyes dilated and the heart within his chest pounded like a drum as the blood raced through his veins. Then they were all thrust back into their seats again as the bus accelerated and shot forward like a racehorse. A little further on the vehicle reached the first of a series of cobbled speed bumps that had been set into the tarmacadam. The driver now seemingly chomping at the bit gave the machine full rein and whipped it up to close on forty miles an hour, in a severely restricted zone mind you. And those passengers who were not outwardly concerned nonetheless felt the muscles in their stomachs instinctively tighten up. The bus thumped into the sudden rise in the road and clattered over the speed restriction like a steeple-chaser. Again he glanced to his right and his gaze devoured her left bosom as it clearly bobbled up and down as if especially for him alone, its weight seemingly unrestrained and free in the material that was supposed to cup its form. He had never ever seen anything as sensual, anything so utterly sexual, in all his relatively uneventful little life. He suddenly, shockingly, felt the sap rising in his loins, and he quickly placed his folded coat in his lap and resolutely fixed his attention once more on the world beyond the bus's window, and upon anything other than her bouncing breasts. But they wobbled and bobbled before his eyes, bewitchingly. They mesmerised him like a snake charmer and it was all he could do to keep his hands folded firmly within his lap. However, events soon took a turn for the worse, or for the better, depending upon how one regards this lowly tale. And as it happened, it was something that he had completely no control over whatsoever.

As the bus approached the fairly modern and decidedly nondescript maisonettes that signalled the beginnings of 'Mill Bank' proper, he was dismayed to see a largish group of people waiting at the bus stop. They filed onto the bus and filled the various empty seats around him, and much to his chagrin, a middle-aged couple took the back seat directly behind him. And even before the vehicle had moved away from the curb, he felt that they were looking at him, scrutinising the back of his head, he felt uncomfortable and shifted in his seat, it was as though they somehow knew what he'd been up to only moments before. He felt the ear-burning guilt of someone who'd been rumbled. And this feeling was further exacerbated by the couple's subdued and constant whisperings, interspersed with the occasional conspiratorial sniggering. It instantly irritated him, so much so, that he had half a mind to turn around and tell them to shut the 'bloody hell' up, or worse still, move to another seat. In the end he did neither. He just continued to wind himself up instead. Then before he'd gathered his jumbled thoughts together, the bus had travelled through the 'Mill Bank' hamlet and turned itself back onto the main 'Halifax Road' where it stopped at the 'Triangle' bus stop and filled itself to capacity. And in that relatively short space of time he had not once glanced over in her direction. Not that it really mattered now, for she was completely obscured from his view by a somewhat rotund person, who had just taken the seat next to hers for virtually the remainder of the journey. And he wouldn't properly see her again until they neared their journeys end and they rose to their feet in order to get off the bus and when fate brought them together face to face.

By the time the 531 was approaching the town centre (as I have already mentioned) it was packed to capacity. The air aboard the bus was stifling and decidedly unpleasant. And when the bus pulled over to the stop just by the indoor market almost three-quarters of the passengers willingly, and gladly, disembarked and the open doors suddenly, gratefully, almost desperately even, sucked in the clean fresh November morning air inside and swilled the somewhat fetid smell of all its humanity out and up into the winter sky. Including the choice odours of the musty couple that had sat behind him all the way from 'Mill Bank', whispering and sniggering. As the bus moved off towards the 'Broad Street Plaza' he suddenly realised that the mystery woman was still sitting there. And although she was now sat alone her profile was now most hidden by the big, padded winter coat she had donned. She too was alighting at the bus's terminus. Those remaining passengers still aboard fidgeted about, some folding away their newspapers or closing their books, others hastily finishing off the umpteenth text message of their journey, and hastily readied themselves to get off. He moved to the edge of the now empty seat beside him and awaited her next move. He had still not seen her face clearly in any sort of detail and wondered what on earth she actually looked like. He wouldn't have to wait that much longer. As the vehicle circled the bus station and eventually pulled over into an empty bay, she almost jumped to her feet and made her way quickly to the front. He followed in her wake and stood not more than a couple of paces behind her. He caught the scent of her perfume. It awakened every sense in his body and he tingled with school-boy like excitement. Close enough, but not close enough to encroach upon her peripheral vision. And then it happened! A pedestrian, obviously completely oblivious to the outside world, stepped out in front of the slowing bus. The driver, ever keen with the pedals, slammed on the brakes and the little bus lunged and screeched to an immediate stop. He unwittingly crashed into her back as they both flew forwards. He grabbed her around the waist (so slender, so tiny!) in an act of self-preservation. Then as the vehicle rocked back upon its suspension, they were both suddenly sent backwards, his arms still firmly wrapped about her waist for dear life. He fell heavily into the seat behind the driver with a resounding thump pulling her with down into his lap. Well, he was absolutely mortified, his face a picture of abject shock and fear. The driver peered around from his seat and apologised profusely. She turned to face him and he saw her face fully for the first time as she quite unexpectedly burst out into the most raucous and uncontrollable laughter that he'd heard for a very long time. (He tried as best as he could to laugh nonchalantly, but he failed miserably!) She was the most beautiful thing that he had ever seen! When in actual fact, if the truth be known, the reality was very different. She was a most extraordinary plain looking woman and her beauty was most definitely in the eyes of the beholder! He smiled dumbly back into her brilliant white teeth and her red-haired freckly face, and his heart was washed overboard and out to sea and was lost forever. They were still laughing, she giggling like a school-girl, as they idled their way through the bus station and subconsciously meandered towards 'Marks and Spencer' for no apparent reason. And amidst all this laughter and aimless chatter he asked her whether she'd care to join him for coffee. She said yes straight away. She'd love to, and his fate was sealed!

The café was small and plain looking and had few redeeming features. It comprised of a number of smallish square tables accompanied by the ubiquitous plastic chairs, (in this case coloured green and grey) and a serving counter somewhat on the small side. The relatively small staff was attentive enough, always on the go, as busy as beavers, as well as friendly and helpful in the extreme towards all those who came before them. Nonetheless, it was altogether quite nondescript. Not much of a café to write home about! But this was the café to which he brought her, as though fatally drawn to it, and so as a café it would have to make do for the time being at least. She breezed up to the counter ahead of him and ordered two large latte coffees and two toasted currant teacakes. Not to be outdone he insisted on paying. She adamantly refused. He was emphatic about it. She was stubbornly phlegmatic and held her ground. The woman behind the counter smiled benignly, looking from one to the other, her hand outstretched awaiting the outcome. He again insisted on paying and she was just about to refuse once more, trying desperately to remove some money from her purse, when someone directly behind her tutted rather loudly and impatiently, and she panicked and capitulated blushing with embarrassment to the roots of her very red hair. He paid triumphantly and so brought 'their' first little tiff to an end. He also took command of the tea-tray as they moved away from the counter and went and sat at a table over against the wall. In his mind it very quickly became their little corner.

The sky above the café had grown dark and ominous. Furthermore, the wind had picked up a strength that was a warning of things still to come about, and so early in the winter it bode no good at all. The leaves still clinging to the trees along the 'Ryburn Valley' relinquished their fragile hold upon twig and branch and fell to the earth below, the last hopes of yet another summer past. Within an hour of the sky darkening, the temperature dropped and the first wary flakes of snow, albeit somewhat wet, flopped to the ground and quickly disappeared. Nonetheless, they had issued their warning. Birds, noticing the sudden change in the atmosphere, stopped their chitter-chatter and looked around in silence, then shook themselves and ruffled their feathers in a pointless protest towards the coming winter months, then winged themselves away about their business. People stared up to the heavens in sheer disbelief and shivered despondently. Surely not so soon! Memories of the 'Indian' summer, still so recent, lingered in the minds of the many peering up skywards that November day. Surely not so soon!

Back inside the café they were warm, submerged in the bright yet cosy fluorescence that had enveloped them, along with the smells of coffee and the hints of cooking food that wafted out from behind the serving counter. They were completely oblivious to what was happening outside, in the real world. They talked. He talked. He talked for most of the time. She smiled and nodded. She acquiesced. She laughed and giggled and her face was transformed and her radiance shot forth and battered him into submission. She had the most incredible emerald green eyes that shone, sparkled, and dazzled him near to death. He fell head over heels and hopelessly in love. His oh so silly heart was lost!

They stayed together for well over an hour and a half. And in all that comparatively short space of time he divulged much and revealed more about himself than he had to anybody else for a very, very long time. And what's more, as he gave voice to his inner-most secrets, he felt suddenly unburdened, altogether lighter, as if a great weight had been lifted from his shoulders. And so it went on. It poured out of him. It veritably gushed. Then just as he was about to launch into another great spate, she suddenly shot to her feet, (having glanced furtively at her watch) aghast in mock horror. Somewhere very close to him indeed alarm bells had already rung their warning! She excused herself and said that she'd have to fly in order to make the appointments she had made. They were very important and couldn't, under any circumstances, be missed. He apologised in earnest for having delayed so long. It was all his fault, she should have stopped him ages ago, he was so very sorry. They hurriedly left the café. The lady who had served them knowingly shook her head, as her fellow colleagues looked on in the same direction, all silently exclaiming, 'and there he goes again'! Then as they were fast disappearing from view they all went about their work like busy little bees in a flurry of movement as their 'supervisor' suddenly popped into sight.

He followed her to the store's main entrance and once again apologised profusely for detaining her so long, he hoped she wasn't angry with him. She again flashed the smile that had so easily won his heart and told him not to be so silly, it was just as much her fault as his. And, she admitted, she had never had a proper sense of time if the truth be known, and that over the years her little peccadillo had got her into all sorts of trouble. There was a slight pause between them. She sensed that he was about to apologise again and so quickly placing her hand upon his arm (her sudden and unexpected touch thrilled him!) told him that she simply had to fly. She simply must go, now! He looked anxious, awkward, and didn't know what to say next, how to say goodbye to the woman he so didn't want to say goodbye to. Impasse! She very quickly gave in for the second time that morning, a decision that angered her, like a petulant wasp, all the way to the travel agents, and then again into the bank where she knew she needed a very clear head in order to complete a number of very important transactions. She agreed to meet him later on at the bus stop. She agreed that they could travel home together. Crisis averted. He beamed and nodded in agreement. What a really great idea. Then she was gone from him. He watched her walk away until he couldn't see her anymore in the mix of colour, jumbled movement and bobbing heads, then he too turned and went upon his way and did his shopping.

His shopping done he got to the bus stop, within the bus station, a good fifteen minutes before the bus was even due to arrive. He was first in the queue. He was on tenterhooks and paced about nervously. Having been inside the warmth of the shops for nigh on two hours he shivered in the freezing November air that seemed somehow trapped inside the shelter's glass concourse. His teeth chattered noisily. He zipped up his coat and fished out his gloves from bottom of his small rucksack and hurriedly pulled them on. By the time the bus was due to arrive the queue had grown considerably and yet there was absolutely no sign of her anywhere. He scanned the surrounding bus station hoping for the merest glimpse of her. Nothing! She had definitely told him that they would travel home together. He felt that she had meant it. He knew she had from the tone in her voice, which he now recalled in its every detail. He couldn't have got it so wrong, surely? He stood on tiptoes, holding onto the metal handrail, and searched the vast throng of people that were all about him. There was still no sign of her at all. He grew jittery. Just as he checked his watch for the umpteenth time the bus suddenly turned up and he felt compelled to board it. He didn't really want to, no not at all, but his common sense told him to do so, it was the best thing to do. He had thought of waiting for the next one, give her another chance, but in the end it was only a fleeting thought, and he was at the front of the queue after all. If she wasn't there then she simply wasn't there and that was all there was to it, full stop! And that only meant that she didn't want to see him again, and that was that! He showed his day ticket to the driver and went straight to the back. The last person in the queue boarded and paid their fare and the bus moved away. He was utterly dejected. He felt the bottom had fallen out of his world yet again. He was oblivious towards everything around him, he saw nothing, and his mind was enveloped in doom and gloom. And so, lost in thought was he that he didn't even notice her boarding the bus at the stop just past the indoor market. Indeed, he wasn't even aware that the bus had actually stopped at all until she suddenly plopped herself down on the seat beside him. He very nearly jumped out of his skin and smiled back into her face inanely, shocked and unable to speak. After his initial shock he very quickly got to his feet and asked her to swap seats. She'd be much happier by the window he told her. For once the bus passed through 'Sowerby Bridge', he reasoned, he'd be able to point out certain landmarks, and places, that might be of some interest to her. She readily agreed with him. They exchanged places with one another. But as it worked out things didn't quite go according to plan. For after some basic chit-chat with each other concerning their respective shopping forays, in which he very quickly told her everything in great detail, where as she divulged virtually nothing in particular that he could even remotely remember later on, he fell fast asleep until the bus braked heavily to allow a passing tractor access to a field on the narrow winding road. He came to with a start. He was absolutely mortified with himself and apologised profusely for having rudely fallen asleep on her. She must think him very ignorant he further blurted out. He simply couldn't think what came over him. He was so, so very sorry! She simply laughed in reply and nudged his arm playfully and told him not to worry about it. It was all quite all right, really it was. She reassured him that she had enjoyed every minute of the journey back, especially looking out of the window at all the beautiful, windswept, and desolate scenery. She had enjoyed it all, especially the peace and quiet. Moreover, at the point where he'd woken up, the bus was only two stops from where she had to get off anyway. As she fastened her coat in readiness she quickly explained that she was staying with her sister who lived at 'The Making Place', at the top of the 'Soyland Town', and hoped to be staying with her family for at least a week or so as she still had other meetings and important things to do in 'Halifax'. The bus was approaching her stop. He stood up to make way and let her pass. He desperately wanted to see her again but suddenly lost the ability to ask her. His tongue somehow stuck to the roof of his mouth and wouldn't budge an inch to help him out and he began to stutter his words. In that split second she sensed his sudden awkwardness and guessed at what he was trying to ask of her. And once again that day she came to his rescue. She very quickly told him what time bus she aimed to catch the following morning, and, if he wasn't busy doing something else, it would be really nice to meet up again for a coffee and a chit-chat, if that is, it wasn't putting him to any trouble. And this time she was paying! She made him agree, she insisted. He nodded his agreement grinning from ear to ear like the proverbial 'Cheshire cat'. She squeezed past him and made her way to the front of the bus just as it was pulling over to the side of the road to let her off. He watched her depart as he re-took his seat. As the bus pulled away and continued its journey down into 'Ripponden' he watched her cross the road and pass through the gated entrance into 'The Making Place'. He continued to watch her and just before he lost sight of her he saw her turn to look at the departing vehicle, and as their eyes met she quickly looked away from him, but in the fast fading light he could well have been mistaken. It could all have been a trick of the light. For some unknown reason the look she had given him (if a look it had been) filled him with a slight sense of melancholy, and he didn't quite know why. Perhaps it was because what he had really wanted was her lovely happy smile, or a cheery wave goodbye? And in getting neither it sort of dismayed him. But never mind, he thought to himself on a more cheerful note, at least he'd be seeing her tomorrow. And furthermore, more positively, wasn't it she who'd actually suggested their meeting again anyway? So it stood to reason that there must be 'something' that she liked about him! Silly fool! He couldn't have been more wrong though. Nothing in actual fact was further from the truth. A truth he would never know, or fully comprehend. When he got off the bus at the 'Ripponden' turning circle he made his way to his favourite pub and had a bite to eat and rather too much to drink. Far too much in fact. So much so, that by the time he reached the place where he lived, he had fully convinced himself that she actually liked him a very great deal indeed, and that their 'falling' in love with one another was beyond question, a mere formality. And yet he didn't sleep at all well that night. His dreams were turbid and grotesquely confused. And he awoke early next morning terribly hung-over and able to remember little, if anything, of the night before.

He met her later that morning as planned. They talked like chatterboxes, almost incessantly, throughout the bus journey as it weaved its way towards town. They must have appeared to those other passengers around them like life-long friends, bosom-buddies, or like two people very much in love with one another. As soon as the bus reached 'Halifax' they made their way straight to 'their' little café where he continued to open up and revealed everything that his life had to offer. And so this went on. For the entire week. And by the following Friday evening he was hopelessly head-over-heels in love. Completely smitten. Incontrovertibly and irredeemably lost! By the end of the week he'd told her absolutely everything about himself. Everything! Whereas she'd told him nothing, or, if anything, very little at all! As on the previous day, after an hour or so in the café, they parted company and went their separate ways to complete their respective errands. Then, as before, they met again to catch the two o' clock bus back to 'Ripponden', except for on the Friday afternoon that is. An unexpected and very important meeting at her bank had been suddenly and hastily arranged. A meeting that couldn't, on any account, be missed or re-arranged for a later date. That meant that they would have to catch a later bus back home on that particular day. It was a minor irritation that unexpectedly threw him off his guard, and he had to make a few little changes to his meticulously planned schedule. But he somehow managed to adapt them nonetheless, and so he visited three extra shops upon that particular day and whiled away his time impatiently. And, moreover, of their four further meetings that week, as on their very first day together, he fell asleep again (much to his chagrin) upon two of them. Embarrassingly, on one of them, he suddenly began to mumble quite audibly, so much so, that in order to shut him up she was forced to give him a good sound poke in the ribs with her elbow which very nearly knocked him clean out of his seat! He didn't dare say a word after that. What on earth could he say to her? His face burned with embarrassment and he felt certain (quite rightly so) that everyone aboard the bus was staring at him. He didn't say another word to her until they reached her stop, where she somewhat reluctantly and tersely agreed to meet him the following day. Friday. The end of the week. The end of 'their' week together. On the Saturday he planned to spring his surprise upon her. He was certain that she would be 'over the moon' when he eventually revealed to her what he had planned for them both. Of that he had no doubt. Furthermore, he was so sure that she would love it, and be clearly overjoyed, that he could already picture her radiant face before his. In his mind's eye he clearly saw her flinging her arms about his neck and he felt a tingling right down his spine.

She very nearly missed the bus the following morning. He saw her darting across the road some little distance in front waving her outstretched hand in order to catch the bus driver's attention. She was laughing her head off, clearly she was very, very happy. Indeed, when the bus stopped to pick her up on that Friday morning, he could clearly tell by the look upon her sweet, fresh face, that his little faux pas of the day before had been entirely forgotten. He was completely forgiven. From the moment she plonked herself down next to him, utterly breathless, a new shoulder satchel plumped upon her knees, she didn't stop talking. She couldn't stop herself. Nearly all of it was trivial chit-chat, meaningless chattering and jibber-jabber. However, she inadvertently let something slip in all that flowing nonsense, a hint of something to come, a bombshell! Whereas he, for his part, wasn't really listening to a word she said, he was thinking about how much he'd already fallen in love with her, and how simply marvellous she was, so he missed it, and as the music played inside his mind it shot clear over his head. For a split second she'd let her guard down, her heart thumped inside her chest and her finger-nails dug into the soft flesh of her palms, and with dismay she stared straight into his eyes for any sign or recognition that she'd let the 'cat out of the bag', but all she saw was blind and dumb infatuation and so she fell silent. For in all her excited gabble she'd let it slip that 'they' had at last arrived, that very same morning, much earlier than expected, and how she simply had to get to the travel agents to pick 'them' up. Unknown to him his bird was ready to fly away. But not just yet, not quite!

By the end of that most momentous of weeks he'd told her just about everything that there was to know about himself. He had told her about his being adopted and the inner turmoil that that had subsequently caused him. Not to mention the failure on his part to form any kind of loving and meaningful relationship with his adoptive parents. He told her (in colourful detail, no holds barred) of his previous failed marriages, and how he felt that they had set him back years, mentally as well as emotionally, and especially, financially! But he added strenuously, they were definitely in the past now. Well and truly behind him. His life was back to normal now and he was back on track so to speak. He could now look ahead positively and he was happily unencumbered, because all of his negative baggage had been jettisoned a long time ago. He was, to all intents and purposes, a 'new man'! He also revealed to her, amidst his tirade, his continuing unhappiness and discontentment within his professional working life. Moreover, what a very bad choice of profession he'd actually made in the first place. Oh how he'd loathed and detested his lot, believe you me. But he'd never let it get him down, he told her. He'd put his head down and got on with it. After all, like most everyone else, he reiterated, he had 'bills' that had to be paid. He wasn't a moaner or a groaner, he was, as a matter of fact, just an ordinary run-of-the-mill sort of man and he'd just had to make the most of a bad job. Like countless others had done, all over the country, near and far. And, on a much more positive note, he could always look forward to a comparatively early retirement and a very good superannuated pension. So you see, he concluded, there was a definite light at the end of his tunnel! She had listened quietly and attentively to the decanting of his very mediocre wine and at the end of it all she asked him only two things. Why hadn't he changed the direction of his life if he was so terribly unhappy, and why on earth hadn't he at least, at the very least, changed his job! Well, he pondered some considerable time over that, and in the end he couldn't really find an answer to give her back, and so he thankfully fell completely silent and neither of them said any more on that particular subject. In fact neither of them said very much to one another for quite a long time after that. Their silence was awkward and somewhat strained to say the very least. But eventually it had ended in more of the same trivial chit-chat, and the cloud between them was lifted.

When she got off the bus later that Friday afternoon the sky was dark and gloomy and he felt that something, something not quite right, was in the air. However, as on the previous days they arranged to meet at the same time the next morning. He watched her off the bus and she stopped this time to let the vehicle pass her by. He looked at her through the big glass window and with a somewhat sad smile upon his face he waved to her a fond goodbye. She waved back but stayed rooted to the spot watching the bus disappear down the 'Stony Lane'. She had never done that on any of the previous occasions. Perhaps then, she did like him as much as he liked her after all, he thought to himself as the bus sped down the hill. Indeed, he was so preoccupied with his inner thoughts that he even failed to notice that his 'favourite' cottage had already been sold. It would surely have posed as a very bad omen if only he had noticed it. But see it he didn't. And now, nearing the end of his journey, he suddenly realised that he still had the 'trick' up his sleeve and it lightened his thoughts a little as he smiled at himself in the glass of the window. He just couldn't wait to reveal the 'big' surprise he had in mind for them both. His 'great' plan! But not to worry now. Tomorrow was another day, wasn't it?

She didn't catch the bus that Saturday morning. And deep down he had known that she wouldn't do so. It really came as no great surprise. And in his heart of hearts he knew that he'd made a complete fool of himself. He'd done it again! When would he ever learn! He winced inwardly and the tears of self-humiliation stung at the corners of his eyes. He furtively brushed them away. Then he grew angry with himself, at his own sheer stupidity! It had all followed a familiar pattern and he knew it well enough. When would he ever learn! All in all, it was an abysmal journey. When he eventually got off the bus in the town centre, he knew that it was inevitable that he would have to make his way, as he always did, to the ('their') little café. He knew that he would have to sit at the very same table over in the very same corner, if it was indeed free, and he also knew that his being sat all alone would inevitably attract the counter staff's attention. Furthermore, he knew that he had to go through with it all, the whole 'charade', again! What he didn't expect and what took him completely by surprise, was that one of the staff would actually approach him this time. He wasn't prepared for that, no, not at all! She was genuinely sympathetic.

"On your own today then?"

He looked down into his large cup of piping-hot tea. He'd not even taken a sip of it as yet. He nudged the spoon with his forefinger. He didn't know how on earth to reply, let alone what on earth to say to her. She then placed her hand tenderly, lightly, upon his shoulder.

"Chin up love, don't worry, there'll be others, you wait and see if there isn't."

And with that she turned away and went about her business. He looked down at his watch. There was still just about enough time to catch the next bus home.

Postscript.

On the following Monday morning, at about the same time that they had arranged to meet on the number 531 bus, amid a spectacularly impressive snowstorm, a wedding breakfast was in full flowing jocularity. It was taking place inside a sumptuous hotel somewhere in the small city of 'Yellowknife', situated in the 'Northern Territories of Canada'. And, as a lone ray of sunshine somehow penetrated through that snow-laden sky, the light sparkled dazzlingly upon the falling crystallised flakes of ice, as did the huge diamond that adorned the slender finger of her left hand, in the brilliant fluorescent light and the white-toothed smiles and laughter that abounded and enveloped all in joy, mirth and happiness.

THE END

COMPLETED TYPING ON 28th JULY 2016

The Hillbeast! (Stewart Utterthwaite Again!)

"Why do you carry those things around with you all the time?"

Asked the young barmaid as she watched Stewart Utterthwaite empty his little leather purse onto the bar-counter beer towel. Amongst the jumble of coins were four different sized ball bearings, things he'd found by the roadside on his many travels. He'd kept them because he liked them, he liked the feel of them, and he knew that one day (like that very day) they would come in useful. They were among his most prized possessions.

"What use are they to anyone?"

She continued, her dimpled chin resting in the palm of her hand, her chubby elbow resting on the bar-top counter. The pub was empty (it was mid-afternoon) save for the two of them. It was still very early as yet, but the pub was sure to be very, very busy later on. It always was. She was a pretty young thing, seemingly full of life, rubicund and robust. He was drunk, and slowly getting himself more drunk into the bargain. But by the heavens he carried it well. He was in fact one of the pub's most regular and most loyal of patrons. A pillar of the public house movement. A bastion of 'Real Ale'!

He moved the silver balls away from the coins with his fingertip until they were lined up in a neat little row, according to their size. Of the four, two were dull and had lost their shine, which, he explained almost eye-ball to eye-ball, was because they had indeed been used, the other two, were as shiny as a new pin, and were as yet unused, as yet untried, but ready to go at a moment's notice, he told her. Brand spanking new they were.

"What are they for?"

She reiterated.

"They're just little silver balls!"

He slowly shook his head from side to side. And with his warm beery breath, in a subdued voice, which was barely audible above a whisper, he explained that they weren't just any little

179

silver balls, they were in fact silver bullets! Her eyes widened perceptibly.

"Silver bullets! What do you want those for?"

He leaned forward that bit closer to her, the tips of their noses almost touching. For killing the 'Hillbeast!' he told her. Her eyes grew wider still. Like veritable saucers! He pulled his head away from hers and stood upright, he tapped the side of his nose with his forefinger and nodded his head in a sign of acknowledged wisdom. The kind of wisdom that is gained only with age, and after a lifetime of drinking fine 'Real Ale', and thus, sometimes, such sageliness is bestowed upon a person of even moderate intelligence! Stewart paid for his beer and went and sat down to read his newspaper in the side parlour away to his left. He abandoned the young barmaid to her 'girly' daydreams as the 'Hillbeast', unbeknown to her, burrowed its way into a miniscule part of her brain and germinated and grew quicker than you could say 'Jack Rabbit'! Within half an hour of his having shown her his silver balls, and which obviously had had a strong bearing on her thoughts, especially his mentioning of the 'Hillbeast', she came waltzing into the room displaying all her comely features and plonked herself down upon the leather buffet by the side of his chair. He looked up from his newspaper and gave her a quick sideways glance, like a cunning old fox. She was looking at him earnestly, straight at him. She required answers, and she needed them fast! Her pupils dilated and her stare was burning holes into the side of his head. She grabbed a hold of his sleeve and shook his arm vigorously.

"Tell me about the 'Hillbeast'!"

He slowly folded his newspaper and placed it carefully on the table next to his pint of beer. He looked furtively all about the room, as though the pub were full of unwanted eyes and ears, scurrilous eavesdroppers, when in actual fact, as I have already mentioned, they were completely and utterly all alone. All alone except, that is, for the subdued piped-music that floated around them somewhere and nowhere in particular, and the motes of summer dust that caught the light and danced upon the circulating air. He suddenly broke the silence. He asked her if she were serious. Did she really want to know? Indeed, could she handle the truth? And, if he did tell her, then she wasn't to go blabbing to every 'Tom, Dick and Harry'! She would have to be very careful; it would have to be 'their' little secret! She quickly nodded her agreement. Her eyes were now grown wide with awe, her face, the perfect picture of innocence, and white-faced gullibility. She was ripe for the taking. And so the tale began in earnest. But once the charade began, both the be-witcher, and his wholly mesmerised listener, were very quickly removed to a world where the bounds of make-believe and reality were so increasingly entwined and enmeshed that they were both very soon bamboozled and lost. Stewart Utterthwaite was in a totally different world now, on another dimension altogether. The barmaid, well she was marooned, lost somewhere within the deep, dark, mystical places of her mind, (a mind that actually wasn't all that deep really) utterly beguiled. What a performance. What humbug. What a load of old codswallop. But as the saying goes, if you are going to tell a lie, well, tell a big one. And tell a damned good one at that! And this is what he told her, in hushed whispers and softened gasps and cries of horror, with bulging eyeballs and outstretched arms, then with white-knuckled hands clasped about the throat, and finally, through clenched teeth and a rubbery saliva-dripping tongue, and this is what he, and she, believed.

He told her that the 'Hillbeast' was old, as old as the hills themselves, even as old as time itself, and maybe even older than that, he added sagely. She slowly nodded her head in wide-eyed amazement and asked him in barely a whisper whether he had seen it, the 'Hillbeast', had he ever seen it for real? Stewart Utterthwaite leant into her apprehensive face, his own eyes now grown as wide as they could stretch, eyeballs bulging like a madman's. Oh yes he said, he'd seen it all right, as clear as the nose upon his face, and it was dreadful! He told her that he'd seen it on at least two separate occasions, he was certain of it, as sure as eggs is eggs! But more than that, he'd heard it, often going about its deathly business in the dead of the night many, many times. And even more shocking, he further told her he'd heard it calling to its long-lost mate, hooting, screeching and sometimes gurgling in its deep and throaty tones. He suddenly cupped his hands to his mouth and produced the strangest set of noises that the inside of that pub was ever likely to hear. The young, and now terrified barmaid, very nearly slipped off her buffet, but Stewart pulled her close to his side and tried to keep her steady. And what's more, he added, he'd listened to its deep soft grunting, almost like a rutting pig, as it rummaged and grubbed around the woods, and in the deep dark shadows of the undergrowth, searching for its next victim. Its next meal! She was aghast with horror!

"So what does it look like?"

She asked tentatively. He asked her whether she had ever heard of the 'Abominable Snowman', his face still right up close to hers. She slowly shook her head. Well then, how about the 'Yeti', or, the 'Bigfoot'? He whispered scrunching up his eyes then suddenly opening them up as wide as he could as if in alarm. She nodded excitedly clasping a hand to her mouth. Well, he continued in hoarse undertones, well it's like that, but a lot taller, and much bigger, and it weighs very nearly two tons, he further explained. He also told her how it could run like the 'clappers', and how it was completely covered, from head to toe, in matted mangy fur that stank to high heaven like something that had been dead for a week! (By now Stewart Utterthwaite's imagination was running riot and fully in control of his brain and he firmly believed every word that was coming out of his mouth! And so did she, more importantly.) And what's more, he said nudging her knowingly, it could change its colour to suit its surroundings, very crafty, so as to be able to sneak up on its prey and eat them raw, bones and all, crushing the victim to its stinking body before ripping them to bits! Nobody, but nobody, escaped from the claws of the 'Hillbeast'!! She leant forward, even closer to him than before, her nose almost touching his, and asked him.

"How did you do it then, escape I mean? Tell me! Tell me now!"

Such a pertinent question. He was quite suddenly taken aback, momentarily stumped. He hadn't expected that one. He took a quick draught of his beer. Then it came to him, as quick as a flash. He explained how the first time he did it; he escaped by climbing up a very tall tree, right up to the very top, knowing full well that the 'Hillbeast' can't climb trees for toffee because they've no real head for heights at all! And there, he said, he stayed as quiet as a church mouse, for very nearly a week, eating bark and twigs and leaves and catching rain drops on his outstretched tongue, until the 'Hillbeast' grew sick and tired of waiting for him to come on down and went away off home sulkily. The second time he escaped was even more cunning on his part he told her, and very, very clever, and on any other day he would surely have gotten himself a medal, he was certain. He then told her to remember 'this one', just in case she ever needed it, as it would surely save her life, no doubt about it, because everybody knew that girls couldn't climb trees as well as boys, didn't they? She nodded her head in agreement. Well, he went on, the second time he encountered the 'Hillbeast' he happened to be caught out in the open, without a single tree in sight, so he'd dropped to the ground like a lead balloon and played dead, holding his breath for close on half an hour, and that he said really worked a treat. It definitely saved his bacon on that particular day. For it fooled the 'Hillbeast' completely, and after it had given him a good long sniffing, and the odd poke or two, and a couple of kicks for good luck, it mooched away in an angry mood leaving him alone and to make good his escape. The trick being, he explained, that the 'Hillbeast' could only eat raw and living flesh, and then drink it down with lots and lots of warm fresh blood! So there you are then. You see! He tricked it pure and simple. And with that he slapped his thigh heartily utterly pleased with himself, smiling his trademark smile from ear to ear, and nodding his head in smug satisfaction. She got up and went back to the bar to work, tut-tutting loudly, clearly muttering something under her breath, but nevertheless with the seed of the 'Hillbeast' well and truly festering in some subconscious region of her brain.

They both happened to leave the pub within ten minutes of one another. The young barmaid, who was now completely on edge, made her way home half running, half walking, along the darkening road back towards 'Rishworth', making well sure that she stayed as much as possible in the yellow light of the street lamps, constantly looking all about her, on her guard, her eyes as big as saucers! She moved as fast as she possibly could even though she was tired out and wearing ridiculously high heels, heels that were totally inappropriate for a quick getaway should one just happen to become necessary. The thoughts of the 'Hillbeast' were now foremost in her mind. Her fear intensified by the hastily growing shadows and the creepy gloom that lay in depth just beyond the dry-stone walls on either side of the main road. She heard noises that were both real and imagined, noises that thoroughly startled her, spooked her completely, and made her jump clean out of her skin. And worse still, she was sure that she saw things, grisly things, terrible things, moving out there in the dark, saw them out of the very corners of her eyes as she cried out in fright. She was now verging on a nervous wreck. A time bomb of irrational fear just waiting to explode, and all it now needed was a catalyst!

Once outside the pub Stewart Utterthwaite walked a matter of mere steps before turning immediately to his left and commenced making his way, albeit somewhat unsteadily, on up the steep overgrown track. A track that he knew like the back of his hand, and a track that would take him up to the top of the hill above, and what he hoped would be the short cut back across to 'Rishworth'. A track that would eventually take him back down onto the 'Oldham Road', and which would lead him home to the apartment that he shared with the 'love of his life', Maggie Habergam. This particular route would cut out the numerous windings in the road, and even though he was very happily intoxicated, and couldn't care less, it would nonetheless save him countless minutes as well as the boring trudge along the seemingly never-ending pavement, or so he thought. The night was warm and pleasant and smelt deliciously of high summer, and just above him all the stars were out to chaperone him home. He felt at 'one' with both himself and with the world at large, what on earth could possibly go wrong? What indeed! (For unknown to both parties concerned, at that very moment, the 'Hillbeast' was up and about and would very soon be ready to make itself known and show itself to the glory of the night!)

As soon as he reached the top of the steep track way, he paused for a few moments in order to catch his breath. His legs weren't as strong as they used to be and he most certainly wasn't getting any younger! Although he wasn't 'old' by anybody's standards, and he knew full well that he didn't look a day over forty-five! He just wasn't a 'spring-chicken' anymore, that's all. When he'd caught his second wind, he lit himself a cigarette (he'd promised Maggie fervently that he'd stop at Christmas!) and continued leisurely on his way. After a little way across the top of the hill he began to hum loudly, then to sing out loud, all the songs off 'The Beatles'' 'Abbey Road', his favourite album of all time. However, down below him, many, many feet distant, the young barmaid, by now terrified out of her wits, thought she heard a voice, or worse, voices, wafting on the growing breeze that was coming through the tree tops. But instead of running away she slowed her pace and listened through bat-like ears for any warning sounds of danger until her eardrums seemed to pound in the stillness, a stillness that was ready to pounce!

By the time they had drawn level with one another, him up high upon the tops and she, way down below upon the pavement, Stewart had come around to 'Ringo's' classic 'Octopus's Garden'. Although for some strange reason he phrased it 'Octopoli's Garden' instead. And when he reached the instrumental part of the song his drunkenness got the better of him and he produced all sorts of weird and wonderful noises to accompany the tune inside his head, some bass and guttural, others high-pitched and positively whining. To the young barmaid down below, the sounds became horribly distorted as they were carried down with the wind through the soughing branches, and sounded to her ears ominously, and unquestionably, animal, and definitely not of this world. She froze in her tracks, her legs and her feet unable to move in any direction. The sounds came again, louder this time, as she tottered towards the wall before her, her eyes as big as moons, and waited for her doom. She tried to scream, but all that emerged from the huge black hole in her face was a pathetic little yelp. Fear had trapped her! However, way up above her Stewart was coming to the end of his 'Octopoli's Garden' when he suddenly broke wind. It sounded more like a prolonged clap of thunder than trapped and escaping air and it even shut him up. It reverberated in the stillness and echoed away into the shadows suddenly alerting those creatures that were up and about their business. So loud was it that it even made him jump very nearly out of his skin. He stopped and had a good hard look all around him, hesitantly feeling at the back of his jeans just in case. But all he saw was the impenetrable black of the night (though the stars were shining bright) and all he heard was the heavy, dense, silence that was all about. Nevertheless, he was sure that something, something bad, something wrong, was very near to him, about to strike, close enough to get its claws into his flesh, as the tiny hairs upon his body shot up on end causing him to shiver uncontrollably right down to the marrow in his bones. He quickly thought about singing the next track. Dutch courage! He stepped backwards. Then it happened! He lost his footing and tumbled down the hill. One moment he was rolling, and then he was running, arms outstretched in front of him, wailing, shouting, moaning. Dry wood snapped and cracked beneath him, bushes, branches and ferns swooshed aside in his crashing wake. What a racket! And then he was down again, and then he was up again, arms and legs all over the place. Rolling and bouncing and then sort of running, like some crazy chimpanzee, his arms waving all around him. His downward momentum was unchecked and unstoppable. But this rolling stone gathered more than just mere moss. Everything stuck to him. Grass, dead leaves, twigs and sticks, sheep droppings and cowpats, cones and berries too, as fern and bracken fronds laced his clothes and ruffled his hair. And on and on he came, like a tumbling dice, coming nearer and nearer by the second to the young barmaid waiting to be devoured.

But all she thought she remembered seeing, and all she thought she saw was a mass of mess crashing through the undergrowth and suddenly exploding into sight and into the wall that stood before her. Like a ball made of rubber it rebounded backwards in confusion. Then up it suddenly popped right in front of her, in all its terrible, hideous glory. The 'Hillbeast'! The scream that burst from her face could well have split rock itself. Piercingly propelled out into the night. The 'Hillbeast' staggered towards her its arms outstretched thrashing the air between them. But before it was able to get its claws anywhere near her raw flesh and windpipe she flew, like the wind, and then she was gone from there. The 'Hillbeast' tried desperately to communicate towards the disappearing form of its prey but Stewart Utterthwaite's mouth was so clogged up with soil and grass, with dried leaves and goodness only knows what else, that any hope of speech was totally thwarted, and all he could do was wail and moan like the wild animal he had in fact become. But by now it was far too late for any sort of sane reasoning. The balloon was indeed up as the saying goes! All hell had indeed broken loose! On up the empty road she went, like a sprinter, heading towards 'Rishworth', screaming blue murder at the very top of her voice, like a speeding bullet. And the scream followed in her wake like a dragon's tail, long after she was clearly out of sight, and her scream rent the air asunder for all it was worth. It was terrible to hear. And those residents in 'Rishworth' who actually heard it (and that was more than just quite a few, so I'm told) prayed that it was indeed the wind they'd heard as they pulled the bedding up around their heads, and hoping to high heaven that they'd not heard the wailing of the banshee!

By the time she had reached the 'Heathfield Preparatory School' both scream and legs gave way to complete exhaustion, and she collapsed, in a whimpering heap, outside the front door of a nearby cottage begging for help and begging for mercy. Suddenly she was bathed in the bright orange light of an open door and was gently lifted to her feet and led, swooning, into a warm and a grateful sanctuary. Police were telephoned. Tea was made and administered. Biscuits nibbled. Blankets fused and smoothed around shoulders. And within fifteen minutes or so a vengeful posse was readying itself to be launched into the night, hell-bent on bloodletting, and armed to the teeth with cricket bat, makeshift clubs, yard brush, rake and spade, as well as including a bit of old garden hose topped off with an ugly-looking brass nozzle.

Vengeance was out there for the taking. And so with garbled intelligence, and amidst sobbing protestations, off they went into the night in search of the 'Hillbeast'!!

Now as soon as the young barmaid had disappeared round the bend in the road and was completely out of sight, he had turned on his heels and dashed, as fast as he could, back up the hill the way he'd just, only moments before, tumbled down. With renewed vigour, and with her scream still ringing in his ears, he clambered up the steep obstacle-strewn incline back up to the top. Once there he dithered. First he took a few steps one way and then a few steps the other. Which way should he go! Then he made his decision. Back to the pub! A safe haven, surely? Well, at the very least, he could get another drink and tidy himself up a little bit, then get himself a taxi home. The funny thing is though, he now felt completely sober. So off he went at a run, back over the tracks he'd made not all that very long before. But this time there were definitely no songs to be sung. As he ran he pulled the bits of debris from his hair and from his clothes as best as he could under the circumstances. And as he ran he kicked himself. He should have got a taxi home in the first place. He knew that now. Had he done so then none of this would ever have happened, that was for sure! Eventually he got himself back down to the bottom of the track way without further ado or mishap, and he reached the pavement just as Maggie Habergam was pulling up in the small pub car park. After she'd carefully parked up she climbed out of her car and came face to face with Stewart, who now stood before her in all his dishevelment, wearing a woebegone look upon his face and accompanied with the pronounced sweet odour of the open field, an odour that clung to his smiling aura like 'Clingfilm'. She was aghast and at first didn't quite know what to say to him. She held out her arms towards him in sheer exasperation.

"And where on earth have you been?"

He offered her no reply, but just smiled dumbly, his own arms now outstretched towards hers.

"Well! Come on, I'm waiting! What the bloody hell have you been up to now!"

He simply hunched his shoulders and told her in his own simple way how he'd been coming home the short-cut way, over the top of the hill, and somehow or other he'd lost his footing and fell all the way down to the bottom, it was, he said, as simple as that.

"I see. Then why didn't you walk back along the pavement then? Why did you go back up that stupid old hill! Well, come on then Mr. Clever-clogs, I'm waiting for an answer!"

He looked beyond her. He looked up towards the top of that fateful hill, a hill that towered above them both in the darkness, and again shrugged his shoulders, still smiling. She then told him fair and square that she didn't believe him. He had been up to no good. And she knew that look on his face like the back of her hand! He should have been home absolutely ages ago. His dinner was ruined. It wasn't fair on her. He knew full well that she worried about him! So she tore a veritable strip off of him, right there and then, in no uncertain terms. Then she ordered him to strip off completely, nude, and be double quick about it! He wasn't getting in her motor-car smelling to high heaven like some farmyard animal that was for sure. He protested vehemently about stripping in public, especially naked! But Maggie was adamant and in no mood for either compromise or negotiation. Strip he must! He was just about to put his foot down when he suddenly heard, away in the distance, the distinct sound of a police siren, and it was heading their way. In a matter of seconds he was as naked as the day he was born. His reeking clothes stuffed into a black bin bag and hastily locked away in the boot of the car. Whilst he was forced to sit on a plastic carrier bag on the back seat, covering up his withering embarrassment with a copy of the minutes from the last 'Lesbian and Gay' meeting that Maggie had only just recently attended over in 'Hebdan Bridge'. Beneath the sheath of papers in his lap he felt the snail of his manhood retreat still further into its shell, and just in time too. For as they rounded the infamous bend in the road a police patrol car flashed into sight, clearly travelling at top speed, and heading directly towards them. Stewart dropped down onto the seat as though he'd been shot dead. She asked him what on earth was wrong, (as if his being naked on the back seat of a car with a whole host of gay people sat in his lap wasn't reason enough!) why was he lying down all of a sudden? Then, as the flashing lights passed them by and quickly receded into the night, he simply told her that he was worn out, and was just having a quick lie down, a little rest, that was all.

He nipped out of the car grabbing hold of the picnic blanket that Maggie had retrieved for him and made a dash for the main door with the plastic bag stuck firmly between the cheeks of his backside. Once inside he scampered along the corridor towards the front door of their flat and safety. With a huge sigh of relief he went straight into the bathroom and had himself a good long shower.

Later on that same evening, as they were drinking their pre-bedtime malt whisky, she asked him what had really happened to him. Stewart couldn't have lied to her even if his or her life had depended upon it. He told her the truth as he always did, and as he always would. He told her everything, right down to every last detail. Including mimes, voices and actions. And she laughed her socks off. In fact she laughed so much that she very nearly lost control of herself. Her bladder was nowhere near as strong as it used to be, nor as resilient. Stewart laughed along with her but it was more out of his keen sense of embarrassment than simple merriment. Much later on that night, in the deep dead of dark, when all was deathly still, they both were subjected to terrible dreams, and their sleep disturbed, as the dreaded 'Hillbeast', who caught them all too easily, roared and slavered and plucked them from the ground crushing them to its reeking chest as it made ready to rip out their gullets and eat their bodies raw!

Not all that very far away from their panting, mumbling slumber, someone else was dreaming strange and terrible things that very same night. Amid her sweaty, rumpled bedding, she thrashed and muttered in a deep and barely discernable tone. Her hair was alive. Her eyes opened and closed. Fingers and toes splayed themselves then clenched tight again. She pleaded for mercy. But in the wildness that seemed to be suffocating her no help came, as truly wicked things were inflicted upon her. The white and delicate throat was left alone that particular night as other flesh of a raw kind was taken as the rightful trophy and deflowered. Suddenly she became quite still, her body relaxed then turned and rolled upon its side. She pulled a fluffy pillow to her glistening naked body and gently, but determinedly, humped it to her warm and sticky self.

The rest of her night's sleep was calm and uneventful, and so, is of little concern to us all.

Postscript.

The police patrol car that had sped past Maggie Habergam, and had put the fear of the gods into Stewart Utterthwaite, had not indeed gone to the pub as he'd first expected. It had gone instead to an isolated hill farm over at 'Pike End', up on the rolling hills above 'The Turnpike Inn'. The farmer there had telephoned and reported that blue murder had been committed in his fields and that he needed help right away! When the police eventually arrived the clearly agitated farmer escorted the officers to the scene of devastation to witness the awful carnage for themselves. Scattered all about were the remains of what appeared to be half a dozen sheep or more and at least, from what they were able to make out, in the light cast by their torches, the remainder of two, or possibly three butchered cows. Their blood and entrails adorned the grass with their slippery red mess. Viscera everywhere. But what made both men retch was the terrible stink of death that pervaded the air all around them, and which lingered in their nostrils and in their dreams for many, many days to come.

And so, with that, a little note to you all. Beware of the dark at all times. Fear its moods and its shadows, its impenetrable gloom, and its language of the nether worlds that lie just beyond our understanding and hair-tingling fears! Beware all of you I say, beware of the dark, especially when you are all alone with nothing and no one to arrest and allay your fears.

THE END
COMPLETED TYPING ON 14th AUGUST 2016

That Gap Before the Bridge! (Autumn!)

Reaching fifty had caused me almost unendurable turmoil. Quite literally, weeks of sleepless nights. Sudden, eyes open wide, an awakening in the dead of night, with the heart-stopping realisation that 'old-age' was just around the corner. In those weeks just before my fiftieth birthday I completely re-evaluated my life right up to that very moment in time. And as I remember now, looking back, I didn't seem to have all that much to show for very nearly fifty years, of what I had been up to then, a wholly uneventful life. Two utterly disastrous marriages. Failed relationships littering the past like useless confetti blown away with time, to be forgotten. Routine and 'run-of-the-mill' occupations that brought neither joy nor sadness, but which just sort of ushered me along (admittedly uncomplainingly) the straight road of my ordinary little life. I neither complained nor objected. I just sort of put my head down (like countless other millions) and got on with it so to speak. I went with the flow as they say. And so ten years passed by, absolutely flew by in the blink of an eye, up and went in a puff of smoke. And now, just before my unruffled gaze, loomed large and bold my sixtieth birthday. A landmark in time, my time! A momentous occasion to be celebrated by family and friends. Toasts and speeches to be given and shared by all concerned and connected with my life. Only there was no one, you see. Really no one. There was absolutely nothing to share with anyone. I was indeed an island. And a desert island at that! Some people are like that, you know, and I'm sure that some of you reading this will have come across someone like that at one time or another. A someone who just sort of muddles through as best as they possibly can, making the best of a mundane and humdrum sort of existence. However, I wasn't always as nondescript, no siree. When I was a late teenager, and throughout my early twenties, I was the life and soul of the party. A veritable ball of electricity, a real live wire. And I can honestly tell you that for quite a long time I was at the top of anybody's invite list. Then, like a rock band that had suddenly had its day, I disappeared completely off the radar for some inexplicable reason, really. Persona non grata! I simply vanished from the scene. I very quickly lost touch with a great many people, as you do, people who'd been all too ready to slap me on the back and buy me a drink, and retreated into my shell. I started to frequent pubs and bars that were none too popular and off the beaten track and very quickly, and very quietly, disappeared from sight. I buried myself in my job, then my marriage, and subsequently my divorce. Very soon the only people I had regular contact with (besides work colleagues) were all linked to solicitors. I even received a Christmas card from one particular legal firm wishing me 'season's greetings' and all the very best for the coming new year. I was genuinely touched, and I think that I might even have shed a tear or two. But let's forget all this for now. I dwell on the past too much, a very bad habit of mine, or so I have been told.

Reaching sixty raised absolutely no complications whatsoever. No anxiety. No anxious moments at all. At most I pondered upon where the time had gone, and had the years been kind to me, especially concerning my looks. Vanity has never deserted me and it is another of my little peccadillos. I have known more than a few who, for one reason or another, haven't got anywhere near to sixty, so I am well aware that I'm extremely lucky, nay fortunate, to have reached the age I now am. And on top of all this, I am relatively a fit and healthy man, not at all bad for sixty. I am still able to do most things in life with relish and enthusiasm and with an undiminished sense of vigour. But anyway, I digress. So where was I? Ah yes, I was very nearly sixty!

I live, or lived that is, in an old converted textile mill down at a place called, very appropriately, 'Spinners Hollow'. I actually found myself to be situated above two fellow 'crown green bowlers' Stewart Utterthwaite and Maggie Habergam. There was never a dark cloud around when one happened to find one's self in their delightful company. Stewart's tales alone were enough to keep one rapt and amused for hours on end, and Maggie's cooking was to die for, and would indeed melt the very hardest of hearts, I can tell you without a word of a lie. I had, only a few months before the 'great occasion', taken to walking down to the 'Slitherow Bridge' (now sadly obliterated) and taking a late breakfast in the little café in the somewhat small, and very old, converted factory complex. After my meal I ventured back outside into the fresh air to rest and digest my food. I sat upon a comfortable bench that stood just before the commemorative plaque that indicated the entrance to the trestle bridge that had led one up to where the old 'Rishworth Station' was actually situated. My birthday being mid-September reveals that this memoir initially deals with the summer months (thankfully which were pleasant) that led up to the anniversary of my birth. As I sat upon the bench that actually had the name of 'Rishworth' carved into its backrest, and I believe still does, and contemplated the 'world' beyond the main 'Oldham Road', I happened to glance over to the tiny sandwich shop that appeared to be somewhat delicately slotted in that gap before the bridge. It was a tremendously busy little place. Like bees around enticing summer flowers people came and went almost non-stop. I, for some reason, I know not what exactly now, decided that on the morrow I would forgo the little café and visit the sandwich shop instead. And so I did. The next morning I wound my way along the heavily wooded banks of the 'River Ryburn' as the summer sunshine filtered through the breaks in the canopies way above my head. In places, here and there, the sun's rays hit the water and stopped me in my tracks so as to gaze upon the dazzling but all too fleeting beauty. The light in places pierced to the somewhat shallow sandy bed and I caught the occasional glimpse of fishes suddenly detected, darting for the cover of shade or deeper water. I wished I could have said what they were, but I knew not. A few names came to mind. Dace, Chub, Roach and Perch, and Stickleback, but if the truth be known they were all the same to me. They might as well have been Sardine or Pilchard for what it was worth. I carried on my way as the river meandered along the other. Eventually I reached my journey's end, at the confluence just below the 'Oldham Road' bridge. I was now directly beneath where the trestled 'Slitherow Bridge' would have spanned the air directly above me. The 'River Ryburn' followed a course straight on and to my right, upon the left came tumbling down the waters from the 'Ryburn Dam'. In my ignorance whether this was in actual fact dam water, or a named 'flow', I could not say to be exact. I made a mental note to find out as soon as possible. In fact I would ask Stewart or Maggie as soon as I saw them next, or better still, knock on theirs, and join them for tea and a piece of Maggie's beautifully baked cake. I climbed the short steep hill and quickly came to my bench. The main road here, as everyone knows, can be very dangerous. Traffic (all too much of it I'm afraid) speeds around this somewhat blind and concealed bend in the road, and all too often has absolutely no sympathy whatsoever with pedestrians of any age, or sex, marooned upon either side. With that in mind I moved along the pavement until I found a much safer place to cross and made my way into the little sandwich shop. It was obviously going to be a good hot summer's day as the shop's proprietor had placed just outside a few metal chairs and a couple of tables a little to one side. I decided there and then that I'd eat my breakfast right there, alfresco, outside in the clean fresh air, and take in the sights all about me. I was indeed lucky. The small shop was empty and I was served straight away. I actually knew the owner in a passing sort of way and we traded pleasantries with one another. I hoped she didn't think that I was a 'spy' from over the way, the competition from over the road. I felt the need to explain my presence, which she laughed and brushed aside without the slightest hint of concern or suspicion. After all, I was just another customer. At the end of the day I was money in the till, wasn't I? As she busied herself with my order her assistant, a plain-looking younger woman, say, no more than 'thirty-ish', came to the counter and asked if there was anything else I wanted. I say 'thirty-ish', because believe you me, I am no expert when it comes to the fairer sex, especially when it comes down to deducing their age, with me I'm afraid it comes down to pure guess work, a shot in the dark and nothing more. She looked me right in the eye and held my stare. Her eyes were big and round and were greyish or bluish in colour and actually shone, no they sparkled, with a sense of warmth and openness and I was instantly drawn into a light, playful, chit-chat with her. I cannot for the life of me, remember what we said to one another. But I will always remember the look in those eyes. I remembered them until my dying day. In fact I know that they were among the very last things that I saw in my mind's eye just before I went away. With a cardboard mug of tea in my hand I went and sat down in the rapidly warming fresh air and waited for my breakfast to be brought to me. Every now and again I turned my head towards the glass window in hope I might catch sight of those captivating eyes once again. But I was out of luck, and then my food was served and the owner joined me at my little table and we chatted away to one another like long-lost friends without word or sight of the younger woman at all.

After that morning I went to the 'sandwich shop' every day. Sometimes strolling along by the river, other times by the less scenic route along the 'Oldham Road'. Sometimes she was there and sometimes she wasn't. But her eyes never left me. Not long after that we were soon on first-name terms and it was she that came out to join me at my little breakfast table. And very soon afterwards we were diving deeper. How and why we did so I cannot really explain. We just did. And this hadn't happened to me since I was a much, much younger man! We were very soon talking about every subject under the sun. I was pleasantly surprised just how knowledgeable my new friend actually was. She could talk on just about anything and everything and was ready to give her opinion with confidence and self-assurance. And then, after a little more than two weeks, our conversations turned inwards towards ourselves. Tentatively at first, wary of each other's feelings, fears and privacies, and above all wary that we each had secrets, and these we respected and honoured. There was no prying and above all no pushing at personal, hidden, boundaries. Our language was, so very soon, intimate, and upon every occasion possible we touched one another, accidental at first, then touched with purpose and intent. We swapped numbers and email addresses and we were very soon in contact with one another around the clock. We were fascinated with one another, utterly obsessed. And all of this a secret from everyone around us. A secret from the world. Our secret! And let me tell you, it was electrifying. It was exhilarating beyond all expectation and belief. We were lovers in all but name, and by the end of the fourth week, our first month 'together', our orbits changed direction, inexorably, and I whole-heartedly believe, inevitably. Our planetary bodies were on an unstoppable collision course.

We arranged to meet at a secret location known only to us. We were very, very careful. Ultra cautious. We arranged the details like silly, excited school children. We giggled. We whispered surreptitiously. We cast each other sly lascivious looks, and when we were able to, we squeezed one another's hands until the fingers blanched white. We, at first, arranged to meet in a town not all that very far from where we both happened to live. I couldn't possibly take the chance of picking her up in my motor-car. That would have been too daring so early on, we might have been seen together, caught out by eyes unseen and unknown. Too dangerous by far. Tempting fate as they say. It had to be some out-of-the-way sort of place initially. Where we were to meet was well connected by public transport, so she had a choice, bus or train, whatever took her fancy, it was entirely up to her. It was agreed that I would pay for the room (casually revealing that my wife was delayed in traffic and would therefore be joining me shortly) and subsequently meet her upstairs. And that is exactly how it transpired. As I awaited her knock at the door I suddenly realised, sitting by the window, that I 'really' knew nothing about her, nothing about her past, her personal history. In fact, much to my consternation, all I actually knew about her was glib, chit-chatty sort of stuff, throw away facts of general information. But now, full to the brim with lusty expectation and deeply lascivious thoughts, that suddenly didn't matter very much and the heavy, furrowed frown that had creased my brow, vanished as quickly as it had come. I pushed my trepidation and all my cowardly doubts to one side.

When the knock came it was loud, over loud in fact, and as bold as brass, and it very nearly made me jump clear out of my skin. For a split second it was a knock of detection, a warning of ambush, and it made my heart pound and leap into my mouth. I shot out of the chair and was at the door in an instant and in that same moment in time she was in my arms, her body pressing with all her might into mine, full of nervous body-tingling pent-up excitement. As we kissed and her snake-like tongue burst into my willing mouth, and before I'd blindly fumbled to secure the door, she was already shedding her upper clothing. She was rampant and the near animal response in my groin was instant and devastating. Copulation was immediate, brazen, frenetic and wildly varied, but most of all it was wicked! We made lots of noise. We must have made lots of noise, (but no one complained or raised the slightest objection) but we didn't care a jot. I certainly didn't care. This was life indeed, my life, my life renewed at all levels. My body was firing on all cylinders, all guns blazing! And I wallowed in all its sweet, sticky and sweaty exultation. I was indeed a man reborn and it was down to her, to the younger woman lying completely dishevelled beneath me, then kneeling in front of me, and above me, and above all to the younger woman that ultimately lay by my side softly panting, utterly sated, her arms hugging the pillow that she'd seemingly pulled to her body in salvation. After our extreme exertion we dozed, lost in deep thought, and then probably slept for some considerable time. When we were both fully awake again, we chatted, giggled, very possibly sniggered, then, still snuggled in one another's arms, we talked meaningfully to one another. She disclosed just more than a little about herself and her life. Her misery. Her lack of fulfilment throughout her adult life.

About the desert, (her words not mine) that surrounded her on all sides, a desert full of un-happiness.

She repeatedly told me how she hated her partner of many years standing. He was despicably mean and thoughtless. She told me how he continually left her all alone and starved her of all affection. She had been left emotionally scarred. He had scared, no chased, away all her friends and left her with very little money with which to enjoy herself, he had stripped her of all her independence. Until now, all that she had left were the four walls around her, a prison, a house full of bitter sadness and her growing sense of depression. And then quite suddenly the coin flipped. Almost in the same breath she told me what a jolly, good, and kind man he had been when they had first met. Well she said, how deep down, well not all that very deep really come to think of it, what an honest and decent and thoughtful man he could be, and would be if only he put his mind to it. And what's more there was no denying it that he was a thoroughly devoted father, a 'bloody great dad', of that she had no doubt. She then began to weep softly. Her body racked by the gentle heaving sobs. I honestly did my level best to soothe her genuine distress. I really wanted to ease her pain. And so I pulled my arm from around her belly and stroked her luxuriant hair and whispered reassuring 'sweet-nothings' into her beautiful ear in between a host of tiny kisses. After a little while this appeared to do the trick as she calmed down and her sobs subsided and she drifted off once more, and so did I, for when we awoke, stretching arms and legs, amid contented and sleepy yarns, the clock was most definitely against us. Time had run away and we were late.

After this first meeting, and after our first coupling, our love-making grew bolder. We began to meet nearer and nearer to where we lived. Flouting the odds of detection. Our love-making exploded in broad daylight wherever and whenever it could. When our carnal desires overwhelmed us, we simply surrendered to them whole-heartedly and without the slightest hint of protest. We were at their mercy! It didn't matter where we were, and it didn't matter what the weather was like, that was all there was to it. We simply didn't care anymore. And this carried on like this for all of the summer and a little beyond that as I remember now. And it was amidst all this wantonness that we inevitably grew more and more daring. And out of daring there followed recklessness, and out of recklessness there came stupidity. We must have been seen, somewhere, I haven't the faintest idea or notion where. But seen we were. Our affair detected. We had been rumbled indeed but we didn't as yet know it. We were now living in imminent danger, and we didn't know that either. Quite suddenly and 'out-of-the-blue' she broke off all contact with me completely. After she didn't reply to my third, fourth, and fifth messages, I knew instinctively that something was gravely amiss. Terribly, terribly wrong! When eventually I ventured into the 'sandwich shop' a couple of days later, the atmosphere was veritably 'Antarctic'. Those eyes, her captivating eyes, looked into mine without the remotest sense of recognition and emotion. My little 'hot-potato' had become the 'ice-maiden' personified. There was no communication between us at all, not even the merest flicker or glint in her eye. She made the distinct point of coming absolutely nowhere near me. Even the slightest of touches were now utterly out of the question. Within the week I abandoned the 'sandwich shop' as a lost cause and walked upon the opposite side of the road. I didn't even glance over in the direction of the 'sandwich shop' as I passed by, not once, not even out of the very corner of my eyes. And once more I frequented the little café of earlier days before I had grown addicted to lust, and our hot and sweaty ways together.

However, this overt lack of communication with her was intolerable. It completely disrupted my life. She kept me awake for hours at night, tossing and turning, and when I eventually fell asleep, she woke me up in the dead of night like a thunder-clap. This couldn't go on like this. It surely couldn't end this way? I had to speak to her. I had to see her, close to, to try and clear the air at the very least.

I eventually trapped her just behind the 'sandwich shop' as she was making her way home. She stood stock-still in the middle of the lane as I addressed her, pleaded with her to speak to me. She glowered at me. There was hatred fizzing in her eyes. Her ram-rod posture un-nerved me and didn't bode well at all. Only her eyes were expressive as flitted glances in every direction but mine and her fluttering eyelashes danced like the wings of caged birds. At last she spoke. Well by that I mean she spoke, or spat, three words. First she said my name followed by the emphatic words, 'it's over'! She repeated these words at every plea I fired at her. She moved to pass me by and I tentatively tried to block her path but she barged past me with a near physical determination. Again the three words were spoken, but this time spat out with venom and were definitely intended to poison me, and any hopes that I had harboured, once and for all. Their loudness made me shrink away utterly dejected, and I slunk away down the little cobbled ramp and made my way back home, back along the river and out of sight, as quickly as I could.

I didn't dare go anywhere near the place again until well beyond the end of summer and autumn had indeed arrived. In fact the leaves had just begun to fall in earnest when next I ventured to visit the place. And as you will presently see it would have been gravely advantageous had I never gone anywhere near that spot ever again. But there I was, you see, drawn to the place out of morbid curiosity. The scar still hadn't healed properly, if at all, was still painful, still wept with the puss of self-pity. But it really doesn't matter now does it as it's all the same to me. As I drew abreast of the 'sandwich shop' (for I was walking along the 'Oldham Road') I quickly spotted that its shutter was down and a 'For Sale' sign attached to the premises. My curiosity aroused; I carefully crossed the road and was soon standing before a white notice placed very carefully inside a plastic wallet fixed securely to the shop's shutter. Basically, it notified all its customers that the business had closed due to unforeseen circumstances, and therefore, would not be re-opening any time within the near future. It ended by thanking everyone past and present for their greatly appreciated patronage, and concluded with a very big 'Good Luck' to one and all. I suddenly wondered if that included 'yours truly' as well? But somehow I doubted that very much. As I re-crossed the main road, I pondered upon what on earth could have happened? Surely to God it could have had nothing at all to do with me? I suddenly shivered right down to the marrow in my bones, it was as if someone, and a someone not at all very nice, had just walked across my grave!

As I reached the middle of the bridge, and for some unknown reason, I decided to peer over the parapet down to where the two hurrying waters converged twenty feet below me. How beautifully bucolic it all looked and yet at the same time how decidedly dank and miserable it was. Coldly wet and damp. The end of summer not long gone, and all of summer's warmth and life. The long hibernation just around the next bend in the river. As I looked at the bubbling waters, rushing over rocks and boulders, as they had done for relentless time, I wondered what kind of winter we would have. Would there be snow this time around, heavy frosts and biting north-easterly winds? All manner of stuff to gladly get wrapped up in. Invigorating to walk without and take in the sharp, fresh air. Hard lonely times ahead no doubt. One thing I did know for sure, we'd have rain all right, lots and lots of rain. Day-long mists hanging about the place like grey heavy shrouds, and squally sheets of soaking wet drizzle that wet you right down to your underwear and socks. Horrid stuff!

I shuddered and sighed as I straightened up and it was then that my end came quite unexpectedly taking me completely by surprise. Out of the blue one might say. I was suddenly, and very skilfully, waylaid. By whom and by how many I had no time to ascertain as it all occurred in the blink of an eye. Whoever it was they had obviously been waiting for me, intent on harm. I had been stalked like prey and hunted down to this spot upon the 'Ryburn Bridge' and caught. Before I could offer even the very slightest of resistance I was manhandled with deft certainty and expertise and rendered useless. Whoever they were (and there were definitely more than two of them, that much I do know) they had cleverly decided to ambush me, and they knew exactly what they were about and I was powerless to stop them in their tracks. And then, before I had the faintest idea of what was going to happen to me next, I was being swung, to and fro, with consummate ease I might add (my assailants were obviously sturdy beggars; I can definitely say that in their favour) like a sack of 'King Edward's' potatoes. I tried desperately to catch the merest of glimpses of my attackers amid my garbled and frantic calls for help. But all I saw was pavement, road and parts of a cloudy sky, just before I was tossed aside like a pancake over the bridge's parapet, and sent flying through the crisp autumnal air like some poor discarded rag doll. And that, I'm afraid to say, was all there was to it. I haven't the faintest of ideas whether anyone saw what was happening to me, whether anyone witnessed my demise. Not that it matters now anyway. It's all purely academic as they say. Alas no one came to my aid and as a result I was well and truly done for!

My fall was broken (and so incidentally was my spine) as I landed squarely on the big river boulder that I had been looking down upon only moments before from the pavement above. There was no pain at all. Nowhere! I felt absolutely nothing. And strangely enough, considering what had just happened to me, I felt no sense of distress. Indeed all that I could see was the cloudy sky soaring directly above my gaze. I distinctly remember noticing just how fast the greyness was sailing across my field of vision. And, if I tried to raise my head, which I could only manage fractionally, I was just able to see the belt buckle at my waist. Of my legs and feet I could see absolutely nothing. I remember panicking a little and thinking that I hoped they were still there, somewhere thereabouts, not that it really mattered because I was never going to use them again. But at that particular moment I had actually no way of knowing that. If my head dropped under its own 'dead-weight' I could see the river waters to my left and to my right. I saw its sparkling silvery bubbles rushing happily past my eyes. But directly below the top of my head I could see nothing at all. In this dire predicament that I now found myself to be in, my hearing became instantly acute. I could hear the leaves all around me detaching themselves from twig and branch, and of their fall, some to the littered ground below, and some to the waters that now completely surrounded me. They sounded like heavy stones crashing through the self-same trees shattering the deathly still and unearthly silence. Then, as their sound faded to somewhere else, the rushing waters all about me grew to be a roar, a gushing torrent pounding past my stricken, lifeless form. And so time passed. 'Rush-hour' approached the living world above and beyond me. I heard cars, buses and lorries on the road above me. And sometimes the faintest of sounds of voices wafting down upon the breeze to where I lay. All so very near, and yet so very, very far away from me. They might well have been upon the other side of the world for all it mattered to me! But more than all of this I was almost deafened, driven close to madness itself, by the sounds of the moving, rushing, gurgling and infinitely busy water. I could even smell it too. In all its myriad forms. Its freshness, its dankness, the soil at its river's edge and of the animals that lived beneath its surface. And every now and again I felt its little tiny slashes upon my face, upon my eyes and ears, my cheeks and lips, tiny little sensations of freezing cold freshness. And then I felt and saw nothing at all for I must surely have passed out as my breathing became tired and strained.

When next I opened my eyes, I was looking up into an amazingly clear and star-laden night sky. I still hadn't moved nor could I budge an inch. In fact, all I could actually do was turn and slightly lift my head. I obviously remained in that position throughout the entire night. Drifting in and out of consciousness I don't know how many times. I think that I might well have called out for help, I might have done this repeatedly, many times, I simply don't know. I could well have dreamt the whole thing up. I do know that my voice was weak, hardly audible above a hoarse rasping whisper. This I definitely do know because every now and then I became suddenly aware that I was singing 'I've got a lovely bunch of coconuts'. How peculiar it all seemed to me. I heard movements all around me, animals I suspect, abroad in 'their' night, foraging, in the act of staying alive, whilst I was well aware that I was in the awesome act of dying. I heard people leaving the 'Indian Restaurant' above and to one side of me, people getting into their motor-cars and driving off and away into their pretty little lives. And when I thought of this I began to cry, and then I wept, uncontrollably. I didn't really want to go, you see, not quite just yet, and most certainly not quite like this. I had thought about my end (as many of us do) many times, but lying all alone, my back irrevocably broken by the fall, attacked and waylaid like some simple being, wasn't at all how I'd envisaged it. This wasn't what I had in mind at all. But when all was said and done at least I wasn't in any pain, none whatsoever. No physical pain that is. The only real anguish was that which raged around the inside of my head. My mind was full with thoughts, all confused, all jumbled, all of them racing about the place hither and thither, no connection, no link to one another as far as I could make out. No physical pain at all. I supposed I should be thankful for small mercies, that at least.

When next I came around, there was the very merest hint of light in the sky. Very slight, very subtle, but there nonetheless. I also became increasingly aware that something, a something that I couldn't quite latch on to, was different in and around me. What was it? It obsessed me and it really made me feel very angry, simply because I couldn't quite put my finger on it. And then my anger turned to worry, an anxious worry that caused me to look about within the strictly limited movement of my head. All I saw was dark bubbling water and trees and shrubbery inky black and lifeless. But something had changed, something was very, very different from before. And very soon my anxious worry turned into a terrible fear. And then it came to me in a flash. The something that was different was an awful pong, a dreadful stench about the place. A bloody great smell that pervaded the air all around me. A pungent odour of very wet goat. It was almost over-powering and I, in my helplessness and newly stricken state, was powerless to evade its scented tendrils. I was its prisoner. It was a smell that I'd not come across for quite some time, but I recognised it now, instantly. Once, quite a long time ago now, when I was staying at an hotel situated just below the slopes of 'The Great Orme' in 'Llandudno', and whilst out walking my little terrier dog in the early hours of the morning, he'd suddenly and quite unexpectedly exploded into a foaming, tugging, straining ball of fury. I smelt the strong animal odour of 'his' would be adversary well before I actually spotted him, perched just above the roadside wall, staring down at us in belligerent, haughty disdain, daring us to challenge him. I picked up my little dog and held his thrashing body to my chest just as the huge 'Billy' goat turned upon deft heels and disappeared back up the hillside and up into the dark night above. And now here it suddenly was again. That near overpowering wet goat smell. A veritable stench! But I could see nothing. Do absolutely nothing. And what's more, the smell didn't go away. It remained as strong as ever. And I knew that its source was very close by me.

In my now very frail state, I called out weakly to whatever might be out there. There came no reply to my pitiful pleas, well, no verbal reply that is. There was a response and it came in the way of a stone, then stones, river bed pebbles in actual fact, aimed directly and expertly at my broken body. Direct hits. One after the other. As these quite obviously didn't produce any response from me the ones that followed next were aimed directly towards my upper body, chiefly my head. As the light was now growing bolder, I craned my neck towards the direction that I believed the stones were indeed coming from. And then I thought I saw it. Something huge, monstrous, moving slowly and carefully just over by the water's edge. It appeared to slip into and out of the dense foliage that lined the river bank. Whatever it was it appeared to be teasing me, testing me, daring me to make a move and run away for help. The next stones that were thrown in my direction hit me in the face and fully upon my head. They hurt me tremendously and I felt the pain of their repeated blows fully. My head fell onto the boulder just beneath and I never raised my head again in this life. I was fully aware now that these flung stones were the final test, and that to whoever had thrown them, it was now blatantly obvious that I was mortally wounded, paralysed and completely at its mercy, whatever its intention. I then suddenly heard a change in the pattern of the running water's flow. I knew that whoever, or more precisely, whatever was out there had entered the river and was slowly, very carefully, but nevertheless, inevitably coming towards me. And then it was there beside me. With all its horrible stench. It blocked out the growing light from the sky above the trees. It bent down, its hideous face only inches above my own, so close that I could feel its breath on the freezing cold skin of my face, so close that when it inhaled the air into its gargantuan body, it pulled the very breath from out of my lungs. It prodded me repeatedly as if expecting me to make a sudden move, a dash for freedom. But when it quickly dawned upon the beast that I was utterly helpless, was at its mercy, it bent down and plucked a huge rock from off the river's bed and straightened its massive form to its full and dreadful height. It raised the rock within its grasp high above its head and knew it meant to smash my skull to pieces. I stared up towards the terrible rock. I wanted to close my eyes but couldn't, I didn't dare. I was fascinated. I wanted to witness my end, my very death. I wasn't scared at all. And even if I had been it was pointless because there was nothing I could do about it, not now, not ever!

The monster didn't hang about on ceremony, no sir-ree. The rock came down with all the speed of a bullet, with all the strength and power that the creature could muster. It hit me just above my eyes. For a split second I saw the grain and texture upon its surface. I felt a sudden sharp excruciating pain that took my breath away and at the exact same time I heard the terrible crack as my skull split open, a sound that reminded me of a coconut being smashed apart. Fibres tearing asunder. There was a strange taste within my mouth, tangy, and bitter. I saw nothing. And that was that. My light went out. It was over.

Now it just so happens that as the 'Hillbeast' raised the rock high above its head one William T. Bunser, aged twelve and a half, chose to lean over the bridge's parapet and so unwittingly witnessed one life's destruction at the expense of another. He was not in the least bit scared. No, not at all, far from it. His round chubby face was a picture, eyes like gobstoppers, bulging and sparkling, and thunderstruck with excitement. His slack, red-lipped mouth continued munching on its pre-school chocolate feast. This was indeed something to brag about before class registration! This indeed was a real 'buzzer' of a thing to see! With his own eyes too! Now, when the rock split the man's skull wide open and a large portion of his brains popped out and slithered down the big boulder upon which he was lain, like some sacrificial lamb, and plopped into the water, he let out a loud gasp of wonderment that resounded through the trees to where the beast stood in triumph stooping over the corpse. In an unhurried movement it straightened and turned and looked directly into the boy's eyes and growled fiercely, shattering the silence, its sudden rage shaking its massive frame in spasms of defiance. It growled so loud that the boy very nearly choked on the mush in his mouth as he ducked back down behind the bridge's parapet and out of sight. After a good few seconds he popped his head above the parapet once more and was just in time to see the creature dragging the cadaver with consummate ease into the deep, dark shrubbery, that masked the far bank of the river and which marked the beginnings of the woodland proper. But just before it disappeared from sight completely it suddenly stopped and turned back towards him. It slowly raised its free arm and pointed a finger directly towards where William T. Bunser looked on, rooted to the spot. And for some reason unknown that silent accusing finger scared the living daylights out of him. And so he fled, as fast as he could run, for the safety of the school, sweating profusely, and as pale as death itself.

No one believed his weird and wonderful tale. No one! Not even the girls. And later that same day, some of the older boys who'd heard his story second or third hand, took themselves off in a gang to the exact spot where it supposedly occurred and looked for any semblance of evidence that just might back up what he'd blabbed about. They found (surprisingly!) nothing at all. Nothing whatsoever. No blood and most definitely no bits of brains about the place. And so the tale was very quickly dispelled and forgotten. Lost in the annals of 'boyish' exaggeration. Quashed forever!

After his vilification, William T. Bunser was never again heard to brag or tell tales about anything, no matter what. Indeed, for a short while after the incident he was thoroughly subdued. And for a long time afterwards, he never walked to school of a morning. Instead he caught the bus and alighted the stop after the school and walked back, and always on the side where people lived in their houses.

THE END
COMPLETED TYPING ON 19th NOVEMBER 2016